Daughter

Also by Kate McLaughlin

What Unbreakable Looks Like

Daughter

Kate McLaughlin

WEDNESDAY BOOKS

NEW YORK

First published in the United States by Wednesday Books, an imprint of St. Martin's Publishing Group

www.wednesdaybooks.com

Library of Congress Cataloging-in-Publication Data

Names: McLaughlin, Kate, 1971– author.
Title: Daughter / Kate McLaughlin.
Description: First edition. | New York : Wednesday Books, 2022.
Identifiers: LCCN 2021044043 | ISBN 9781250817440 (hardcover) | ISBN 9781250817457 (ebook)
Subjects: CYAC: Serial murderers—Fiction. | Victims of crimes—Fiction. | Publicity—Fiction. | Family life—North Carolina—Fiction. | Fathers—Fiction. | Raleigh (NC)—Fiction. | LCGFT: Novels. | Thrillers (Fiction)
Classification: LCC PZ7.1.M4623 Dau 2022 | DDC [Fic]—dc23
LC record available at https://lccn.loc.gov/2021044043

Our books may be purchased in bulk for promotional, educational, or business use. Please contact your local bookseller or the Macmillan Corporate and Premium Sales Department at 1-800-221-7945, extension 5442, or by email at MacmillanSpecialMarkets@macmillan.com.

First Edition: 2022

10 9 8 7 6 5 4 3 2 1

For Keith

Thank you for showing me that a man doesn't have to contribute his DNA to be a father.

Thank you for being there when I didn't know I needed you, and especially when I did.

I could write an entire book on all the things you've done for me and it still wouldn't manage to convey the impact you've had on my life.

Thank you. For everything.

Oh, yeah—I love you. ☺

Chapter One

2006

Dayton Culver was well aware he was trespassing when he and his golden retriever, Lulu, veered off the path in the woods. If he had known the nightmares the transgression would bring him after that horrifying spring day, maybe he wouldn't have strayed. Lord knew he was going to spend the rest of his life wishing he'd *never* climbed that hill.

The forest had grown up so much in the last couple of years that the PRIVATE sign that marked this particular corner of the property was mostly obscured—enough that he could plead ignorance if discovered roaming around.

His family had known the Lakes for decades. Dayton's older sister, Cadence, had gone to school with Jeff Lake, who had taken over the property when his daddy died a few years back. Jeff visited more often than his parents ever had. Mostly he'd come up to check on the place, but sometimes he'd bring that good-looking wife of his with him. The two had made a lot of changes to the cabin, the most recent of which was an outdoor hot tub. That was why Dayton had a pair of swim trunks and a towel waiting in his backpack. The Lakes wouldn't be there on a Tuesday and he could have a soak with no one ever being the wiser.

He let Lulu run ahead. He rarely had her on a leash, since she wouldn't hurt a fly. She was a good girl with a sweet disposition.

She did, however, love to dig, and when he spied her digging at the ground about a hundred yards from the cabin, he hollered at her to stop. Jeff Lake had started a new landscaping project—he was always planting something—and Dayton didn't want the dog to ruin anything. But when he reached the retriever, he realized she hadn't dug up a shrub.

She'd dug up a body.

"Jesus Christ," he whispered as horror threatened to shake his bowels loose. He knew the girl. Knew *of* her. He'd seen her on the news the other night. She was missing from a nearby town.

Dayton grabbed Lulu by the collar, pulling her away from the body as his trembling fingers fumbled in his jeans pocket for his phone. Reception out here wasn't great, but the nearest cell tower was close enough that he ought to be able to reach someone.

He called Daniel, his cousin who was on the local police force. He knew the cops believed the girl had been taken by a predator—the kind of monster no town ever wants to believe it could house.

Daniel told him to sit tight, so he sat, frozen on the steps to the cabin, far enough from the body that he didn't have to see the girl's empty gaze. Lulu sat with him, occasionally giving a low whimper, as though she sensed his distress.

A short while later, Daniel arrived, along with the sheriff.

Daniel eventually drove Dayton and Lulu home and told him to keep quiet about what he'd found. Dayton called in sick to work the next day so he wouldn't be tempted. The day after, it was all over town that Jeff Lake had been arrested. Police had caught him "revisiting" the body—whatever that meant. Dayton didn't want to know.

Soon word got out that he'd been the one to find the girl, and Dayton became something of a local celebrity. When the police found more bodies on the property—some of which had been there a long time under the landscaping Jeff Lake obsessed over—the horror of the situation became all too real. Dayton didn't want to be a celebrity, let alone a hero. And he didn't want to think of those murdered girls being fertilizer for rosebushes and Japanese maples.

After that, anytime someone praised him for finding the girl, he told them it was Lulu who was the hero. He did this hoping that eventually he could pretend he'd never been there at all. Maybe then he'd forget that poor girl's face.

Dayton gave several interviews after Lake's arrest. His mother was so proud and recorded every news show he was on, clipped the articles from every paper he was in. They quoted a lot of things he said, but the one that got used the most was something that years later he would wish he had never said, or at least had phrased a little differently. He'd said it in response to a reporter speculating about Allison's involvement in her husband's crimes and what that might mean for her daughter.

"That poor child's going to grow up knowing her father was a monster," he said into the microphone held in front of his face. He was too nervous to look into the camera, so he kept his attention focused on the reporter. "What kind of life is she going to have? Everywhere she goes, people are gonna talk about her behind her back—if she's lucky. To her face if she's not. Her father's crimes will haunt her for the rest of her life. God help her. I don't reckon she'll ever get a moment's peace."

Chapter Two

I swear to God I'm going to *kill* someone.

"Change the song!" I yell over the chart-topping pop tune blaring from the speakers. The singer's voice chafes my already-raw nerves.

It's Saturday and my best friend Taylor and I are sitting on the kitchen counter at her boyfriend Mark's house, sharing a bottle of sweet white wine. The party's just getting started, and about twenty of our friends from school are there. Some-one's smoking a joint out on the back deck, and the hot tub has been started up. It's early February in Connecticut, and we're jonesing for a little fun. There's been too little sunlight and too much snow. We're all sick of the snow, and counting down the remaining weeks till spring break.

I'm so sick of this fucking song. "Oh, my God! Change the music!"

"Okay!" Mark yells as he comes into the kitchen. "Jesus, keep your pants on." He's tall with broad shoulders and short hair. All the football team shaved their heads at the beginning of the year, and he's just finally starting to *not* look like he signed up for the military when we weren't looking.

He fiddles with his phone, and the song stops. I barely have time to say thanks before Lil Baby starts up. It's loud enough to fill my head, but not so loud a neighbor's going to call the cops. Not this early.

"You know," says Keith Hamilton, also on the football team and possessing nearly no neck, as he approaches. "If you weren't sitting there, we'd have more room for snacks."

I burp. "You know, if *you* weren't standing there, we'd have a better view." Taylor snorts, spraying wine.

He throws the bag of Doritos at me. I catch it with the hand that isn't holding the wine bottle. "Bitch," he says before walking away.

"Asshole," I reply, handing Taylor the bottle. I rip open the bag, grab a couple of chips, and shove them into my mouth. *Mmm.* "Want some?"

She grimaces. "If I puke later, the last thing I want coming back up is Cool Ranch."

I shrug. "Whatevs. More for me." I plan to be so drunk I don't care what comes back up. I take the wine from her and down another long swallow. The white of my hand is still covered in orange Dorito dust.

"Scar, slow down," she cautions, her dark eyes wide. "Neal's supposed to show up."

Seriously, at the moment I don't care if Neal Davis shows his face. I've lusted after him since the beginning of the year, and he asked if I was going to be here tonight. My excitement lasted all of, like, five minutes because then my mother lost her mind when I asked if I could go on my film class trip to New York next week. She said no, like always. She doesn't trust me to go on a supervised trip, and she sure as hell doesn't trust me to date. I am so done with her being a control freak. What's she going to do when it's time for me to go to college? Come with me?

Oh, hell. She might.

A little voice in the back of my head cuts through the raging static. *Snap out of it,* a whisper tells me. *You don't want Neal to see you fall down, puking drunk. And you're not letting your mother ruin your life.*

I hand the bottle back to Taylor, who sets it on the counter by her hip. "Maybe your mom will change her mind," she suggests, understanding my mood.

"Yeah," I agree, but I don't believe it. Mom's not mean, she's just . . . protective. Overly protective. Like, to the extreme. She had to meet Taylor's entire family before we could even start hanging out and that was in elementary school. The Lis were really cool about it, though. She did a background check on my last boyfriend, who was also my first real boyfriend. He'll probably be the only one I have before college because I'm pretty sure dating me isn't worth the hassle. She sends me to a private school, and I think she monitors my internet activity. She's a lot.

She's also the only family I've got and I'm hers. My father took off when I was a baby, and Mom's estranged from her parents—and her in-laws. We moved to Watertown, Connecticut, when I was two or something. I don't think she's dated more than three guys my entire life, and I never met any of them. There have been times when I've wondered if we're in witness protection.

It's not only me she's paranoid about. Something happened to her to make her this way, but she'll look me in the eye and lie rather than tell me about it. I guess it must have been pretty bad for her to be like she is. That's reason enough to cut her a little slack. And usually, I do. Tonight, though, I'm feeling stingy.

Once, Taylor made a joke about Mom abducting me as a child. "Maybe she's not even your real mother." She had laughed when she said it. It was just a joke. I look a lot like Mom except for my eyes. But I didn't laugh, because it was something that I'd wondered about before.

She very well might follow me to college. Or stop me from leaving. She wants me to go to Wesleyan, but I've applied to every decent college outside of Connecticut with a film school I can find. I suppose she could refuse to help me pay tuition, but that college account has my name on it too, and once I'm eighteen, I have access to the money in it.

So far, I've been accepted to two of the schools I applied to.

I'll be eighteen in August. Only another six months and I can control my own freaking life. I can run off and join the circus if I want and there's nothing Mom can do about it.

"It's important to me. I'm going on that trip," I tell Taylor, my jaw clenched.

"Okay." She doesn't sound convinced, probably because she knows I'm talking out my ass. "Oh, hey—Ashley and Sofie are here." She hops off the counter and I follow after her. Ashley and Sofie are two other friends from school. The four of us hang out a lot. Mom's met them and their families too. She probably has dossiers on them hidden in a box under her bed.

There are times I almost hate her for humiliating me like she has. I mean, it's a small school. Thanks to my one, pathetic ex-boyfriend, everyone knows what she's like. She didn't do me any favors sending me there. Honestly? She didn't do me any favors letting me date that asshole either. Obviously her detective skills aren't as good as she likes to believe.

Some of my anger fades at the sight of my friends. Taylor and I have been friends the longest, but we've hung out with Ashley and Sofie since middle school. Watching the three of them hug is like some kind of *Charlie's Angels* thing. Tay is Korean American and petite with dark hair and dark eyes, while Ash is tall, mixed race with curly blond hair, bright aqua eyes, and Sof is a short and curvy green-eyed redhead. She's white—so white. The kind of white that burns if she's out in the sun for more than five minutes. My hair is brown, and my eyes are kind of a bluish gray. I'm not quite as tall as Ash, but I'm not short either. In other words, next to the three of them I feel lamely average.

I join in the hug. Ash pulls a bottle of tequila from her bag and we all make some noise. Wine and tequila. Shit-faced here I come. I'm going to be so sick tomorrow. I hope Mom can tell. I want her to know I went out and had fun and she wasn't able to stop it.

She knows I'm staying at Taylor's tonight, but she doesn't know about the party. I'm not stupid.

Ash has limes, so we cut those up in the kitchen. By this time more people have arrived, and things are getting loud. Around me people are pouring drinks into red plastic cups, filling the air with the scents of their vapes—vanilla, tobacco, and something fruity . . . mango, maybe? It's hard to tell when the smell of pot keeps wafting in from outside.

"I'm soooo going in the hot tub when Sam gets here," Ashley informs us, flashing a bit of the bikini under her top. I've always been envious of her skin, darker and way more flawless than mine could ever be. She gets it from her former-model mother, who seriously looks like a cross between Tyra Banks and Rihanna. I don't think she's ever had a scar or a zit in her life. "He looks so good wet."

Let's just say Sam's a swimmer and he can really pull off a Speedo. I mean, those things leave next to nothing to the imagination.

Taylor goes through the cupboards and finds us four shot glasses, lining them up on the counter like a pro. Cardi B comes on over the sound system and I start rapping along, and so does Ashley.

I'm sucking on a wedge of lime after a shot of tequila when Neal arrives. Neal Davis. Tall, lean—built like the track star he is. He's got jet-black hair and hazel eyes and the most amazing thighs I've ever seen. Too bad it's winter and he's wearing jeans.

I yank the lime wedge out of my mouth and throw it in the garbage disposal, hastily wiping my mouth with the back of my hand.

Mark greets him with a bro hug. Neal sets a six-pack on the island in the middle of the kitchen and pops one free. "Hey, girls," he says to the group of us, but he looks at me. My heart skips a beat.

"Hi," I say, drowned out by the other three. Doesn't matter—he saw my lips move.

"Ta-kill-ya," he jokes. "Pour me a shot?"

"You do it, Scar," Taylor suggests with a coy smile before drawing Ash and Sof away, leaving me standing there with Neal, alone as we can get in a house full of people.

"I didn't know you drank," he says as I pour tequila into a clean shot glass.

"I'm full of surprises," I quip. I cringe as soon as the words leave my mouth. What a stupid thing to say.

Neal grins and sprinkles salt on the back of his hand. "I guess you are. Aren't you doing one too?"

Sure, okay. I fill my glass and let him put salt on the back of my hand.

He counts. "One . . . two . . . three." We lick our hands, down our shots, and each bite a wedge of lime. I laugh at the face he makes and the way he shudders.

"How can you drink that?" he demands. "Holy shit, that's rough."

I shrug. "I guess I'm just tougher than you." I smile as I say it.

Neal's grin widens. "Pour me another shot, tough guy."

We have another drink. He offers me a beer and I take it, even though I don't really like beer. I need to slow down—Taylor was right—and a beer is something I can just sip.

He pulls a vape pod from his pocket and inhales from it. I like the smell, but I don't have one of my own. The only time I've ever vaped was to get high. I don't really have any desire to become addicted to anything. Plus, Mom would have a fit. She's always citing articles on the dangers of vaping, smoking, drinking, and drugs. Oh, and sex. And strangers. Life in general.

The wine and tequila start to hit, warm and shivery. The music sinks into my bones, urging my body to move. Slowly, I begin to dance, hips swaying to the beat. Suddenly, Taylor, Ash, and Sofie are there with me and the four of us throw ourselves on the mercy of the music, drinks in the air.

Sweat dampens my hairline as I dance, but I don't care. I feel good, free. When Neal joins us, I immediately turn toward him with a smile. Sober me would feel awkward and self-conscious, but not now. I'm not quite drunk, but almost. I'm right on the cusp of fucking amazing. I want to stay right here, teetering on the edge.

We all know the song, but I can't remember the name. It doesn't matter; I sing along as I dance. We all do. Neal and I sing to each other and laugh. Beer spills down my arm. I take a deep drink from the can. I'm thirsty. The song changes but we keep dancing. I close my eyes and keep moving. Sweat trickles down my back. I take another drink; the can is empty, and I set it on a nearby table.

When the song changes again, it's a slow one. Neal pulls me close without saying a word, and we sway together as my arms wrap around his neck.

This is happening. I focus on this moment—enjoy it. If it goes beyond this, my mother will eventually find out and look into him. She'll ask me a million questions and want to meet him, and he'll see what a psycho she is. He'll probably ask me about it. Maybe he'll be cool with her, and maybe he won't. *Maybe* he'll decide I'm worth it.

But none of that matters right now. Mom doesn't even know Neal exists, and he doesn't know about her. He's my gorgeous secret. I sigh as our legs brush together. His hands press against the small of my back. I look up and meet his gaze. Neal smiles. He's going to kiss me, I realize.

My phone buzzes in my back pocket. It's Mom. I know it. She's checking in like she always does when I'm out. If I don't respond within two minutes, she'll text again, and if I don't respond to that within sixty seconds, she'll ping the GPS on my phone. I should have left it at Taylor's. Shit.

The song ends. I step out of Neal's arms. "I'll be right back," I say. I pivot on my heel and head for the downstairs bathroom. Thankfully, it's available.

I use the toilet while reading Mom's text. It's the standard "Just checking in" she normally sends. I type back: All good. Watching a movie.

I flush and wash my hands. My phone buzzes again.

Mom
<3 you.

Me
<3 you too.

My stomach rolls as I type it. Despite how she's made me have to lie to her in order to have any kind of social life, I really do love my mom. In all other ways she's awesome. She's always been there for me and I've never wanted for anything. She just worries too damn much.

Another wave of nausea hits. Shit. Maybe it's not guilt after all. Maybe it's that beer, tequila, and wine aren't meant to get dumped into the same bucket of stomach acid.

Oh, God.

Taylor and I drank that whole bottle of wine, and if I'm honest, I have to admit to drinking most of it. I don't know how many shots of tequila I had, and that beer Neal gave me was a tallboy.

I manage to get my hair in my hand and hold it back a split second before lurching for the toilet. The liquor burns as it comes back up. Some of it splashes on the seat. I'm going to have to clean that up. My stomach heaves again. Some comes out my nose. Oh, fuck. That stings.

Eventually, I'm empty. There's nothing left to come out. The nausea subsides. I lean over the sink and wipe my mouth, then rinse with mouthwash I find in the cabinet.

I wipe down the toilet with TP before flushing the whole mess and spray a little air freshener to cover the stink. After, I check my face in the mirror and clean up the mascara smudged beneath my eyes. I blow my nose, reapply my lip gloss, and fluff my hair. There. No one would ever know I'd just puked up half my stomach.

When I walk into the living room, people are still dancing, but I don't see Neal. I turn and enter the kitchen. There he is, drinking a fresh beer, talking to Chelsea Chatterton, one of the more popular girls at school.

My heart sinks. Is he really *that* easily distracted? All he needs to see is a smile that costs a fortune and boobs too big to be natural?

I walk by them to the counter where the bottle of tequila waits. It looks like other people have helped themselves, but there's still some left in the bottle. More importantly, there're limes. I cut one into wedges and then pour myself a shot. My empty stomach accepts it with a slight clench.

Where did those Doritos go?

"Are you ghosting me?"

I throw the lime wedge in the garbage disposal and turn. Neal stands before me, his expression serious.

"No," I say.

"Because you took off on me."

"I had to use the bathroom."

"And then you walked by me like you didn't even see me."

"You were having a conversation."

He steps closer, lowering his head to speak so only I can hear. "I was waiting for you."

I raise my gaze. His face is very, very close to mine. I can see the swirls of green and blue and gold in his eyes.

"Oh," I say. Stupidly. "Thanks."

"I'd like to kiss you," he says.

The air rushes from my lungs. Thank God I had that shot, because there's no way I'd let him kiss me when I had puke-and-mouthwash breath. "I'd like that too."

His lips touch mine, and my brain shuts off. His mouth is warm and damp and so oh-my-god incredible. He tastes like beer, which mixes with the tequila in a way that reminds me of the bathroom, and my stomach rolls. I ignore it.

When Neal finally lifts his head, we're both breathing a little hard, breath mingling.

"Want to go somewhere a little quieter?" he asks.

In my head I hear my mother warning me about going off with strange men and boys. I ignore that too. Neal isn't a stranger, and I've never heard any girls talk about him being the least bit rapey. I like him. I trust him. So, I nod.

He offers me his hand and I take it, following as he leads me out of the kitchen, down the hall to the stairs. No one pays any attention to us. There are people making out in the hall—waiting in line for the bathroom. Neal and I go upstairs. He's one of Mark's best friends, he knows the house. He leads me to a bedroom that looks like a guest room, shuts the door, and locks it.

My heart kicks my ribs. What if I'm wrong? What if he has done bad shit to girls and no one's ever talked about it because they're afraid?

He leads me to the bed. The only light is what comes through the window, so he's cast mostly in shadows. I sit down beside him on the quilt.

"We won't do anything you don't want to do," he whispers.

"Okay." I want to believe him. I do. I hate my mother for making me so paranoid too.

He kisses me again—deeper this time. More urgent. My

stomach flutters and I lean into him, wanting more. Neal lies back on the bed, taking me with him so I'm stretched out on top of him, his body warm and hard beneath mine. His hands roam my back as my hair falls over us like a curtain, blotting out the moonlight. There's only me and him and the sound of our breathing as music thumps and muffled laughter rings out in the distance.

We're in our own secret world. We can do whatever we want, and no one has to know. At this moment, with him, I can pretend this is how my life is. Pretend I have control over any of it.

I don't ever want to leave.

February 12, 1996

In Wake of Recent Abduction: Police Urge Women to Be Vigilant

The recent disappearance of three women in the Raleigh area has police urging women, particularly ages 18 to 24, to exercise caution when out alone, especially after dark.

Heather Eckford, 23, of Raleigh is the most recent disappearance from the area in the past five months. Miss Eckford was last seen at Mystique Gentleman's Club, where she began work last Sunday morning just after midnight. After finishing her shift, Miss Eckford was last seen exiting the back door of the club into the parking lot. Her car and purse were found in the lot the next morning. Witnesses say Miss Eckford was seen talking to a man with medium-length blond hair wearing a backward baseball cap and glasses earlier in the evening.

Prior to Miss Eckford's disappearance, Kasey Charles, 19, and Julianne Hunt, 21, went missing in October and December of last year, respectively. Miss Charles, a student at NCSU, had been out with friends when she disappeared from a bar after meeting a man with blond hair. Miss Hunt, a waitress at an all-night diner, was last seen on the evening of December 13. Witnesses say she'd been her usual self that evening and had been happy over a large tip left by a "golden-haired handsome stranger." Like Miss Eckford, her vehicle and belongings were found in the parking lot the next morning. She is still missing.

Police have not confirmed that the disappearances are related, but all three women having been seen talking to a blond man is enough for them to issue a statement urging women to take extra safety precautions, especially those who work night shifts or may be out alone late. Authorities urge women to ask someone to escort them to their vehicles and, if out socializing, to travel in groups.

Chapter Three

"Did you have sex?" That's the first thing Taylor asks when we wake up the next morning. Both of us completely passed out when we got back to her place after the party. We're still wearing our clothes.

"No," I confess, grimacing at the taste in my mouth. "He didn't have any condoms." I need coffee. And water. And a tongue transplant. Oh, and some bacon and eggs to fix the sourness in my stomach. Toast too. Maybe a bagel.

"Don't you have an IUD?"

"Yeah, but that's not going to protect me from herpes or chlamydia." I'd gotten the IUD to help with heavy periods. That it's also birth control is just a happy coincidence. Mom made me read a pamphlet about STIs a couple of years ago and it scared the hell out of me.

Taylor makes a face as she gets out of bed. "Neal doesn't have herpes."

She doesn't know that. Only Neal knows that, and while he's hot, he's not risk-getting-infected hot.

I slept in the other bed in her room. It used to be her sister's until Vikki went to college. Slowly, I peel back the covers. "Anyway, no. We didn't have sex." We did do just about everything else, though. I smile at the foggy memories. Hopefully Neal had a good enough time to come back for more.

"I'm going to grab a shower," she says. "Feel free to use the loo down the hall."

"Loo." I don't know where she picked that up, but she's said it forever. Normally I'd wait for her to finish and use her en suite, but I really need to clean up. I smell like booze and definitely have mascara rings under my eyes. Sleeping in my clothes makes me feel like crap.

I take my overnight bag with me and as soon as I'm in the bathroom with the door locked, I strip off my clothes and start the shower. Then, I brush my teeth—twice—making sure to scrub my tongue.

I wash off my makeup under the spray, shampoo and condition my hair, and scrub myself with a puff until my skin tingles. It was a good party, so why do I feel so much better with all traces of it washed away?

Taylor's not in the bedroom when I return, so I leave my bag and head downstairs. I'm dressed in thick leggings, a big sweater, and fluffy socks, and my wet hair is twisted up into a bun on top of my head. I find my friend in the kitchen making breakfast, dressed in an almost identical outfit.

I help her cook. I'm scrambling eggs when Mom checks in. She wants to know when I plan to be home because she has to go in to the pharmacy for a few hours. She's the pharmacist, and while the pay is awesome, she has a lot of responsibility.

I tell her I'll be home around one.

"Wanna come over?" I ask Taylor. "We can binge-watch something on Netflix."

"Sure. Mom and Dad will be home soon anyway, and I really don't want to hear all the gossip from my great-great-aunt's funeral."

"You sure?" I pour egg mixture into the hot frying pan. "You might miss out on something juicy. Like that boy toy of hers made a pass at your grandmother."

She rolls her eyes. "Oh, my gawd, you're so funny. What's taking the coffee so long?"

I cast her some side-eye. Usually making fun of her great-great-aunt's much younger boyfriend gets a smile out of her. "Someone's grumpy. Guess you didn't get any last night either, huh?"

"No," she replies with a scowl. I'm oh for two trying to make her smile. "Mark practically ignored me for his friends all night. I think he wants to break up but doesn't have the balls to do it."

My eyebrows go up as I reach for a spoon to stir the eggs. "Seriously?" It's the first I've heard of this.

"Yeah. Didn't you notice how much he talked to Aliah? She practically had her boobs in his face, and he didn't mind at all."

I hadn't noticed, but I'd been too busy with Neal. "What are you going to do?"

She swipes away a tear with the back of her hand as she opens the cupboard where the mugs are. "Dump him before he can dump me. And then move the fuck on." She flashes me a bright smile. "Travis asked me out."

Laughing, I shake my head and stir the eggs. I'd be concerned if I didn't know from experience that she'd be fine. Once Taylor decides to move on, she's gone. "How do you do it? You've had more guys this year than I've had since starting high school." For someone with such a low opinion of guys, she certainly seems to like them, and they seem to like her.

Taylor sets two mugs on the counter. "It's because I know my worth. You're shy—and you think you're lucky when they pay attention to you when it's the other way around."

I can't be insulted by her assessment when it's true. I am shy, and didn't I feel like the luckiest girl when Neal flashed that smile in my direction?

We continue talking about the party while we cook. After we eat breakfast and drink the entire pot of coffee, we leave for my place.

"Huh," Taylor says as we're about to get into her car.

"What?" I ask, glancing at where she's staring.

"See that black SUV? It looks just like one that was parked outside Mark's last night."

"Lots of people own black SUVs, Tay. We live in New England. It probably belongs to a neighbor."

"Yeah," she agrees. "Probably." But her frown indicates she doesn't like me dismissing her theory. Seriously, the girl watches too many crime shows. Not as many as Ash, though. That girl's a walking encyclopedia of all things serial killer. She wants to study abnormal psychology in college, and I have no doubt she'll excel at it.

We get in the car and back out of the driveway. I glance at the SUV as we drive past, but the windows are tinted, so I can't see in. There's nothing special about it. Honestly, it could belong to a drug dealer or a soccer mom.

"So, are you going to tell your mom about Neal?" Taylor asks as we drive.

I shoot her an incredulous look. "Are you still drunk? No, I'm not telling her about Neal. I'm not telling her anything if I don't absolutely have to."

"She'll find out."

I shrug. "What's that saying? I'd rather ask for forgiveness than permission, especially when she isn't likely to give it. Besides, you saw how things went with Chase."

"Chase is an asshole. He didn't need to be like that and embarrass you like he did."

"Mm." But he had. Told everyone about my "unstable" mother. Told everyone I wasn't worth it. He still got laid, though, so there's that. Anyway, he graduated last year, so I haven't had to deal with him since.

"If you think Neal is anything like Chase, why do you even want to date him?"

"I don't think he's like Chase. I just don't want to take the risk. Not yet."

Taylor nods as though she understands, when we both know she doesn't. Her parents are reasonable. She does whatever she wants. That old jealousy rises in my stomach, but I push it aside. She's not to blame for my life.

Mom's gone when we get to my place, and I'm glad. I really can't deal with her right now. I throw my dirty clothes in the wash and grab a couple of sodas from the fridge while Taylor finds something on Netflix for us to watch in my room.

We lie on my bed, propped up on a mountain of pillows, curtains drawn. Mom says spending all my time in the dark is a recipe for depression. She's probably right, but I like it. It's peaceful.

Taylor's phone buzzes halfway through the second episode of the British baking show we're watching (her idea). She hesitates before sending it to voicemail. Must be Mark.

"I'll call him later," she says, looking at the TV.

I pat her arm but don't say anything. She'll do what's right for her. I've known her long enough to know if she wants my advice, she'll ask for it.

We watch six episodes before Taylor decides to go home.

Mark hasn't called again, and I know it bothers her. He used to call and text her all the time. Then again, she used to answer when he called.

"I'll talk to you later," she says, giving me a hug.

I hug her hard, then close the door behind her. Sighing, I go to the fridge for another soda. Mom should be home soon, and we'll decide what to do for dinner. Maybe she'll feel like pizza. She's not really much of a cook, and I haven't eaten since breakfast. After watching the baking show, I'm tempted to make cupcakes. Too bad I can't bake to save my life.

I glance out the window above the kitchen sink, watching the brake lights of Taylor's car as she pulls out onto the street. The streetlights illuminate the driver's side and I see the glow of her phone. She's calling Mark, I bet. Hopefully the cops won't see her talking and driving.

There's something else. I almost miss it, but my brain clicks in about a second later. Soda in hand, I turn back to the window, my focus on the lights across the street—just a few houses down.

And the black SUV parked beneath them.

My high school is a big, redbrick building that looks more like a sprawling old estate than a school. It's been around for more than a century, and while the inside has been kept up-to-date, they apparently like the "old money" exterior. There are some kids here that buy into that whole "exclusive" thing, but most of us realize it's our best chance at getting into a good college. Schools like ours have money behind them, and with that comes clout. The website has a list of "Notable Alumni," and the names belong to politicians, business moguls, celebrities, and even a couple of sports figures. Bottom line is that people who go to our school are expected to excel, and that's what colleges want, right?

It's an awful lot of pressure.

Neal's waiting by my locker Monday morning when I arrive. How he knew which one is mine is beyond me. He would have had to ask someone. I like thinking that he went through the effort to find me. He's wearing jeans and a black sweater that makes his eyes look really green.

Heat fills my cheeks at the sight of him. Saturday night is a little foggy, but I remember being with him. I remember the things we did. I remember how good he was at them. . . .

"Hi," he says, eyes sparkling like he knows what I'm thinking.

"Hi," I parrot.

"I had a good time at the party."

"Yeah." I avoid his gaze, so I won't embarrass myself. "Me too."

"You didn't text me yesterday."

I spin the combination lock. "You didn't text me either."

He leans his shoulder against the locker beside mine. "Yeah, but you said you'd text me."

I glance up at him as I open the locker door. "I did?" I don't remember saying that.

He nods. "When I asked if I could text you, you said you'd text me. Did you forget?"

"Um, yeah. Sorry." I take the books I don't need out of my backpack and put them in my locker.

"You were pretty wasted," he says with a chuckle. When I look at him his smile fades. "Hey, you wanted to hang out, right? Or am I an asshole who's read this whole thing wrong?"

He looks horrified. It's kind of nice. Most guys wouldn't care, I don't think.

"No, you're not wrong," I say in a low voice. I look around

to make sure no one can hear. "I just feel bad for forgetting." Actually, it's a little upsetting. I can hear Mom's voice in my head listing the dangers of drinking too much and how it affects memory and judgment. I thought she was full of shit, but . . . I mean, I really *don't* remember telling him I'd text.

I don't remember saying goodbye to him that night either. God, I don't even remember how Taylor and I got back to her place.

He nudges my arm. "It's okay. I was feeling pretty good too. I thought maybe I messed up."

I shake my head and close the locker door. "You didn't."

"Does that mean you'd like to do it again sometime?"

I can't believe we're talking about hooking up like it's lunch, or something. I take a breath. I want to tell him I'm not interested in being casual, but I don't want to seem thirsty for a relationship either. "Yeah," I say. "Sure." So why did I hesitate?

Neal grins. "Maybe we can hang out some night this week? Catch a movie or something?"

Like a date? Something inside me breathes a sigh of relief. Maybe he's *actually* interested in me. I don't mean that in, like, a totally desperate way, either. My experience has involved several crushes that never looked at me sideways. It's hard finding someone you like who likes you back. "Sounds good."

He looks at me for a moment, still smiling. "So, some of us are going to Myrtle Beach for spring break. You should come."

"Myrtle Beach?" I frown. "South Carolina?"

"Yeah. We've got rooms booked and everything." He leans closer, lowers his head. "I have my own."

Not going to lie, his breath against my ear sends a shiver down my spine. Taylor told me yesterday that she plans to go, even though she broke up with Mark five minutes after she left my place. She, Ashley, and Sofie have their own room. I could crash with them.

Yeah, right. Like Mom would ever go for it.

"I'll see if I can make it," I tell him.

He frowns. "What else do you have going on?"

I sigh. There's no point in lying—I'm not good at it, and he's no doubt heard the stories Chase spread. I might as well give him the chance to run away before I get too involved. "Look, my mom's pretty paranoid. I'm not sure she'll let me go."

"For real? Or you just don't want to go?"

I have to step closer as someone wants to get into the locker beside mine. I lower my voice. "You think I'd make up something that embarrassing if I didn't want to go? No, my mother is super strict and anxious. I'd tell you I was going to Europe or something if I didn't want to go."

Neal laughs, "Your whole crew's going. She likes them, right?"

She does. "I'll ask, but I make no promises."

Another nudge. "You could always sneak out."

I raise a brow. "You really want the South Carolina state police showing up at your hotel room? Because she's that level."

His eyebrows pull together a bit, like he's trying to figure everything out. "Is it a sex thing? Like, is she super religious or something?"

"She's not a friend of Jesus, no. More like she's worried I'll be carried off by an ax murderer."

"There's really not much chance of that happening, statistically speaking. Like, you have a better chance of falling down the stairs or being in a car accident."

It's nice that he doesn't overreact. Less embarrassing. I

don't feel like he's judging me. There have been so many people who think I should stand up to my mom—like, openly defy her. That's not an option. I love Mom. I don't want to fight with her, but I'm also aware of how little power I have in our relationship. Where am I going to go if she gets pissed? I don't have anywhere to run, unless it's Taylor's, and I can't expect her parents to take me in. Until I'm eighteen, I have to do what Mom says—or find a way to sneak around it.

I can't think of a way to sneak around Myrtle Beach.

"I know. I think she knows too. It's just . . ." I sigh. "I'm all she's got."

"Only child?"

I nod.

"Single mom?"

Another nod. "No family in town either."

"Shit." He looks perplexed, but his eyes sparkle. "You in witness protection or something?"

I laugh. "No!" It sounds ridiculous out loud.

Neal's grin is back. "Not like you could tell me if you were."

The bell rings. Crap.

"Which way are you going?" he asks. I gesture down the hall. "Me too. I'll walk with you."

Is it just me, or do people look at us as we walk by? I'm not exactly Miss Popular. I do okay, but most of the school knows who Neal is. Do they think I'm the flavor of the week? Maybe I am, but I'd rather have him temporarily than not at all.

God, that makes me sound desperate. I know he's dated a lot of girls. Maybe I am just new and shiny to him, but I'll take it.

He walks me to the door of homeroom. "Maybe I'll see you at lunch?" he asks.

"If it's nice, I usually sit by the window," I reply.

A little smile curves his lips. "I'll find you. Save me a seat."

"I'm pretty popular," I joke. "There might be a line by the time you get there."

He hitches his backpack up on his shoulder. "I'll have to make sure I'm there first, then." He gives me a little wave before turning to walk away.

I watch him go for a second—those shoulders and butt are hard to resist—then head into class. People who have never paid attention to me before this look at me as I walk to my seat. Suddenly, I'm interesting.

It's funny how having your name attached to someone else's can immediately alter your social standing. Humans are so fickle. I sit up a little straighter in my seat and pretend not to notice the looks, but inside?

I *like* the attention.

When Mom gets home from work, I'm waiting for her with a glass of white wine and a smile.

Her blue eyes narrow suspiciously even as she smiles. Her lipstick is dark red, and it looks fabulous with her sleek blond hair and pale skin. She always looks perfect for work, but I know what she looks like when it's just us, and it's nothing like this.

"What have you done?" she asks with a lift of her brow as she removes her coat and boots.

"Nothing," I reply. "Can't I just be happy you're home?"

"You're seventeen. You should never be happy I'm home." She's still smiling, though. She takes the glass and sniffs it. "Is it drugged?"

"Seriously?"

She laughs. "Okay, out with it."

I could hedge—drag it out a little longer—but what's the

point? I pick my glass of soda up from the counter and take a drink. "There's a bunch of kids from school going to Myrtle Beach for break. They asked me to come."

"Myrtle Beach?" She says this with enough wistfulness that I wonder if she's been there.

"Yeah. Taylor's going."

Mom shakes her head. "I don't think it's a good idea, Scarlet. A lot of predators use popular vacation destinations as a hunting ground." Most mothers would worry about sex or drinking or drugs, but no. My mother worries about serial killers and rapists. What's weird is I have never seen her watch any crime show—fictional or based on real life. Never seen her read a book about that kind of stuff. Part of me wants to ask what happened to her, but I'm afraid of what she might say.

"I'll be with a group." I try another tactic. "Please, Mom? It's senior year. I might never see some of these friends again. I'll give you all their names."

That softens her, I think. "Scarlet . . ."

"Just consider it," I interrupt. "Please."

Hesitantly, she nods. We both know she'll probably say no, but for now I can at least hope. And maybe I can convince her to let me go if I'm extra good. If I can show I'll be careful.

I set my glass by the sink. My gaze lifts to the window out of habit. For a second, I forget about Myrtle Beach. "Huh. That black SUV is back."

"What?" Mom steps up beside me and looks in the same direction. She frowns. "How long has that been there?"

"I noticed it yesterday morning. Hey, you think Mr. Grant's going to get busted for stealing Mrs. Daily's rosebushes?" It was a neighborhood scandal—not that we talk to our neighbors that often. I heard Mrs. Daily yelling at Mr. Grant about it one morning.

Mom doesn't laugh. Doesn't smile. I don't know if she even heard me. She stares at the vehicle. God, she really is paranoid. There has to be a reason why, but I can't imagine what.

Unless we really are in witness protection.

"Is there something you want to tell me?" I ask with a smirk, trying to distract myself from the unease building in my stomach.

Her head whips around. "What?" Her tone is sharp. Her breath smells like sweet wine.

I nod at the window. "Black SUV. Acting squirrelly. Are you dealing out of the pharmacy?"

"Of course not." She's scowling. "How could you even ask me something so foolish?"

Wow, her good mood has totally gone to shit. "Because you're obviously freaked out by a car on the street. And you pulled the blind." She had, denying the kitchen of what little sunlight the day had left to offer.

"I'm not freaked out by a car. I'm aware of strangers in the neighborhood. And I pulled the damn blind because the sun was in my eyes."

I arch a brow. "Right." Seriously, what the hell is up with her? I'd wonder if she was off her meds if she took any. The only thing she takes is a multivitamin in the morning, and magnesium so she doesn't get migraines. "It was a joke, by the way."

Her shoulders sag. It makes her look frail. She's always been thin—like a model. I used to envy it, but the sight of her shoulder blades, sharp and jutting beneath her blouse . . . I can't look away. She could break so easily.

The fingers of her free hand curl around my wrist, cool and dry. A gentle squeeze, that's all I get before she lets go. It's not much, but it's enough.

"I have a bit of a headache," she tells me. She sets the glass of wine on the counter beside my drink. "I'm going to lie down for a bit. We'll get Chinese for dinner. And then we can talk about spring break."

I shrug, defeated. "Sure." I'm not that upset, because I never even hoped she'd say yes in the first place. I know better.

She stops in the doorway and turns. "Scarlet, sweetie?"

I meet her gaze. "I know. You love me. You just want me to be safe."

Mom smiles, but it's sad. "Yes, but that's not what I was going to say."

"What, then?"

She opens and closes her mouth before saying in a rush, "Oh, hell. I can't stand to see you look like that." She sighs. "It's not going to be much of a surprise now, but I was thinking you and I could go to England for break. Like we used to talk about."

England? Is she kidding me? Neal's definitely going to think I'm ghosting if I tell him this. Actually, he'll probably think the same thing I am—that my mother will go to almost any lengths to keep me from being out of her sight.

And you know what? I don't fucking care. It's *England*. I've wanted to go for years.

"Mom," I say, unable to hide my excitement. "That would be *awesome*."

She smiles and I see the relief in her face. "Good. We'll start making plans over dinner. You order, okay? Anything you want. You know what I like."

"General Tso's. Got it." I watch her leave the room as I reel from the shock. What the hell just happened? Is Mom really so paranoid she'd take me to another continent to keep me close? Fuck it. I don't care. I'm going to England. Oh my God, I'm going to do so much shopping in London. And maybe we can go to the Tower and see where Anne Boleyn died. And the ravens.

I have to tell Taylor.

My mind spinning with plans, I turn curiously back to the blind and raise it, looking out onto our street.

The black SUV is gone.

Chapter Four

Tuesday night the weather people call for a huge late-winter snowstorm that's supposed to last into Wednesday morning. School is canceled. Taylor comes over that night so we can use the snow day to "work on our history essays."

In actuality, she's scored some of her brother's medical kush and we're going to dye my hair, chill out, and eat until we can't anymore. I'll be sober by the time Mom gets home from work, but in the meantime, I'll get a little stress relief. Sometimes life feels like a lot. Maybe I make it harder than I need to, I don't know. What I do know is that I spend a lot of my life feeling like I need to look over my shoulder, though I have no freaking idea what I expect to find chasing me.

We vape on the back deck and watch people shovel and snow-blow their driveways. The snow stopped around eight, just before Mom went to work. I have a plastic bag over my hair and a towel over my shoulders. I'm wearing sweats and big fuzzy slippers. No doubt I look hawt. I can't wait to see my hair when it's done, though.

"Are you seriously going to England?" Taylor asks, passing me the vape pen.

"I guess so." I suck in a deep breath and shudder. I absolutely hate the taste of pot, but I love how it makes me feel. The burnt taste of the vape hits the back of my throat. I hold the breath, then slowly exhale. Tension slowly releases in my neck and shoulders. "Mom usually keeps her word."

"Wild." Taylor shakes her head. "Hey, at least you get to go on an awesome trip."

I shrug. "Neal will probably hook up with someone else."

"Then he's an ass," she replies, releasing the vapor from her lungs. "This stuff's good."

"Mm." My head is light, my brain slow. I'm not thinking about much at all, and I'm not worried about anything. "Dude, I can't wait to do the Jack the Ripper tour." Mom actually agreed to go, and I am holding her to it. It's the history and mystery of it that's appealing.

Taylor laughs and hands me the pen again. "Ash is going to be so jealous."

One more toke and I'm done for the time being. I'm at that perfect place where I just want to go sit somewhere and ponder the wonders of the universe. I want to feel this safe and slow forever.

I need a drink, though. My mouth tastes like skunk and my tongue feels furry.

Back in the house we check my hair—it still needs to process for a bit, so we listen to music and eat chips, then I rinse my hair in the kitchen sink. The water runs dark red. I put in a deep conditioner—also with a shot of color—from tips to roots. A shower cap goes on top of that. It's a good look for me, I think.

"Let's start the movie," I suggest. "I'm going to leave this in for a while."

We get drinks and snacks and head to the living room to veg on the couch in front of the TV. Chips and chocolate chip cookies—the food of stoners everywhere.

I never used to smoke much, but this year has been rough, and I don't want to tell Mom about the anxiety I've been having in case she decides I shouldn't go to film school next year because of it. Most of my worry stems from how I think she's going to sabotage my plans. So, it's either suffer or get high. Seems like an easy choice to me. I have pills my doctor prescribed, but Mom would know if I was taking more of them than I should. Sometimes her being a pharmacist is a real buzzkill.

We're halfway through a Marvel movie when the doorbell rings.

Taylor and I exchange a questioning glance that only the sublimely high can share.

"You expecting anyone?" she asks.

"Nope." I haul myself off the couch, stumbling as I round the coffee table. I probably shouldn't answer the door, but Mom sometimes gets packages delivered. She wouldn't be impressed if I left them out in the snow.

I open the door to find two serious-looking men in suits standing on the freshly shoveled veranda. One is a white guy probably a little older than Mom and tall AF. The other is Black with close-cropped hair and beard. They're both wearing suits under long wool coats.

"Miss Murphy?" the tall one asks.

My heart is beating in my throat. I'm suddenly anxious, for no reason other than these men look so . . . official. And that I'm stoned. "Who are you?" I ask. My tongue feels two inches thick and dry as an old rug.

"Special Agent Richards," says the other. His beard is so perfectly manicured I can't stop staring at it. "I'm with the

New Haven field office of the FBI. This is Special Agent Logan from Raleigh."

I have to tilt my head back to see the slight smile that doesn't quite reach Agent Logan's dark eyes. He has a kind face, but he looks tired. Like, bone-tired. "Hello," he says.

I blink. I need to sober up. Thankfully, the pounding of blood through my veins seems to be helping. I'm standing there like an idiot with a shower cap on my head. "Can I see your badges, please?" I ask. It sounds like "badthas, pleath?" through the static filling my head.

"You're diligent," says Agent Logan, reaching into his pocket. He has a slight Southern accent. Guess that's Raleigh, North Carolina, then. "That's good."

"Ted Bundy pretended to be a cop," I say, taking the badge he offers. I smell cigarette smoke. Can he smell the pot on me? "And John Christie was one." I sound like Mom, I realize.

Agent Richards's gaze narrows a little. "You know a lot about serial killers."

Because I know the names of two? He clearly hasn't met Ashley. Honestly, I only know about Christie because of her. "I'm a young woman," I say. "It's kinda my job. Know the enemy, right?" I look at the badge and hand it back. I wouldn't know if it was fake or not anyway. Besides, the black SUV is in the driveway. It's the same one that's been around since the weekend.

This is serious.

"Right," Richards agrees, but there's something off in his tone. "Know anything about a guy named Jeff Lake?"

"Everybody does," I answer. "Sam Claflin won an Oscar for playing him." The movie is a little over-the-top and speculates on the number of total victims, but Claflin's performance is incredible. We discussed it in my American Cinema class at the start of the year.

Both of the agents stare at me. Unease slithers down my spine. "What's this about?" I ask. I'm tempted to shut the door.

"Miss Murphy, do you know your mother's maiden name?"

"Has something happened to Mom?" Oh my God. I'm having a panic attack. I can't breathe.

Agent Logan puts his hand on my shoulder. "Let's go inside, Scarlet. Is that okay?" At my nod, he steps inside, guiding me forward. He pulls one of the stools out from underneath the kitchen breakfast counter. "Sit down, sweetheart. Your mom is fine."

Oh. Air rushes into my lungs so fast the room spins. "Delvigne," I tell him. "She was Gina Delvigne."

The feds exchange a glance.

I'm on the verge of a total freak-out. I pull the shower cap off my head. Damp, slick hair thumps against my shoulders. "I'd really like to know what's going on."

"Call your mother," Agent Logan instructs. "Tell her we're here."

Is Mom in trouble? No. Mom has never done anything wrong in her entire life. Shit, if a cop even glances in her direction, she gets super paranoid.

Oh, hell. She is in trouble. Maybe she *is* dealing out of the pharmacy. Or one of her employees is. My knees are too weak to make it to the living room. "Tay," I call. "Can you bring me my phone?"

A second later, my friend walks into the kitchen. Her hair's in a messy bun and she's wearing sweats two sizes too large for her. It's obvious she's high. She stares at the men with a derpy smile that turns into a nervous chuckle.

"Hi," she says dumbly.

Agent Logan smiles at her and takes my phone from her hands. "Hi there. And you are?"

"This is my friend Taylor," I say as he hands me the phone. He makes conversation with her as I dial Mom's number. She picks up on the third ring.

"Hi, sweetie. Can I call you back? A customer needs a consult."

I swallow. My throat burns it's so dry. "Mom, the FBI is here."

Silence, then, "What?" It's a tone of voice I've never heard her use before.

"They asked me what your maiden name was." I'm staring at the agents as I say this. They stare back.

"What are their names?"

What the hell difference does that make? "Agents Richards and Logan."

"Fuck," Mom whispers. My heart skips a beat. She hardly ever swears like that. "Scarlet, give the phone to Agent Logan."

"Mom . . ."

"Just do it, sweetie. Everything's going to be fine."

My body is jerky and uncoordinated as I offer the phone to the taller of the men. He looks silly holding my sparkly phone case that says BYE BITCH to his ear. "Hey."

Hey? Like they're old friends. What the hell? Oh my God. *Are* we in witness protection? I might need to sit down. Wait. I am sitting down. *Shit*. I'm messed up.

"Yes," Agent Logan continues, his gaze locked with mine. I can't make out Mom's words, but her tone is stressed. "It has been a long time. . . . Yes, she's fine. . . . No, I haven't. . . . Of course I won't. . . . See you soon." He lowers the phone and hands it back to me. "She's on her way."

I'm shaky. "What's going on?"

Agent Logan gives me a friendly smile. "I promised your mom we'd wait until she got here to discuss it. My guess is she'll make the drive faster than she ought to."

"She never speeds," I tell him. "She doesn't like dealing with police." He just smiles again, as if he knows something I don't.

"Since we're going to be waiting a bit," Agent Richards says, clapping his hands, "how about some lunch? You girls like pizza? My treat."

I turn to Taylor, who is staring at me with eyes wide as coffee cups. This can't be happening. It's a joke. A trick.

But I know in my churning stomach it's not a trick or a joke. And I know after today my life is never going to be the same.

August 26, 1996

Parents Ask for Public's Help in Finding Daughter

CHARLOTTESVILLE (AP)—The parents of a University of Virginia junior who was last seen walking home from a party on August 1 say they believe their daughter was abducted and are asking for anyone who might have information to please come forward.

Mr. and Mrs. John Ford of Waynesboro plan to also make a televised appeal for the return of their daughter, Jackie, 21.

"Our daughter isn't the type of girl to run off," Mr. Ford said over the phone yesterday evening. "She calls a couple of times a week and visits every Sunday. She's real focused on her education and her future. She wouldn't walk away from all that, especially not without telling us first. She wouldn't purposefully put us through this kind of torment."

Jackie, who is 5 foot 6, 120 pounds, with long brown hair and green eyes, was last seen in the area of Thomson Road just after midnight. She was wearing a pair of cut-off denim shorts, a cropped red T-shirt and sandals. Anyone with any information is asked to please call the Charlottesville Police.

My mother arrives sooner than I expect. Agent Logan opens the door when we see her pull in. She stares at him a moment, then says something I can't hear. He hugs her.

The FBI agent is hugging my mother. They fucking know each other. How do they know each other? *Why* do they know each other?

Mom comes for me next. I stand up. Her hair bobs around her jaw as she walks toward me. Her cheeks are flushed with cold as she catches me in her embrace. I smell Agent Logan's aftershave on her hair. I don't like it.

"Are you okay?" she asks, holding me at arm's length like she's inspecting me. I really hope I don't smell like pot.

I nod. "Mom, what's going on?"

She arches a brow. "They haven't told you anything?"

"They wanted to wait for you."

"Good." Some of the tension in her jaw eases when she releases me. "What have you done to your hair?" She looks horrified.

"I dyed it. You hate it?" I rinsed the conditioner out after calling her and blow-dried it. It's a gorgeous burgundy. I think it looks good.

"No. You look like . . . someone I used to know." She shakes her head. "You didn't finish your lunch."

I glance at the half-eaten slice of pizza sitting on a plate on the counter. "I couldn't."

"You should try. Is there coffee?" She turns to Agent Logan as she asks.

"I'll get you a cup," he offers. "You still take it black?"

She nods.

"Mom," I whisper when he heads into the tiny kitchen. "How do you know him? And why is he here? Are you in trouble?"

"Shh." She takes my cold hand in hers. "It's going to be okay. Sit down with me so we can talk." It's the voice she used with me when I was a little kid and had a bad dream.

Numbly, I sit on the stool, clinging to her hand like I did when she'd comfort me back then. She sits next to me.

"Do you want me to leave?" Taylor asks.

I open my mouth to say no.

"Yes," my mother says. Her expression softens at Taylor's hurt look. "Sweetie, we're going to be talking about some very private things. Scarlet can tell you what she thinks is appropriate after, but do you mind leaving us for now?"

My friend grabs her phone and keys. "I'll get my stuff later," she tells me, flushing. "Call me."

This is so messed up. When the door closes behind her, I realize I'm the odd man out. Everyone else here seems to know each other, but I don't know any of them—not even the woman sitting beside me.

Agent Logan returns and gives Mom a cup of hot coffee.

Then he and Agent Richards sit down on the stools across the counter from us.

"What's this about, Andy?" Mom asks him.

My shoulders stiffen. *Andy*?

Agent Logan smiles slightly. "You're a difficult woman to find, girl." He says it with a degree of respect.

"Obviously not difficult enough," she replies.

"What's it been? Fifteen years?"

"About that. But you didn't come all this way to catch up."

Watching my mother talk is like watching an actress play a part. She looks familiar, but she's a different person. There's a sharpness to her that's strange to me.

She's scared and trying to hide it. She's pale AF.

Agent Logan runs a hand over his smoothly shaved jaw. "Lake's dying."

"Lake?" I echo, glancing at Mom. "Jeff Lake?" Is this why they asked me about him earlier? To see how much I knew?

My mother looks me in the eye. Her gaze glints like polished stone. "Yes. Jeff Lake."

"Mom, were you one of his victims?" I'd heard stories about a couple of girls who got away from him. *Oh God, that would explain her paranoia.*

"Yes," Agent Logan says when Mom is silent. I don't like the way he looks at her—like she's important to him. Like they share a secret. "She was one of his victims."

I pull her into a hug. She's stiff against me. "I'm so sorry." I don't want to lose it in front of the agents, but I know what Lake did to those girls. The idea of him hurting my mother . . . And I've been such a bitch to her about being so strict.

She eases out of my arms, holds me away from her. Her arms tremble. "What's killing him, Andy?"

"Pancreatic cancer."

"Good." Mom's voice is so cold a shiver runs down my spine. "When you see him, tell him I hope he dies nice and slow."

"It won't be as slow as either of us wants, Allison."

Allison? I glance at my mother. Wait, she can't be . . .

"It's Gina now. Why did you say it won't be as slow as either of us wants?"

"He's offered us information on the other girls."

My mother shakes her head so violently her hair whips my face. "No. Jeff never *offers* anything. He wants something in return."

"The girls we haven't found, Al—Gina," Agent Logan says, his voice rising. "You know what that would mean for the families."

"No!" she shouts. I wince. "I won't see him, Andy. I won't."

A pained expression pinches his face. "Not you, no."

Mom turns as white and still as a marble statue. Is she going to faint? "No," she whispers. "No, not that."

Suddenly, I'm tired and pissed at sitting here feeling like a stupid idiot. "Someone needs to fill me in. *Now.* Mom, are you—are you Allison Michaels?" It's almost too much to wrap my head around. If she's Allison Michaels, Jeff Lake's wife, then . . . then I'm . . .

No.

It's Agent Richards who continues. "Jeff Lake has offered to tell us about the rest of his victims—who they were and where to find them—but he'll only give that information to one person." He glances at my mother.

Mom shakes her head again. She looks like she's on the verge of tears. I can't look at her—it's too horrifying to see her like this.

"You can't make her see him," I tell them. Mom might

drive me crazy sometimes with her paranoia, but it all makes sense now. She's still my mother and I love her. I'm not going to let anyone hurt her. Us.

Agent Logan sighs. "It's not your mother he wants to see."

I want to stick my fingers in my ears like a little kid. Lalalalalala. Can't hear you. There's this roaring noise in my head, like when you hold a seashell to your ear. They're not saying what I think they're saying. They fucking can't be.

"Please, don't." Mom pleads as she looks at him. "Don't do this."

"He'll only tell his daughter," Agent Richards says, looking at me like he's swallowed something bitter.

"No," I say. I know exactly where this is going and it can't be right.

When Allison Michaels left her husband and disappeared sixteen years ago, she had someone with her—her baby. All the chips and soda I ingested earlier threaten to come back up as revulsion twists in my stomach.

I am *not* the daughter of a serial killer.

Chapter Five

"I didn't want you to find out this way."

I turn my head toward my mother. We're alone. Agents Logan and Richards left a few minutes ago, after deciding Mom and I needed time to talk. They waltzed in here, turned my life upside down, and walked right back out. I kind of hate them both for that.

I don't know what to do with this information. My name, my life—*me*—it's all a lie. I'm numb. I should feel something, shouldn't I? Instead, I'm slumped on the couch. Half-eaten bags of potato chips litter the coffee table. Shit, Taylor's vape pen is there. Thankfully, Mom hasn't seen it. I hope there's something left in it, because I might need a hit later. I shove it in the pocket of my sweats.

Jeff Lake—the Ted Bundy of the nineties and early 2000s—is my fucking father. He's one of the most notorious serial killers in American history, certainly of the twenty-first century. Half my genetics came from him.

Regardless, this man—this "American Monster," as some

outlets have called him—has decided he wants to see me. As he's dying. He forced the FBI to jump through his hoops if they want the names of his remaining victims.

And if I don't visit him—if I don't breathe the same air as him—those girls will never be located or identified.

"We're up against a ticking clock," Agent Logan had replied when I told him I needed to think about it. "I'm going to ask you to think quickly, please and thank you."

Maybe this is shock, this hollowed-out feeling. This experiencing everything as if from behind a glass partition. Maybe I'm still stoned. I just cannot believe this is happening.

There's this pinched throbbing behind my eye. Am I having a stroke? An aneurysm, maybe? That might be better than whatever this feeling is.

Mom's looking at me, waiting for me to speak. Right.

"You should have told me before this." My voice is calm—too calm. It's almost like I can feel my brain trying to work through all this new information and make sense of it.

She nods. Looks sheepish. "I wanted to wait until you were old enough, and then I just kept finding excuses not to."

A tickle of belligerence tracks the pit of my stomach. "Why, because you didn't think I could handle it?" I'm some fragile kid? Isn't that the reason she's basically wrapped me in Bubble Wrap and kept me on a leash my entire life?

She's surprised. "No. Because I—I was ashamed."

That's not what I expected. I don't know what to say. My mother has always had an air of superiority around her—like she thinks she knows better than anyone else. Better than me, especially. Shame is not an emotion I'd expect her to ever feel.

"How was I going to explain to you that I married a killer?" she asks, her voice cracking on the last word. "That I was stupid enough to believe in him until it became impossible, and the entire country thought I'd been part of it?" Emotion makes her voice raw and rough, so that she doesn't even sound like herself. There are tears in her eyes. I've only seen her cry a couple of times in my entire life.

My mother is Allison Michaels. Lily Collins played her in the movie with Claflin. They portrayed her as loyal and sweet. Gullible. I remember the scene in the courtroom when she discovered that the necklace her husband gave her—the one she wore at that very moment—had come from the neck of a dead girl. She broke down. Bailiffs had to escort her from the courtroom. She screamed the entire time.

During our class discussion, I'd suggested she knew what her husband was, that she wanted to ignore it. She didn't want to know.

Bile rises in my throat, bitter and acrid. I take a drink from my glass of soda. I have to hold the glass with both hands because I'm shaking.

I don't know what to say to her, or how to reconcile the woman in the movie with the woman I know. There's no way my mother would have stood by a monster.

My mother isn't stupid. And she certainly isn't gullible. Not anymore, at least. So, either she had suspicions about her husband and ignored them, or he really had fooled her like he fooled everyone else.

That would be the kind of thing that could make a woman totally paranoid, wouldn't it? Make her doubt her judgment. Make her want to keep her daughter from making the same mistakes.

So much about her makes sense to me now. She's spent my whole life warning me about monsters because she knew it was only a matter of time before the one chasing us caught up. No wonder she drilled me about being careful.

But she didn't know about him. She couldn't have. My mother is not a monster. She wouldn't have stayed with him if she'd known. She would have gone to the cops. Unless he threatened her. I wrap my arms around my middle, hugging myself. "I don't think you could have explained it," I allow as my brain struggles to make sense of all of it. "Not in a way I'd understand, because I don't understand at all."

She shakes her head. "I wanted to, and then you watched that damn movie in your class. I thought for sure you would figure it out on your own when they showed those clips of the real us."

"You're not a brunette," I say dumbly. How many times have I seen pictures of her as Allison Michaels and not recognized her? I don't want to even try to count. It will make *me* feel way too stupid.

"My hair's the same brown as yours, actually." She touches a dark-wine lock. "I dyed mine a very similar color once."

Right. Allison Michaels had long, dark hair. When I picture her, she's so much younger than my mother, innocent-looking. There's a sweetness to her that Mom lacks. My mother looks smart and sharp. Whoever does her hair is good because you'd never know she wasn't a natural blonde.

Honest to God, my mother looks nothing like Jeff Lake's wife. Allison Michaels had a rounder face and a curvier figure. And she smiled a lot. Or at least she used to. Mom is so thin, and her smiles are guarded. I have seen her genuinely happy. I've seen her laugh.

I guess I've just never really seen *her*. I can't judge her for not seeing him. Not fairly, but I can feel it in the back of my brain. There is a part of me that wants to make this her fault. I want to rage and scream, but . . . I can't. I'm too numb.

"Is my name really Britney?" I ask. I thought they made that up for the movie.

"Not anymore." Her tone is so cold a shiver races down my spine. "Your name is Scarlet Murphy. Britney Lake doesn't exist. It was never my choice to name you that."

Okay, she really hates the name Britney. Point taken. I lay my head against the back of the couch. "I keep thinking this is a dream. It can't be true. It's like a bad movie."

She tucks a strand of hair behind her ear. She looks tired. "I'm so sorry, sweetie."

I nod. Maybe the anger circling the back of my mind will fight its way forward, but right now all I can think is that I'm glad I didn't grow up knowing what my father was. That kind of stuff damages a kid, I think. I wish I still didn't know.

What am I supposed to do with this resentment I've been building between us? I still feel it, but it seems petty and stupid now. I'd have to be a real asshole not to understand why she lied. I don't like it, but I appreciate it.

I have no idea how I'm supposed to feel.

"I suspected that my father was a douche. I just wasn't expecting this level of douchery." I shift uncomfortably against the cushions. "He killed fourteen girls."

Mom's expression darkens. "Those are only the ones they found. It was more than that, I'm certain." Her gaze looks haunted, and I know better than to ask any questions.

I study her face, looking for that girl. "If he dies, they'll never find them."

She shakes her head. "That doesn't mean you have to see him."

I laugh—roughly. "No? The FBI disagrees."

Scooting closer, she takes my hand in hers. Her fingers are like ice. "Scarlet, I left everything I knew—everyone I loved—so you didn't have to grow up in Jeff Lake's shadow. I didn't do that just so he can try to fill you with his poison. He's doing this to hurt us."

"You mean, like, revenge?"

"Honey, if he wanted to confess out of decency you wouldn't need to be there. He wants you to know him—see him for what he is. And he wants me to have to live with that. Giving up those girls, that's his gift to the FBI, but seeing you? That's my punishment for leaving him."

I stare at her. "That's fucked-up."

She doesn't even chastise me for swearing. A breathy sound escapes her—a chuckle or a sob, I'm not sure. "No shit. God, I could use a cigarette."

I'm quiet. There are so many things I want to ask, but I don't know where to start. I want to know how they met, what she liked about him. How she felt when she realized what he was.

"Did you ever worry I'd turn out like him?"

Her fingers tighten around mine as she looks me in the eye. "No. Not for a second."

Okay, that's one down. "Your parents aren't dead, are they?"

"No," she admits with a shake of her head. "I figured out years ago how to send letters to them that no one would suspect came from me."

I swallow against the pressure in my throat. I have grandparents. Family. She hasn't seen them for sixteen years. She hasn't called or visited her own mother. All to protect me. "I want to meet them."

Her mouth thins. "Okay, but, honey . . . if the press finds out I'm alive and that you are too, our lives are going to change. As soon as it gets out that Jeff is dying, it's going to dredge everything up. You'll become a focus of morbid fascination for a lot of people, some of whom will try to contact you. Maybe even hurt you."

Unease slithers along my spine. "Is that what happened to you?"

Mom nods. "I got death threats. A woman walked up to me in a grocery store and slapped me in the face. People would drive by the house and throw things. . . . There was no part of my life that was private or mine anymore. And when I found out that one of your day-care workers talked to the press about you, that the reporter took your picture . . ." Her jaw tightens. "I decided we had to run."

Fuck. The movie didn't really go into a lot of that—some, but not a lot. I remember thinking it was what she deserved. My classmates made jokes about how "Baby Britney" would turn out. I swallow a bubble of maniacal laughter. "I can't imagine what that must have been like."

"It was horrible." She lifts her chin. "I would do anything to spare you that kind of attention. I thought I had until you called and told me Andy was here. Jesus."

"You knew him before?"

"He was one of the agents who figured out Jeff was the Gentleman Killer—stupid name. He was one of the few people who was nice to me. More so once he realized Jeff had fooled me most of all. I think he took pity on me." She shakes her head. "If he came here, he must honestly believe Jeff's offer of a confession is sincere."

"Why would Jeff lie?" I can't make myself refer to him as my father.

"Because he enjoys it. His whole life has been a lie." Red splotches stain her cheeks—the first sign that she is getting angry. "He gave me a dead girl's necklace, looked me in the eye, and lied. Even when I confronted him, he told me it wasn't true. He lied to the police, lied to the jury. And he lied to those poor girls. He gets off on deceiving people."

"If he's such a liar, what makes them think he won't lie to me?"

Her gaze meets mine, so full of fear and weariness. "He will lie to you. He'll also want to make an impression. His ego demands it. So, he needs to brag a little maybe. But more than anything, he wants to see himself in you—even if it's just your eyes. And he'll get one last moment in the spotlight before he goes. That will make up for having to give up his secrets. And then he'll leave you there, dealing with the glare."

I'm his legacy. "Fuck," I whisper. I can't see him. What was I thinking? I can't be face-to-face with that kind of evil.

But . . . I want to meet him. He's my father. I want to know where I come from. And there's a part of me—a part I don't want to think about too deeply—that wants to know him.

And I want to help the FBI. I'm supposed to help them. Like, it's my duty or something, right?

"You look exhausted." She lets go of my hand. "Guess this killed your buzz, huh?"

I'm too overwhelmed to even be mortified that she knew I was high. "It's a lot to process."

She kisses me on the forehead. "Go lie down. We can talk more later if you want. I'll tell you whatever you want to know."

"You don't have to go back to work?"

"I'm not leaving you."

I push myself off the couch. My legs wobble beneath me as I make the short walk to my room. I close the door behind me and crawl onto my bed.

If people find out who we are, there's no need to lie any-more. When Jeff dies, there's no reason for us to be paranoid and hide. Maybe it will be rough for a bit, but . . . there's no reason for Mom to stop me from going on trips or out on dates. She can lighten up, right? I mean, eventually people will find something else to talk about. Times have changed. People have really short attention spans now thanks to social media.

My laptop is on the bedside table. Reaching out, I pick it up and place it on my stomach. I start it up and immediately open a web browser. I type "Jeff Lake" into the search bar.

So. Many. Hits. I start at the top and work my way down. Some of the articles are repeats, some are plain garbage. A few are . . . upsetting. I start with Wikipedia, because it feels familiar:

Jeffrey Robert Lake (born January 17, 1971) is an American serial killer and necrophile who kidnapped, raped, and murdered numerous young women between 1992 and 2006, possibly earlier. He was tried for the murder of 14 women in North Carolina after their bodies were found on his family's property, but authorities believe there to be additional victims whose remains have not been found or identified as Lake's victims.

Witnesses and victims described Lake as "charming" and "handsome." Lake exploited these traits to get close to his victims in singles bars and online dating sites. He would take his victims to his cabin in a secluded area of North Carolina, where he would keep them for days, sexually assaulting them before finally killing them. He would revisit them afterward to groom them and perform sexual acts until putrefaction made such interaction impossible. After, he would bury them in his yard or in the woods. He kept mementos of his victims, often giving their jewelry or belongings to his wife, Allison Michaels.

Lake was arrested in 2006 when he returned to the site to visit one of his victims' bodies after a hiker found the remains and reported it to the police. Even though he was found with the body, Lake insisted he was innocent, and has maintained that plea throughout his incarceration.

Lake's wife maintained his innocence into his trial, but when she realized many of the gifts he'd given her had come from victims, she filed for divorce. Shortly after, she disappeared with her daughter by Lake, and while people claim to have spotted her over the years, none of the sightings have been confirmed.

Lake is currently on death row in Central Prison, Raleigh, North Carolina.

Necrophile. Oh, my God. They didn't go into that in the movie. Or, if they did, I missed it. What kind of fucking monster has sex with a corpse?

My stomach tightens. The monster who married my mother. The monster who fathered me.

From there I go to YouTube. There are a lot of videos about Jeff there. Mostly they're snippets from news shows or true crime exposés.

There's an interview with him.

I grab my earbuds from the table beside me and plug them into the computer before playing the video. It's not great quality, but it's good enough. There he is, about to be interviewed by Barbara Walters in prison.

He's charming and at ease, speaking with a low, Southern accent. He's handsome; I can see why Mom would have been drawn to him. He doesn't talk like a monster. Doesn't look like a monster.

I do have his eyes, I realize. And our smiles are similar. Weird, to see bits of yourself in a stranger. In a killer.

"Jeff, tell me about your childhood," Barbara says.

He shifts in his chair. "Well, I was born to a single mother who liked the bottle more than she liked her son." He says this with a slight, self-deprecating smile. "I found out later Mama couldn't stand the sight of me because I was the result of her being raped at a college party."

Oh, my God. Is that true? And how could he say that like it was nothing? He goes on to talk about being raised by his grandparents and how strict his grandfather was. His grandmother was a religious woman who believed in a vengeful God. She would not allow her grandson to sin as her daughter had.

Jeff Lake never stood a chance. If he hadn't been born a killer, his immediate family took great pains to make sure he became one. They were supposed to love him and instead they despised him. They warped him. It would be easy to feel sorry for him if he wasn't what he is.

If he wasn't the reason that I've never been allowed to have a normal life.

He spends most of the interview insisting he's innocent, but he does it coyly, almost like he's flirting.

Or joking.

Later, Barbara asks, "Do you have any regrets?"

"Other than my past behavior making people think I'm capable of such depravity? Yes, ma'am, I do. I regret all that, of course. I regret that I made it easy for these heinous crimes to be pinned on me, that I made myself open to being framed by a monster. I regret that those families think I robbed them of their cherished daughters. Most of all, I regret hurting my wife so horribly that she chose to divorce me and take away my little girl. Allison and Britney are the only good things that have ever happened to me. I miss them terribly."

Breath catches in my throat. He sounds so sincere. His expression looks regretful. It's tempting to believe him, to empathize. How does he do that? I focus on his eyes, because that's where the truth is. If you didn't pay attention, you might miss it, but the way he really feels is in that sharp gleam. No regret. Those memories are all he has.

Jeff Lake knows exactly what he is, and he embraced it with all his heart. He doesn't regret killing or causing pain. He only regrets getting caught and being forced to stop. It's obvious when I can press pause and freeze him on-screen, but how would I know if he was lying to my face? And what would I do if he looked at me with those cold eyes that look so much like my own?

I close the laptop. I'm so pissed I can't watch anymore. Lying there, I close my eyes, but rage claws and churns in my stomach. No—not just rage. Fear too. That sharp wriggling along my nerves that means I'm close to panic. I open my eyes, reach over, and open the drawer in the bedside table. In there is the prescription my doctor gave me a few months ago when I'd had trouble with panic attacks and anxiety. I open the bottle and shake two yellow pills into the palm of my hand. I dry-swallow them before I can reconsider, put the cap back on, and throw the bottle back in the drawer.

I lie back once more. Close my eyes and wait. In my mind I see my fath—*that man's* face and that stupid smile of his.

I don't want to give him the satisfaction of getting what he wants—his revenge on Mom. I don't want to be in the same room as him. I don't want to know him. What I want is for him to die the slow, painful death he deserves, and to pretend none of this ever happened. That's what I want, but like so much of my life, I don't think what I want really matters. And do I really want to spend the rest of my life regretting that I didn't help bring peace to the families of his remaining victims? No.

I sigh. At least I get the satisfaction of knowing that no matter what I do, he'll still get the slow and painful death.

Chapter Six

Newsweek.com

What Happened to Allison Michaels? The Strange Disappearance of Jeff Lake's Ex-Wife

BY **JOSIE DURAN** 6/28/12

Many people were surprised when seemingly all-American Jeff Lake was arrested on suspicion of being the Gentleman Killer in 2006, but few were as shocked as Lake's wife, Allison. For the next year she would proclaim her husband's innocence almost as resolutely as Lake himself, until his trial for the murder of 14 North Carolina women killed between 1992 and 2006.

Lake and Michaels met in 1999 in Raleigh, North Carolina, where Michaels was a student at Duke University, and Lake worked as a lawyer. Michaels would describe Lake to friends as "old-fashioned," "sweet" and "dependable." The two dated for a year before Michaels moved to New York City to continue her education. Lake asked for a transfer and went with her. The two moved into an apartment in Brooklyn, where they lived for two years before returning to the South. They were married in 2001, and their daughter, Britney, was born in the summer of 2004.

Family friends say Lake was a "doting" father and husband. He appeared to be totally devoted to "his girls," as he called them. One family member remembers Lake lavishing Michaels with gifts, many of which are now known to have belonged to his victims, including the youngest, 19-year-olds Kasey Charles and Patricia Hall.

The prosecution reportedly showed Michaels photographs of her husband's crimes. When Michaels was confronted by the gruesome evidence stacked against her husband, including proof that he'd given her several "gifts" of items from his victims, her faith in Lake's innocence broke. She filed for divorce during the trial and testified for the prosecution. Many believe she played a pivotal role in Lake's conviction. He was found guilty at midnight, November 4, 2007. Because of remarks Lake made to authorities and evidence found in his possession suggesting more victims, Lake has been held on death row since his sentencing. He remains incarcerated at Central Prison in Raleigh, North Carolina.

During the high-profile trial, those close to Michaels say, the media scrutiny became too much. She was constantly harassed by those wanting to know how she missed the signs of her husband's psychopathy, and she received hate mail from women who were "fans" of Lake, calling her unworthy of his devotion. (To this day, Lake continues to refer to her as his wife.) Michaels withdrew her daughter from day care after reporters talked to one of the teachers. Fearing for her daughter's safety, she began to work from home. Not long after, she called in sick to work and was never seen again. Even her family claim not to know where she and little Britney escaped to. More than five years later, they continue to maintain complete ignorance of Michaels's whereabouts.

The new graphic novel from XTZ Comix titled *The Gentleman,* written by John Deacon and illustrated by Sam Smith, has renewed interest in Lake's crimes and curiosity as to the fate of his wife and daughter.

There have been sightings of Michaels in New York, Seattle, Boston and additional cities, but none have been confirmed. Since she was never charged in connection with the murders, police are not actively searching for Lake's ex-wife, who is believed by most to have been nothing more than a pawn in her husband's murderous game. Though some less scrupulous news outlets have offered rewards for information on her or her daughter, so far no one has been able to claim them.

"You're fucking kidding me." Taylor's eyes are so wide I can see the entirety of white around her iris.

I turn my phone so I can see her better. "Yeah, sure. I'm lying to you because I think it would be hysterical to convince you my father is a psychopath. Would the FBI have been here if this were a joke?"

She stares at me, as if trying to figure out if I'm trying to trick her. Oh my God, is she still stoned?

"You're serious," she says, finally. Some of the color drains from her face.

"Look up a photo of Allison Michaels if you don't believe me."

She shakes her head. "I believe you, but I can't believe it. This is insane."

"Yeah. I know. Apparently after reporters showed up at my day care, Mom pulled me out of school, got us fake IDs, and left North Carolina." I'm not even a real New Englander. I'm from the South. God, I hope I don't have family that still flies the Confederate flag.

Right, because I can deal with a psycho-killer father, but not a family of bigots. FML.

"Scar, are you okay?"

I'm not sure how to respond to that. "I'm . . . somewhere between numb and freaked. Look, Tay, you can't tell anyone about this, okay? No one."

Her expression turns defensive. "I won't. I can keep a secret, you know."

I fight back a sigh. "I know. I just had to say it, okay?"

"This must be such a mind-fuck for you. I can't imagine."

"You have no idea." The jumble of thoughts in my brain threatens to unravel, and I have to exert real effort to keep from losing myself to them.

"How'd she get the IDs?" my friend asks after a few moments of silence.

Leave it to Taylor to ask *that* of all possible questions. "She wouldn't tell me. I guess she doesn't want me getting any ideas." As if a fake ID for drinking would be a priority for me right now. Although, it *would* be awesome.

"So, he's saying he'll only talk to you?"

"Yep." I rub my hand over my face. "He's dying and they're all horny to find the rest of his victims." A little voice in my head whispers that I'm being disrespectful of those girls, but fuck it—this is *my* life. They're dead, so what does it matter?

It matters, the voice whispers.

"What are you going to do?"

"No idea." My conscience protests, but I ignore it. "Can you imagine if this gets out?"

I watch her type something.

"What are you doing?" I ask.

"Googling Britney Lake," she replies. "That's your name, right?"

"No. Yeah. I guess." I fucking hate it. "I'm never going to

be Britney." In movies, Britney's always a blond cheerleader that has perfect teeth and a tan.

Taylor's jaw drops on the screen. "Scar, do you remember the name of Lake's first victim?"

I frown. "No." Does anyone remember the victims? It's harsh, but true. Everyone remembers the killer, not the people they killed. The only people who remember the victims are friends and family and maybe the real aficionados.

Are there people out there still wondering about me and my mom? Do people search our old names like Taylor just did? I'd bet all the money I've got that Ashley has. Are there websites devoted to trying to find us? Ted Bundy has a daughter people still wonder about, and she would be forty-something now. Probably has kids of her own.

"Her name was Britney Mitchell."

No wonder Mom reacted the way she did. My father named me after a girl he killed. A girl he probably violated after she was dead. Bitterness floods my mouth. "Tay, I'll be right back."

I jump off the bed and race to the bathroom. My knees hit the tile floor hard, and I get the toilet lid up just in time to puke up the entire contents of my stomach. *Shit*. My stomach seizes and I retch again. And again. Bile this time. I shudder.

I've seen pictures of Britney Mitchell. I just didn't remember her name. I know what Jeff Lake did to her. The entire world knows he named me after the first girl he destroyed.

Once I'm sure I'm done, I flush, get up, and rinse my mouth at the sink. Taylor's waiting when I come back.

"You okay?" she asks.

"Nope." I laugh shakily. "This is so fucked-up."

"Do you want me to come over?"

"No. Mom doesn't know I told you yet. There's still stuff she and I need to talk about. Thanks, though."

"Just know I'm here for you."

We hang up a few minutes later. On my laptop I log into my Netflix account and search for *The Gentleman*. It comes up immediately—a shaded photo of a menacing Claflin. I'm about to watch it when I stop myself.

Taking the computer with me, I go to Mom's room. She's sitting on her bed, looking through what looks like an old binder.

"Hey," she says, glancing up. The lipstick is gone, and her hair is tucked tight behind her ears. The darkness of her roots peeks out. "I'm looking through some photographs. I thought you might like to see some of your family now that the secret's out."

I want to be angry at her. I really do. I want to blame her for this, but I can't. Does that make me a good person or an idiot? Both? I don't know. What I do know is that she looks like a huge weight has been lifted off her shoulders. She's been carrying this by herself for a long time.

"I would like to see them. Also, I have something I want you to do with me."

"What's that?"

I sit down beside her. When she sees what's on the screen, her expression wilts. "You want to watch it?"

"I want you to tell me what they got right and what they got wrong. It might be easier for us both if it's done through a Hollywood filter."

She looks at me strangely. "That's . . . insightful."

It's also because I'm a coward. A coward who wants the truth even though it scares her. If I watch a movie, I can pretend it happened to other people.

"Can we watch it?"

She nods. Using the remote on her bedside table, she turns on the flat-screen on her dresser. We lean back against the headboard of her bed, supported by fluffy pillows. When she offers me her hand, I take it.

The opening shot is a girl's pale face covered in dirt and leaves. A tanned male hand brushes them away.

"Yes," Mom says, answering my unspoken question. "That's how they found him. He went back to *visit* her."

Shit.

I've always enjoyed a good thriller. It's one of my favorite genres because the bad guy usually gets caught or some kind of punishment. Occasionally, they want you to cheer for the antagonist. Who doesn't love a great villain?

This isn't one of those times. And even though Jeff Lake gets caught and sentenced to death, I can't feel any satisfaction. All those dead girls. All those ruined lives and devastated families.

The worst part is seeing how my mother's character is treated. I have to revisit those scenes where I'd made comments about her before I knew the truth. . . . Each one is like a punch in the chest. Seeing Lily Collins lose it in the courtroom when she realizes the truth about the necklace is especially painful because Mom starts to cry. She doesn't make a sound. I glance over at her to get her reaction and see tears run down her cheeks.

"No," she says, swiping at her eyes with her free hand—her other still holds mine. "They got this part wrong. It was much worse. Especially when the press swarmed me on the steps."

On-screen, several FBI agents and family members protect Allison from reporters yelling questions. "Did you know?" "How could you not know?" "Did you help him?" "Where are the other bodies?" "Do you still love him?" "Do you feel stupid?" "Did Jeff ever ask you to play dead in bed?"

Ben Affleck—playing the FBI agent who arrested Lake—pushes the reporter out of the way and gives him a filthy look.

"That's Agent Logan," I guess. They changed his name in the movie.

Mom gives a slight smile. "It is. I don't think I would have survived the trial without him. He wouldn't let me take responsibility. He made sure I knew that everything I told them would help put Jeff away. Would help the families. He let me give Jennifer Stuart's necklace back to her mother personally. She thanked me."

"That's not in the movie," I say, my voice not much more than a whisper.

She sniffs. "No. There are a lot of things that aren't in the movie, sweetie. A lot of things."

I put my head on her shoulder and don't ask any more questions. She obviously doesn't want to talk about it, and honestly? I don't think I want to know.

Wednesday morning, I return to school as though my life hasn't been turned completely upside down. Everything there is exactly the same. I'm the only thing that's changed. I wait for someone to out me, but no one does.

There's been no mention anywhere—at least that a web search was able to find—of Jeff Lake being sick. Obviously, the prison or the FBI is doing a good job hiding it. I suppose it could be a ploy to get me to do what they want, but why would Lake give up names he's kept to himself for sixteen years without a reason? And why ask to see me now? No, I don't think I'm being played—at least not by the FBI.

Since Ashley is our resident serial-killer expert—she wants to be a profiler for the FBI—I ask her about Lake at lunch. We're sitting in our usual spot by the window. Neal's sitting with his friends a few tables away. He glances over at me and smiles. I smile back. It feels fake.

"Jeff Lake?" Ash pops a french fry in her mouth and chews as she thinks. "No, I haven't heard anything about him lately. He's been pretty quiet since 2017."

"What happened in 2017?" I ask.

"He was in a documentary about women who marry dangerous criminals. They interviewed his wife too."

I frown. I know that wasn't my mother. "He remarried?"

She looks surprised that I don't know. "Yeah. Everly Evans. They got together in 2015. She'd been writing him letters for a year or two before that, I think. She's like, twenty years younger than him. Kinda creepy, because she has a similar look to his victims."

Yep, definitely creepy.

"I never understood that whole thing about women who fall in love with killers," Taylor comments as she unwraps her sandwich. "Besides the obvious ew factor, it's not like you can ever be with them. What's the point?"

"It's an attraction to supreme-alpha personality traits," Ashley informs her. "It's like a mental illness. The women are attracted to the danger more than the man."

Taylor wrinkles her nose. "Still ew."

Sofie shakes her head, bright red curls bouncing everywhere. "Even if you could be with him, I could never have sex with a guy who killed someone."

"Is that your only condition for hooking up?" Taylor asks with a grin. "No psycho killers?"

Sofie sticks her tongue out at her.

"Ash, do you know the names of all his victims?" I ask.

"Oh, yeah. Sure." She rolls hers eyes upward, as though looking at a list in her brain. "Let's see, there was Britney Mitchell, Kasey Charles, Julianne Hunt, Heather Eckford, Jennifer Stuart, Tracey Hart, Nicole Douglas, Kelly King, Wendy Davis, Tara Miller, Patricia Hall, Nina Love, Dina Wiley, and Lisa Peterson. Those are the confirmed victims. There are others that people *think* might have been his, but unless it's confirmed, it's no good." She smiles. "It's important to remember their names, I think. I can name all of Bundy's victims too. You want those?"

"No," I say quickly. At least *someone* knows all their names. I bet Agent Logan does too. *See,* the voice in my head whispers, *they matter.* "Did they ask Lake about his victims in the documentary?"

"Nah. It was all about the women the killers married. The only thing Lake said was that he never thought he'd find love again after Allison broke his heart." She rolls her eyes. "As if he's capable of love."

"Did they mention anything about him being sick?"

She looks confused. "Mentally? Oh, yeah."

"Physically."

"No." She frowns briefly before her expression turns to wonder. "Scarlet, have you heard something?"

"Me?" I make a scoffing noise that rings so fake in my ears. "No. Mom and I watched *The Gentleman* last night, and she said she thought she'd heard something, but maybe it was about someone else."

"Must have been. That movie's so great, though. Sam C. isn't as good-looking as Lake, but he did an excellent job nailing his mannerisms and voice. Collins was good too. Has to be hard to play a woman like Allison Michaels and make her sympathetic."

I stiffen. "What do you mean?"

Ash shrugs. "She was so blinded by her love for the guy she didn't see him clearly. A lot of people believe she was faking it, but Collins really sold that naive belief. I think Allison really wanted to believe in Lake. She didn't want to believe that she could have married a monster." Another fry. "Why the sudden interest? You normally tell me I'm morbid for liking this stuff."

I want to defend Lily Collins. I want to defend my mother, but I don't. "Like I said, Mom mentioned something. I thought if anyone would know it would be you."

She grins. "I am *the* psycho expert. Has your mom forgiven me for telling her she looks like Allison Michaels?"

"What?" This is the first I've heard of it. My heart pounds so hard it hurts.

"I guess it was a couple of years ago. She picked us up from a party or something. The way the light hit her face I told her she looked like Allison Michaels. I had to tell her who that was. I don't think she took it as a compliment, even though I meant it as one. Allison was really pretty."

Sweat moistens my armpits and hairline. What would Ash say if I told her I was Jeff Lake's daughter? She'd probably lose her damn mind. She'd think it was awesome. She'd probably want to study me like a lab rat.

At least I'll have her and Taylor if word ever gets out.

Yesterday I hoped people would find out. I thought it would make me free. Now, I'm starting to realize just how crazy things might get, and I don't know what I want.

"Enough about killers," Sofie chirps. "I demand a change of subject."

Oh, thank God.

"Let me guess what you want to talk about," Ash drawls. "Spring break?"

"Damn straight. Who's going to Myrtle Beach and who's *not*?" She shoots me a pointed gaze when she says "not." Like it's my fault. She's such a jerk sometimes.

"Not." I smile sweetly. "I'm going to England instead."

The look on Sof's face is priceless. Ever since she had a crush on Harry Styles in middle school, she's been a total Anglophile. I admit, it started the same for me, but then I discovered Guy Ritchie films and Brit TV and fell in love with their style of visual storytelling.

"Bitch," she declares. "For reals?"

I laugh. "Yeah. For real." Because I'm absolutely *not* spending my spring break visiting a serial killer on death row. And if I've ever needed a trip to London, it's now.

At the end of the day, I walk home. When I walk up our drive, I notice a rental car parked beside Mom's. She's supposed to be at work.

My pulse throbs in the base of my neck when I walk in the door. Sitting at the breakfast island having coffee are Mom and Agent Logan. Just the two of them, like old friends. Mom's looking at something on Logan's phone.

"I can't believe how grown-up he is, Andy," she says. "And so good-looking. He's what, eighteen now?"

"Nineteen," he replies before looking at me. "Hello, Scarlet."

At least he doesn't call me Britney. "Hi," I mutter. "What's going on?"

"Agent Logan came by to talk," Mom explains, a sad expression settling over her face. I hate it. I want to slap it off her face and I feel like shit for it. So much for me thinking I understand her. I don't even understand myself. I'm all over the place.

"I already told you I need to think about it," I remind him—more sharply than I intend. "Why are you hassling us?"

"Scarlet." Mom's surprised at my behavior.

"Is that what you think I'm doing?" Agent Logan asks in that low drawl of his. "Hassling you?"

"Aren't you? If you keep coming here, the neighbors are going to notice and start talking. You'll get to go back to your job, but eventually people are going to find out who we are and then where are you going to be? Not here."

Mom touches his hand. "Andy, she's still in shock."

"She's right, though," he allows, and meets my gaze with one so direct I have to grit my teeth to make sure I don't look away first. "You and your mother will be risking the life you've built here to help us. The only stake I have in this situation, Scarlet, is giving peace to the families of the remaining victims. I'll be honest with you, that's enough for me. I hope it's enough for you." He slides a folder across the counter toward me. Mom looks at it like it's a snake.

"What is it?" I ask.

"His victims. And people we think might have been his victims. Don't worry, there's nothing gory in there. Just headshots. You want to know why I'm here. Look at them. Some were your age. Most, not much older."

I don't want to. This is a trick, I'm sure of it. I turn to Mom. "It's your choice," she says. After years of overprotection, I'm surprised she doesn't try to stop me.

My fingers touch the file. It's thick. "Have you looked at them?"

She gives me that awful sad smile again. "I don't have to, sweetie. I still dream about them."

Fuck. I open the file. I see the vaguely familiar faces of Lake's known victims—the ones I saw in the videos I watched yesterday. After them is a stack of more girls. Some have been missing for more than twenty years.

"There's a lot of them," I whisper. More than what I've seen before.

Mom and Agent Logan share a glance. "Yeah," Agent Logan says. "A lot of girls whose families don't know what happened to them."

I laugh without humor. "You don't have to play me. I know you want me to see him, and why."

"I'm not playing you," he replies. "I just want you to see how important this is. I wouldn't be here if it weren't."

But he is here. How did he get here? I meet his gaze. "How did you find us?"

"We're not called the Federal Bureau of Investigation for nothing. It took a while—a few months, actually. I was fortunate to have some idea of where to start looking."

"How?"

"Because I told him," Mom replies, not looking at me. She's upset with herself. "I told him places I wanted to visit."

He gives her a gentle smile. "You missed living in New York and the seasons. I knew there'd be too many memories there, though. I figured you'd settle someplace within visiting distance."

A look passes between them—an understanding I'm left out of.

"Did you two have an affair?" The question tumbles out of my mouth before I can stop it.

Mom looks horrified—so does Agent Logan. It's Mom who answers, "No. Agent Logan is a married man. A *happily* married one."

I shrug, but heat fills my cheeks.

"You and your mother didn't deserve what happened to you," Logan tells me, holding my gaze. He's not all that impressed with me and doesn't bother trying to hide it. "I felt partially responsible for some of that. I may have *inadvertently* given her advice. . . ." He stops. I guess neither one of them wants to say too much that might get either of them in trouble. "At the time I had a child not much older than you, and a newborn. I wanted to help you. End of story."

"Because you knew this day might come."

He nods. "Yes."

"So, it wasn't out of the goodness of your heart that you helped us."

Mom slaps her palm against the counter. "That's *enough*."

She's shaking. That freaks me out more than the brittleness of her tone.

Logan holds up a hand. "It's okay." He leans forward, pointing at the girl on the page, but his gaze is on me. "Kim Jackson. She was the same age you are, only she didn't have a great mom. She lived on the streets. She worked on them too. We think that's how Lake found her." He flips the page. "Michelle Gordon. Eighteen. A runaway. She fits the profile of his preferred type. Her mother still makes her bed up fresh every week just in case she comes home. Ann MacKean, a single mom. She also fits the profile. Witnesses saw her talking to a handsome blond man one night after work. She was never seen again. Her daughter was put into foster care, where she was abused and eventually committed suicide. But they're ones we just suspect to be his. I can keep going if you want."

"No," I whisper. "Please, stop." There's no writing on any of the pictures, he simply knows their stories by heart. Not just the ones he knows Lake killed, but the others as well. This is so much more than another case to him. I'm such a jerk.

Mom's hand settles over mine. "All I ever wanted was to protect you," she says, her eyes wet. "But I can't hide the past anymore. Jeff only has a few months left at best, and I have no doubt that he will take the names and whereabouts of the rest of his victims with him when he goes. I would rather die than let him near you."

"You want me to do it," I say, betrayed, but also relieved to have the decision made for me.

"I want you to do what you know is the right thing," she says. "I want us both to. Together. I'll be with you every moment. I want to live my life without looking over my shoulder every damn day."

Blinking back tears, I stare at her, realizing what she said—how she feels. She's willing to be in the same room with the man who ruined her life for this. The man who made her a public joke. If she's willing to do that, I should be too.

I look at the photo of Ann MacKean. What if Lake had killed my mother and I'd ended up in foster care? What if I had been abused and broken? Would there be anyone who would want to try to make that right? Probably not, because Mom had been stupid enough to marry him. Some would say she deserved it, just like they'd say Kim Jackson knew the risks of being a prostitute. Mom was as much one of my father's victims as any of the girls in these photos. Someone needs to do right by *her*.

And by me. Jeff Lake took away my life too. All the things I was never allowed to do because Mom was afraid of someone like him getting ahold of me.

"All right," I say, turning my gaze to Agent Logan's. "I'll do it."

Chapter Seven

We're on a plane for Raleigh at noon on Friday. It's only a two-hour flight from Hartford. It took us an hour just to get to the airport, and that was with decent traffic. Taylor is my only friend who knows where I'm really at and what I'm really doing. I texted Neal to let him know I'd be gone, but he hasn't replied. I'm kind of glad he hasn't. I don't know what I'd say if he asked questions.

Agent Logan is with us. He sits across the aisle on the plane. Mom lets me have the window seat. I've only been on a couple of planes in my life. Once was a trip to Disney World when I was ten. The other was a class trip to Washington, D.C., a couple of years ago. Mom was one of the chaperones. It was the only way I could go.

I took one of my pills before getting on the plane. Not so much because I'm afraid to fly, but because my emotions were all over the place this morning, and, well . . . I wanted to turn them off. Even now, sitting next to Mom, I resent her for this.

I resent her even as I feel sorry for her. I guess because I'm feeling even more sorry for myself.

I wish she'd never hidden me.

I wish Agent Logan hadn't helped her.

I wish I were selfish enough to believe my life was more important than all the lives my father has taken.

I wish . . . I wish I weren't so fucking scared of what's to come. Of a man I've never met. Of how much of him might be in me.

But I haven't gotten to the point where I wish I hadn't been born. Maybe that'll come later.

It's funny what finding out about yourself does. Sofie's mother did that whole ancestry thing and found out she's 4 percent Native American. All of a sudden, Sofie's interested in Native rights and missing indigenous women. She was never interested before, but now it means something to her. I've never once in my life worried about being some kind of psycho, and now I am.

I know I'm not a psychopath. And I know I'm not a sociopath. I *know*. But that doesn't mean I don't have some of that monster lurking in my DNA, right? I mean, 50 percent of my genetic makeup came from him. That's good odds for some kind of psychopathy.

I don't want to look into his eyes and see my own looking back.

Mom says I'm nothing like him, but how well does she really know me? Not like she read him that great. How could he have fooled her for so long? And so well?

I feel like Jodie Foster about to be tossed into a room with Anthony Hopkins. At least my father never ate any of his victims.

He just had sex with them.

I lean back against the seat and close my eyes as my stomach churns.

"You should have taken a Dramamine," Mom says, mistaking the source of my nausea. "You got sick on that flight home from Washington too, remember?"

I got sick because a few of us drank a bunch of vodka before getting on the damn plane. She never figured that out either. I had wanted her to. Wanted to make her mad, but all I got out of it was puke in my hair.

The flight attendant comes by with drinks. Mom gets me a ginger ale, which helps. I sip it while reading an interview with Tarantino on my phone. It's a good distraction.

The anxiety med kicks in. After finishing the article, I feel mostly calm and relaxed. That's when Agent Logan and Mom trade seats. I glance at the agent. He takes up so much more space than my mother. The scent of tobacco and soap follows him.

"Nothing to be alarmed about," he tells me in that low drawl of his. "I just want to have a little chat before we land. I want you to be prepared. That okay?"

I appreciate that he asks, but I don't think me saying no would stop him. I nod.

He relaxes, seems to melt into the seat. He's a very big man. I wonder how he finds shirts with long enough sleeves. Does he have to get his clothes specially made? What must it be like to be so tall and strong? Powerful?

"Great. I want to talk to you about what happens when you speak with Lake, all right?" He looks at me and waits.

"Okay," I say, my voice almost completely lost in the drone of the jet engines.

"You don't have to do anything you don't want to do—that's the first rule. If you start feeling uncomfortable, there will be someone nearby to get you out of the situation. Me, probably. Lake will adapt to whatever boundaries you set before he tries to break them down."

I swallow. I hadn't thought of that. I agreed to this to help the FBI, but I hadn't really thought about what sitting down with a serial killer was going to be. "Am I going to be in danger?" I ask.

Agent Logan shakes his head. "Honestly, I believe you're the last person Lake would hurt physically. Right now, you're useful to him. You're a part of him. He will honor that as much as his antisocial personality will allow."

Physically. He won't hurt me physically. Doesn't mean he won't do his best to mess with my head.

"Don't try to draw information out of him. You're not a cop, and you're not there to interview him. Just let him talk. You don't have to tell him anything you don't want to, and you are allowed to lie your ass off to him if you want." He smiles slightly at this. My lips smile back, as though I have no control over them.

"Won't he know if I'm lying?"

"If you can make your mother believe you were truly at a sleepover last weekend, you can probably make anyone believe just about anything you want." He chuckles as heat blooms in my cheeks. I forgot he'd been watching the party.

"Also, don't believe everything he tells you. These guys like to lie and brag themselves up. They can't seem to help it. We'll have the room wired with both audio and cameras, so we'll be the ones to parse through what he tells you. Your only job is to listen. And to engage him, *if* you want. Remember, he wants you to be interested in him. He *needs* you to be interested in him. And that gives you the upper hand, doesn't it?" It comes out as *dunnit?*

My eyes narrow. "Agent Logan, are you intentionally trying to good-ol'-boy me into relaxing?"

He laughs. It changes his face. He's pretty good-looking for an old guy. When he speaks it's with a very strong, very put-on accent. "Why, yes, ma'am. I suppose I am tryin' to put your mind at ease. Is it workin'?"

I smile. I like this guy. I really don't want to, because, well, he's a fed. But he seems like a nice guy. And Mom really seems to trust him. She doesn't trust anyone.

"A bit," I admit. "So, all I have to do is let Lake talk at me?"

He nods. "Obviously, things will go a lot smoother if you engage him in conversation, follow his leads, but I don't want you putting yourself at risk. As much as I want the names of these girls, I don't want you to feel like you're being thrown to the wolf, so to speak."

"Okay."

"The most important thing for you to do is to stay as calm as you can, and don't let him get to you. He may try to fool you into thinking he's got the power, but he's a dying man with nowhere to run."

And there it is. Lake may have been a monster at one time—something to fear—but he's not anymore. I wonder if Agent Logan knows how much he's just made this whole situation easier for me. "I'll remember that," I promise.

"Good." He smiles slightly. "I've got some work to do before we land, so I'm going to give your mom her seat back. And in case I haven't said it enough already, though—thank you, Scarlet. You have no idea how much I appreciate you doing this."

"Thanks."

He gives my arm a pat—a very parental gesture of approval—before unfolding his large frame from the seat. He can't even stand completely straight in the middle of the aisle. Flying has to be such a pain in the ass for him.

Mom slips into the space he vacated, and I feel the sudden exchange of air. The lingering scent of tobacco gives way to the smell of her shampoo and body lotion. It strikes me as funny how well I know her scent, but I have no idea of my own. Do I smell as much like home to her as she does to me?

She drives me crazy with her rules, and I'm still conflicted over her lying to me my whole life, but I love her. I can't imagine what she's gone through, and she's done it alone. Not like I was any kind of support.

I put my hand over hers. She looks surprised but glad. I keep my fingers entwined with hers for the rest of the flight. She doesn't make a big deal of it. Doesn't even mention it. She just holds my hand like I'm five and we're about to cross the street. I know she won't let me go.

We land minutes after two. Our bags are carry-on, so we skip baggage claim and head straight to ground transportation. It's sunny in Raleigh, and there's no snow.

"It's a little chilly," Agent Logan says. "Right around fifty."

He thinks fifty degrees is chilly? He hasn't spent much time in New England. I know kids at school who'd wear shorts on a day like this.

We're picked up by another agent. "We'll go to Central first," Agent Logan explains. "Then I'll take you back to the house for the evening." We're staying with his family for the weekend. He probably thinks I'll bolt if he doesn't keep an eye on me.

"We're going to the prison *now*?" I try to keep the fear out of my voice.

Mom's hand settles on my arm. "It's okay."

"It's like a Band-Aid, kiddo," Agent Logan says. "Better to rip it off and get it over with."

I glare at him. "What the fuck do you know about it?"

Mom's fingers tighten. "Scarlet, you do *not* talk like that." Then to Logan, "Andy, I'm so sorry." My cheeks burn with shame. He was so nice to me on the plane and I was just an ass to him.

"It's okay, Gina," he says. "Scarlet, I don't know anything about having a father like Jeff Lake, you're right. But I've met more monsters than you can imagine. I would have been stupid not to be wary of every damn one. You're smart to be scared, but waiting another day isn't going to make it any less scary. It's only going to give you more time to think about it."

He's right. I hate that he's right. "I'm sorry," I say, looking away. Mom's grip loosens. She gives me a squeeze.

"You've done nothing to apologize for," he says, "but thanks all the same." Then he and Mom start talking about how much—or how little—things have changed since we left. It's obviously not a conversation I can join. I have no memory of this place.

This is where I was born. I guess it's technically home. I wait to feel some kind of connection, but it doesn't happen. It's just a new, strange place.

There's traffic, of course. Raleigh's a city, after all. I tilt my face toward the sun and close my eyes. Not like I'm going to miss much scenery on the highway, and the sun is so very, very nice.

Even with the delay it doesn't take much more than thirty or forty minutes to reach the prison. By the time we get there my butt is sore from so much sitting. It's pretty much all I've done for the last five hours.

"He's in the prison hospital," Agent Logan explains. "So, you won't have to visit him in the actual visitation areas. It'll be a little more comfortable for you."

I nod. If he says so.

"More privacy as well," he continues. "Y'all won't have to deal with nosy people."

It was decided that we'd try to do this as quietly as possible to keep the chance of word getting out to a minimum. Agent Logan made it very clear that he takes our privacy very seriously. He wants us to be able to return to our lives and go on living as Gina and Scarlet. That's nice of him, I guess, but we really can't go back now, can we?

Beside me, Mom fidgets. I never thought how nervous she must be. Fuck, I'm a real princess today. To me, Jeff Lake's a monster, like Dracula or Buffalo Bill. He won't be a real person until I see him, but to Mom . . . well, he's what she's been running from for the last sixteen years. He was her husband. She loved him. Somehow. Finding out the truth about him must have been awful and painful.

What's weird is that she looks more rested than I've ever seen her. It's like finally having me learn the truth has allowed her to relax.

I take her hand in mine and squeeze. Her fingers are like ice.

"We'll get you checked in and then move on to the hospital," Agent Logan says as we pull up to the main gate. "My office has already made arrangements, so it oughtn't take long."

The gate slides open for us, and as we pass through, I'm struck by a feeling of dread. In film class we talk about the hero's journey and story structure. If this were a movie, I'd be on the threshold right now, about to step into a magic new world where I, the hero, will face several trials and meet many friends and foes. In all the ways I imagined my life playing out, never once did I entertain visiting a prison as a defining moment.

Central Prison is where they send the worst of the worst, I

read online. The state doesn't send you here unless you've got a sentence of ten years or longer—or you've been sentenced to death. Jeff Lake had been given the death penalty by the state of North Carolina, but they never got around to killing him—mostly because they were hoping he'd eventually give them the names of the rest of his victims. They probably could have gotten this information out of him years ago just by threatening to end him. I'm glad they didn't. There's no way I could have done this at eleven, or even fifteen. I can barely do it now and I'm almost eighteen.

The prison could be a school—beige brick all over with a sprawling campus. Only the high chain-link fencing with wire along the top gives it away as something more sinister. An old stone wall with a guard tower on it looks weirdly out of place.

"That wall's all that's left of the original prison, I believe," Agent Logan says, like he's a freaking tour guide. I don't say anything, but Mom makes a little "mm" sound.

"Have you been here before?" I ask her.

She gives a rueful sigh. "This is where he was held while awaiting trial, and during. I visited him here a lot, at first. But it got more and more difficult as the press coverage increased. Plus, they thought I'd helped him try to escape that time. Remember that, Andy?"

Agent Logan raised a brow. "He got ahold of a pair of scrubs and tried to sneak out with a pharmacy tech. They thought you might have gotten the scrubs to him."

"They searched me every time I came in. There was no way I could have gotten them to him."

My heart pounds in my ears. "He didn't get out, though."

Mom squeezes my hand. "No, sweetie. They caught him."

"That wasn't in the movie."

"Well, I suppose the powers that be didn't want to look

bad." She says this with a slight smile. Her voice has changed since we landed. There's a drawl in it. Is this how she's supposed to sound? How much of herself has she changed to hide from her ex-husband? Isn't that like a prison itself?

The medical center is another nondescript beige building. We park in the lot and get out of the car. I'm sweating under my sweater. My legs feel unsteady as we walk across what little bit of parking lot separates us from the building. Agent Logan presses a buzzer to be allowed inside. The guard with us speaks into the intercom—tells them who we are. When the door opens, he holds it for us. I have to force myself over the threshold—literally and metaphorically.

Inside, we have to go through a metal detector and give them ID, even though Agent Logan is with us. He has to turn over his gun. A female guard is there to pat me and Mom down—it's not as embarrassing as I thought it would be, but she doesn't look me in the eye. No one's looked either one of us in the eye since our arrival. Maybe they do that with every visitor, or maybe it's just us.

"Any underwire in your bra?" she asks me.

"No," I respond as her fingers brush under my arms. "I was told to wear one without it." There'd been a whole list of things we weren't allowed to wear.

"You're good," she says, and moves on to Mom.

"No touching," another guard instructs me as we walk. Mom is beside me—she wouldn't let me come alone. "If the inmate tries to give you anything, do not take it."

"I won't." It stinks in here. I want to breathe through my mouth, but I'm afraid I'll taste whatever it is. It's antiseptic, but also like years of dirt and blood and shit and death have soaked into the concrete. It's awful.

"He's restrained," the guard continues, "but you should

keep out of arm's reach regardless. There will be a guard stationed outside the door in case you need assistance."

We nod when we're asked if we understand. Shake our heads when we're asked if we have any questions. Mom takes my hand as we approach the door to the medical ward. I haven't held her hand this tight since I was a kid.

"Is he expecting her?" she asks the guard.

"He was briefed just before you arrived. We didn't want to give him a chance to plan anything."

Plan anything? What would he have planned? A mariachi band? A welcome banner?

The guard unlocks the door and leads us through, down a corridor that has a light flickering overhead. I hear a buzzing sound, but I'm not sure where it's coming from. There's another locked door and then we're in the actual hospital section. I expect it to look like the movies—an armed guard posted outside the room, all kinds of high-tech security to keep the monster inside.

There's really nothing. Just a door. I mean, there are guards around, but it's not what I expected for someone who has done everything Jeff Lake has.

"If there're any problems, call for the guard," we're told.

"Is he sedated?" Mom asks, her fingers tightening around mine.

"Depends on if he's having a good day or a bad one," the guard explains. "Painwise, it seems to come and go. Given the circumstances, we thought it best to give him a little extra to keep him calm." He smiles at me, but it does nothing to make me feel better.

The door is thick and there's a small window that lets me see inside. A man lies in a bed. His body looks thin and frail beneath the blankets. His cheeks are sunken in and covered in blond and gray stubble. His hairline is receding, and his skin has a weird yellow color to it. If I have to assign him a monstrous form, I'd say he looks like a fresh zombie. The rot has started, but it hasn't taken over.

I don't feel anything as I look at him, though I should. I should be afraid or disgusted, or even a little anxious, but instead I'm completely numb as I stare at Jeffrey Robert Lake, one of the most notorious serial killers of the twenty-first century. My father.

"Ready?" Mom asks.

I glance at her. Her face looks as pale as mine feels. I smile weakly. "Time to rip the Band-Aid off."

I just hope I don't hemorrhage.

Chapter Eight

The guard unlocks the door.

"Last chance," Mom whispers, her cool fingers slipping through my clammy ones.

I shake my head. Ripping off the bandage. "I'm ready."

I don't know what I expected. I guess I thought I'd go in alone? But I'm not. The guard enters first, then me and Agent Logan. I'd forgotten he was even with us; he's been so quiet. Gone is the nice man who sat with me on the plane. He's all agent—intimidating and serious. Mom stays outside. I miss the comfort of her beside me, but it's better that she doesn't come in. No one wants to give her ex-husband the chance to use me against her.

Jeffrey Robert Lake—serial killers apparently like to use their full names?—opened his eyes as soon as the lock clicked. Either he's a light sleeper or he was faking.

His gaze is bright. Too bright. Maybe it's because he looks gaunt and gray—so close to death—except for those glittering eyes. He looks at the guard, at Logan, and then . . . me.

My heart clenches. His eyes widen ever so slightly when his gaze falls on me. Are the tears that suddenly well up real, or did he conjure them from some sense of how a father *should* react to seeing his daughter for the first time in years? It just doesn't feel sincere to me.

"Britney," he whispers. His voice is a low, gravelly drawl. Sandpaper and velvet.

"Scarlet," I correct, forcing myself to stand up straight. Agent Logan stands beside me, a looming support.

"Right," Lake corrects himself. "Forgive me."

I expect a cutting remark, but nothing comes. He wipes his eyes with the backs of his hands and makes a good show of pulling himself together. "Would you come closer, darlin'? I'd like to take a better look at you."

I move farther into the room, noticing the sounds of medical equipment and the smells of sickness mixed with industrial cleaner. Lake has an IV, and there's a bag hanging off the bottom of his bed half filled with a brownish liquid. Piss, probably. It would be easy to think there isn't any monster left in him. So easy to dismiss him as frail and useless, if it weren't for those fucking eyes of his. I can't dismiss those.

I stop at the foot of his bed. Agent Logan's presence is solid behind me. Supportive. I feel even worse for snapping at him earlier.

Lake smirks over my head. "You gonna hover like a mama bird the whole time she's here, Andrew?"

"Until she tells me she's comfortable by herself," Agent Logan replies in a neutral tone. "How are you feeling today, Jeff?"

Lake tilts his head. "Oh, you know. The pain comes and goes, but that doesn't matter now that my little girl's here."

His eyes glitter like sapphires as his gaze returns to me, taking me in from head to toe. "Look at how beautiful you are. You're almost the spitting image of Mama. It is so good to see you, darlin'. So good. I imagine this must be pretty strange for you, huh?"

I nod, trying to ignore the pinpricks of sensation running down my arms. There's nothing to get panicky about. I'm safe. I'm not in danger. He can't hurt me.

Lake's gaze narrows. "They tell you why they're finally letting me see you?"

Another nod. He's going to see how terrified I am if I keep this up. I clear my throat. "Because you said you'd give me the names and locations of your remaining victims."

He grimaces. "I don't like how that sounds."

"Neither do I, but it's true, right?" I force myself to look him in the eye and not look away.

A little grin curves his lips. He looks something like a hawk about to gobble up a mouse. "Such spirit. Yeah, there's some Lake in you all right. Allie didn't manage to squeeze it all out. Where is she anyway? I was hoping to say hi."

A little shiver runs down my spine at his hopeful tone.

"She's not far, Jeff," Logan replies. "But seeing her wasn't part of the deal, remember? You want that, we're going to have to renegotiate."

So cool. So clipped. As if my mother and I are components of a business transaction instead of people. I know that's how he needs to talk to this man, but it feels so detached. Reminds me that Mom and I don't really matter. We're just game pieces for Lake and the FBI to use against each other. Pawns. Agent Logan's just more up-front and nice about it.

Lake makes a *tsk*ing noise. "Allie would never agree to see me."

"She might if I asked her to," I hear myself tell him. We're only a few minutes into our first meeting and already I have to remind him I'm here.

And remind him that how this goes is up to me. Not him. Not going to lie, it's a bit of a power trip to suddenly see that change in his expression when he looks at me. When he realizes that I could get him what he wants.

He must think I'm so stupid and naive. Does he really think I'd just offer my mother up to him so he can finish destroying her?

"Yes," he agrees. "She'd do anything for you, wouldn't she?"

He's jealous of me, I think. Maybe he even blames me for her leaving him. I need to remember that. "She would," I reply.

"You are a pleasant surprise, Bri—Scarlet." Lake smiles. He knows what I'm doing. The biggest mistake I can make is think I'm smarter than him.

"Should I take that as a compliment?"

"You should." He nods. "You should. You missin' school to be here?"

"I'll make it up."

That smile grows. His teeth look too big for his mouth. "I bet you're a smart one, huh? Honor roll?"

I shrug. "I do okay." Actually, I do freaking great. Mostly because I know Mom will cut me some slack if I do well in school.

Lake chuckles. "Yeah, you're a smart girl. What do you want to do with your life? Law, maybe?"

He'd like that, wouldn't he? It's what he studied. "Actually, I want to make movies."

He sits up a little straighter. "Really? What kind? Not like that garbage they made about me, I hope?"

"Yeah, Mom said they got a lot of things wrong."

He arches a brow. "You watched it?"

I probably shouldn't have said anything. Or was it the right thing? I have no idea how to talk to him, despite Agent Logan's prep on the plane. I don't know what will please him and make him more cooperative and what might make him angry. I'm doing most of the talking and I'm supposed to be listening.

"I did."

"Before or after you knew it was about your old man?"

"Both."

That seems to please him. "I bet knowing the truth lent a whole new dimension to the viewing experience, didn't it?"

"Yeah."

He leans forward slightly. His collarbone juts out beneath the neckline of his hospital gown. "Did it make you see your mama differently?"

My heart rate jacks up. I draw a calming breath. "It made me feel sorry for her."

"I imagine it would. Certainly made her out to be the injured party, didn't it?"

"One of them," I reply, looking him straight in the eye.

He laughs. For a second I think he's mocking me. "What spirit! Oh, Logan. Thank you so much for bringing her to me." He leans back against his pillows, gazing at me with an expression that looks like tenderness but feels predatory. He lays a long hand over his heart. "I've never felt fatherly pride before."

He's playing me, right? Lying is what he does, but his words cut clean through me, laying open a place in me that always wanted a father. A place that always wondered if the phantom dad I'd created in my head would be proud of me.

I don't need this man's pride.

I don't want it.

He probably doesn't even really feel it. I'm just a reflection of him. A mirror.

He watches me. Waiting. I smile. That's what he wanted. My stomach twitches, but I'm okay.

Suddenly, Lake's expression darkens. He turns that freaky gaze of his to Agent Logan. "Stop hovering, you damn ape. You're not her father, I am. I want to talk to my daughter alone."

"Scarlet?" Agent Logan asks in that careful monotone.

My heart pounds against my ribs. Anxiety flutters in my stomach. But he'll be right outside the door. I just want this to be over.

"It's okay," I say. "He's my father." It was the right thing to say, I think. I'm supposed to play to his ego when I can. Keep him agreeable. Keep him talking.

Agent Logan's hand touches my shoulder, warm and strong, then disappears, leaving behind a cold patch beneath my shirt. I don't turn to look at him, but I hear the door open and close as he walks out. He'll be able to watch through the window with Mom if he wants. And I know they can hear everything that's said in this room, but I have no idea where the microphone is. There's a camera in the far corner of the ceiling. Every moment, expression, and word are being recorded and documented.

We're alone, me and Lake. I don't know when the guard left, but it's just the two of us. I grip the edge of the railing at the foot of his bed. The metal is cold against my sweaty palm. So nice. It's hot in here. My underarms are damp.

"Are you scared of me?" Lake asks, assessing me from his pillows. I can't read his expression.

"A little," I admit. "Do you want me to be?"

He seems surprised that I've asked—like it's not polite. "Of course not. I'm your father."

I tilt my head. "I'm not sure they're mutually exclusive."

"Well, listen to you. You sure you don't want to be a lawyer?"

I've pleased him. I don't like how the realization resonates with my sense of pride. "I'm sure."

Silence falls between us as we conduct a battle of wills through a staring contest. Waiting. Which one of us will give in first?

Lake yawns after what seems like an eternity. "Whew! I am bushed! Sorry, darlin'. Can we pick this up another time? Maybe tomorrow?"

That's it? I try to hide my surprise, but I'm sure I do a suck job of it. He hasn't given me a name. Hasn't given me anything.

Did he just want to get Agent Logan out of the room? Was this all about seeing if I'd be alone with him? Or did he want to get me to admit that I was afraid of him? I don't understand.

"We're done!" Lake calls out. "Logan!"

I glance around, still confused, as the door opens and Agent Logan appears. He doesn't look surprised by the turn of events. "Come on, Scarlet."

"Bring her back tomorrow," Lake instructs him.

I want to tell him to go fuck himself, to shove his games up his decaying ass. I don't, though, because it would give him way too much joy.

"If she wants to come back, we'll come back," Agent Logan tells him. His palm settles against my spine.

"You want to come back, don't you, Scarlet?" Lake pins me with the weight of his gaze. The whites of his eyes have a yellow cast to them. It's the cancer, I imagine. What's it like to know you're approaching your expiration date and still feel like you need to exert control by playing games with everyone around you? Feels pretty desperate to me.

I shrug. "I guess. If you feel up to it." I can play games too, asshole.

"I'll be fine," he replies in a clipped tone.

"We'll check with the nurse tomorrow morning," Agent Logan informs him.

"Take care of my girl, Logan." It sounds like a warning.

"Oh, she's in good hands, Jeff. Both of them are." There's no denying the intent behind his smile. Lake's jaw tightens. The clenched muscle stands out in stark relief beneath his lean cheek. "Come along, Scarlet."

"See you tomorrow, *Scarlet*," Lake says.

I flash him a smile. "Bye, *Dad*." The word tastes like shit on my tongue, but it's worth it to see Lake look like he's been punched in the face.

As the door closes behind us, Agent Logan gives me a gentle push toward Mom, who's waiting down the corridor, chewing on her thumbnail.

She rushes toward me, opening her arms. I throw myself into her embrace. I'm shaking.

"Are you okay?" she asks, her hands smoothing my hair.

"She's more than okay," Agent Logan says, his voice full of so much pride I look up at him in surprise. He smiles down at me. "You were fucking brilliant, sweetheart."

Psychology Today

Manners and Rage: An Examination of the Crimes of Jeffrey Robert Lake

April 3, 2020

Few serial killers capture the American imagination as Jeffrey Robert Lake has. Despite being relatively "new" to the cabal of notorious murderers the media holds in fascination, Lake has risen to the ranks of Bundy or Dahmer in the 14 years since his arrest in April 2006, a feat that bears examination given how almost banal serial killers have become in our society. Perhaps this popularity is due in part to *The Gentleman*, the Oscar-winning biopic about Lake's life and crimes, or perhaps it is his cover-model good looks and Southern charm. Regardless, there is no denying that his story sells.

At the time of his arrest, Lake was in his thirties, a lawyer with a lovely wife and baby daughter. Everyone who knew him described him as a "good man." He was held in high regard by his colleagues. Even more so than with Bundy, the truth of Lake's nature seemed to shock and devastate those close to him, who saw only what Lake wanted them to.

In reality, Lake was a wily and charming psychopath who kidnapped, raped and murdered at least 14 women in North Carolina from 1992 to 2006. Lake would charm women, convince them to go to a second location with him or force them into his vehicle. He would take them to a secluded area where he would rape—sometimes repeatedly—and kill them. He would often return to the site to perform sexual acts with their bodies. All 14 bodies were recovered from property belonging to the Lake family, but authorities believe there to be more victims based on the times of the killings and the months Lake spent living elsewhere.

Lake's cool composure and lack of empathy helped him elude capture and made him an efficient predator. He had no remorse. In fact, he denied having done anything wrong for years after his capture, until finally admitting to his crimes. To this day, he has withheld information about remaining victims from police as a way to maintain a position of power.

In terms of classification, Lake is a power/ control killer who has a need to dominate his victims. Because of this need, his killings were not about lust or attraction, but a desire to be in complete control. This is what led him to rape and sometimes torture his victims and gave him the power to decide when and how his victims ultimately died. This need also explains his engagement in necrophilia, the act ultimately allowing him to have complete control.

Lake has never openly discussed his desires, or the feelings that would follow giving in to them. He has been very careful about what he has allowed others to know, which, again, allows him to maintain control, even though he is in prison and hasn't been able to kill for almost a decade and a half.

Lake would give trophies from his victims to people he cared about, most notably his wife, Allison Michaels. Seeing the trophy on his loved one's person allowed him to remember the moment, recapture the fantasy and sustain the enjoyment of the murder.

If his looks, charm and complete lack of remorse and empathy allowed him to become such an efficient killer, his need for control and to revisit his victims is what got him arrested. After all, had the victims not been found on his family land, and had he not gifted their belongings to others, it is highly unlikely that anyone would have ever believed him capable of such atrocities. He often took pains to avoid leaving behind DNA evidence, but enough was found on several victims to strengthen the case.

By the same token, that need for control and power is what has kept Lake alive. He received the death penalty, but by admitting to the authorities that there are other victims, he has effectively kept himself alive and relevant. The skills that made him a fine lawyer are now being used against those who would uphold the law. There are those who think there aren't any further victims, that it is all a ploy by Lake to stay execution. However, many investigators believe there are more victims, and they are determined to find them. Meanwhile, Jeffrey Lake continues to exert his control at every opportunity. His antisocial personality disorder combined with his looks and charm made him an almost perfect killing machine— one that continues to fascinate us and make us question ourselves to this day. The question remains: Will Lake eventually give up the names of those remaining victims? Or will his need for control and power cause him to take them with him to the grave?

Chapter Nine

Mom has a million questions for me when we leave the prison. Thankfully, Agent Logan answers most of them. He's also the one who tells her that we're coming back tomorrow.

"I knew it wouldn't be easy," she says with a sigh. "It never is with him, but I hate the idea that he's going to drag this out as long as he wants."

"No," I say, turning away from the window. "As long as *I* want. If I say no, he's got nothing."

Agent Logan gives me a smile, but Mom's expression is one of worry. "Oh, honey. Never get in a pissing contest with a skunk."

I stare at her. Firstly, she's gone full-on Southern, and secondly, I'm not sure what the hell she means.

"You can't beat him," she tells me. "Don't even try. Just protect yourself. Andy, you tell her."

Agent Logan gives a little shrug. "Your mother is right, Scarlet, but so are you. It's not that you're not capable or smart—you were brilliant in there today, I want you to know that. But you're not a psychopath. He is, and his brain simply doesn't work like a normal one. Without the proper training, you can't possibly go toe-to-toe with him and beat him at his own game."

"I know," I inform him—them. "But he still wants something, right? If he thinks he's not going to get it, won't he give in?"

"He might. Or he might decide that taking the names to his grave is the ultimate power kick." Agent Logan gives me an apologetic look. "I don't have expectations of getting all the names, but I have to hope that he'll give you enough."

"How many is enough?" I ask.

"At this point, I'd settle for two." He shakes his head. "I meant what I said, though. You did really good in there. You came across as smart enough to be wary, but strong enough not to be cowed. You piqued his interest."

His interest. Wow. My father hasn't seen me since I was a baby. Doesn't even know me, and I've "piqued his interest." Meanwhile, I know exactly what kind of monster he is, and I still wanted his approval.

Fuck.

"What did you say to him?" Mom asks.

I shake my head. "Nothing important."

I catch Agent Logan looking at me, but he doesn't say anything about me saying I could get Mom to visit Lake, or even that I called him "Dad." It makes me like him a little more. Makes me trust him.

"I hope the two of you like pot roast," Agent Logan remarks, totally changing the subject. "Moira informed me that's what she's making for dinner."

I haven't eaten since the pretzels on the plane—hadn't felt like it—but my stomach growls at the thought of a home-cooked meal. Mom and I aren't much for cooking. Usually, we order takeout. Sometimes one of us will cook, but it's nothing fancy.

Now that I've seen Lake—and survived—I'm starting to feel like myself again. And I'm hungry.

Agent Logan shoots me a smile in the rearview. "Y'all want to stop for a coffee or something? Dinner won't be for a while yet."

He steers the SUV into a drive-through. I get a chai latte and a scone that ends up being almost as big as my head. I'll probably ruin my dinner, but I don't care. It's delicious.

I've just finished eating when we reach Agent Logan's house. The neighborhood is nice, with a lot of old houses. We pull into the driveway of a large Queen Anne–style house that's a pale fawn color with cream trim.

"You've painted," Mom remarks.

"Moira's idea. Some of Luke's friends started a house-painting business a few summers ago. We were one of their first projects."

"They did a good job."

"After I fixed all their mistakes, yeah. They did." He flashes her a grin before getting out of the car.

We get our bags out of the back of the SUV. I have a week-ender and my backpack with my laptop. No way was I leaving it at home.

Mom glances around, squinting in what's left of the afternoon sun. She's checking to see if anyone's noticed us, I guess. No one seems to pay us any attention, though.

We follow Agent Logan up the steps to the wraparound porch. The screen door is opened from the inside by a woman who is shorter than Mom and a few years older. She's pretty, though, with auburn hair and hazel eyes.

"There you are!" She greets us with a bright smile. Agent Logan bends down to give her a kiss that's a little deeper than I want to witness, and then she opens her arms to embrace Mom.

"Sweetie," she says. "It's good to see you."

"You too, Moira," Mom replies, returning the hug. We step inside, the door closing behind us. "Scarlet, this is Moira Logan."

"Look at you," Moira murmurs, giving me a once-over. It's so weird, all these strangers looking at me like they know me. I mean, come on, a baby has very little personality. I was like, what? Two when Mom bolted? There's no way any of them could have any idea of who or what I am.

"You're gorgeous," she says. "I'm going to hug you. I hope you don't mind."

"I don't." That's true. It's kind of nice, to be honest. She is soft and warm, and she smells like vanilla and nutmeg. What's not to like?

"Come in, come in. Luke! Come say hello and get these bags!" She rolls her eyes at us. "Boys."

"Oh, we can carry our own luggage, Moira," Mom tells her. "Don't bother him."

"Hello," comes a deep and unfamiliar voice.

I turn my head; so does Mom. Standing just inside the doorframe—the frame he had to duck to walk through—is a guy that I can only describe as gorgeous. Like, so gorgeous that the sight of him is like walking into an invisible wall. *Whack!*

He's built like a football player—wide shoulders and narrow hips. Long, denim-clad legs and biceps that bulge beneath the gray Henley he wears. His hair is dark brown with a touch of red and his eyes are just a little lighter. Strong jaw. He'd look amazing on camera, I bet.

"Hi," I manage.

Mom smiles. "Lucas. I cannot believe how grown-up you are."

He offers her his hand. "Nice to meet you, Ms. Murphy." His voice is like warm butter and sugar.

Mom accepts the handshake. "This is my daughter, Scarlet."

He offers me his hand too. I don't think I've ever shaken anyone's hand before—certainly not someone my age. His fingers are warm and strong.

"Hi, Scarlet."

Before I can respond, his mother shoves Mom's luggage at him, and my weekender as well. "Show Scarlet to her room, sweetie. I'll take Gina up. Feels strange to call you that after all these years, but I suppose I'll get used to it. Gina. It suits you."

I stop listening when Luke turns to leave the room. I am a sucker for a nice back, and, well . . . he has a really nice back. Wow. I don't even feel bad for appreciating him, 'cause it's not like Neal and I are officially a couple or anything. I just watch Luke move as I follow him through the house—which looks like something out of a magazine. Lots of antique and traditional furniture and light-colored walls.

He leads us up a large, winding staircase to the second floor. Then, down a hallway on the right. First door on the left is open, revealing a bright and sunny guest room with gauzy curtains and an ivory-colored quilt on the bed. He sets Mom's bags on the floor as she comes into the room, still chatting away with Moira.

"C'mon," he says to me. "Once Mom starts talking, she has a hard time stopping."

He leads me to the end of the hall, this time a room on the right side. Its walls are slate blue, and the curtains and bedding are rich shades of plum and wine with gray accents. I like it. It feels calming. Safe. Like I could make it as dark as I want.

Luke sets my bag by the desk and turns to look at me. "Did you meet him yet?" he asks.

There's really no need to define "him," is there? I nod.

"That must have been pretty weird."

I laugh. "That's one way to put it, yeah."

He considers me for a moment and then says, "I'm picking my sister up in about half an hour. We usually go to a park and hang out for a bit. Chill out. Want to come?"

There's something unsaid there. It takes me a minute to figure it out. *Chill out.* Is he asking if I want to get high with him and his sister?

"Or you could stay here," he adds. "With my mother. And yours." He smiles.

The smile is what does it. If I have to deal with a psycho father, I might as well bask in this gorgeous guy's company as much as I can. "No," I say. "I'll come with you."

"Great. Meet me downstairs in twenty minutes." And with that, he's gone.

Twenty minutes. That gives me enough time to clean up and reapply some deodorant and lip gloss. I feel like I've melted since landing. I've just pulled on a fresh shirt and brushed my hair when Mom knocks on the door. She takes one look at me fixing my makeup and arches a brow. "You're going out with Luke, huh?"

"And his sister," I remind her. I tense, waiting for her to say no.

"Have fun," she says. "I'll see you at dinner." And then she's gone, leaving me standing there, holding an open tube of lip gloss, wondering what the hell just happened.

Luke's car is a red RAV4 that looks like it's been around awhile. It's clean, though. Like, no fast-food wrappers on the floor or other garbage. I get in the passenger side and immediately end up with my knees pressed against the glove box.

"The lever for the seat is down there," he says, gesturing.

I ease the seat back into a more comfortable position. "Who's tiny? Your sister?"

"No."

Something in his voice makes me wince. "Sorry. Ex?"

"Yeah." He starts the engine, and we back out of the drive onto the street.

"Um, thanks for letting me tag along. If your mom or dad put you up to it, I'm sorry."

He shoots me a surprised glance. "No one put me up to it. I just figured you might want to get away from it for a while."

"Well, you were right, so thanks."

"No problem. Dad's a good guy, you know? But this case—Jeff Lake." He shakes his head. "He's been obsessed with him for years. I can only imagine what it's been like for you."

"I only found out this week."

Another glance. "No shit?"

I nod, smiling slightly. "Yep. Right after your dad showed up on our doorstep. Boom—bomb dropped."

"Harsh."

"I still can't believe it. I've literally looked Jeff Lake in the eye and I still can't believe that it's real."

We brake at a stop sign before making a left turn. "Can I ask what it was like? Being in the same room as him?"

"At the moment, 'weird' is the best explanation I can give you. Creepy too, I guess. He wasn't what I expected, but it's not like meeting your father should be."

Luke makes a scoffing sound. "I bet. Were you scared?"

"Yeah, sure. Mad too, though. 'Resentful' might be a better word. I don't know. I need to sort it all out, but I really don't want to think about it right now. It's a little much." I've already said enough that I'm second-guessing whether or not I should have.

"I hear you. Would you like me to give you a tour of the neighborhood, then? You can ask me questions."

I smile. "Like, how does the son of an FBI agent manage to get away with smoking pot?"

He laughs. "He gets away with it because he's careful and doesn't go home baked out of his mind."

True to his word, Luke plays tour guide. I see his former elementary school and the local library.

"That house right there is where my first girlfriend, Emmaline Beatty, used to live. Girl broke my heart."

That's a fairly vulnerable thing to admit. "How old were you?"

He gives me a wink. Somehow he makes it seem cute rather than cheesy. "Seven. Not sure I'm over her to this day."

"Probably just as well that it didn't work out with your last girlfriend, then," I quip. As soon as the words leap out of my mouth, I want to take them back. "Sorry, I—"

"No," he says, giving me a faint smile. "I was joking about Emmaline, but I think you're right. You know, everyone else has been telling me how sorry they are that we broke up, and every time they do I feel like an ass because I don't really feel that bad. No one else has said that maybe it was for the best."

Huh. I guess my inability to censor myself came in handy for once. "Well, it can be for the best and still hurt, I guess.

I don't know. I don't have a lot of experience with dating. Mom's been pretty overprotective."

"Marrying a serial killer will have that effect, I guess." He says it so matter-of-factly that I can't help but laugh. I laugh harder than I probably should. Certainly longer. It's the funniest thing I've heard in a long time.

"You all right?" he asks when I check for running mascara. "Thought I broke you there for a minute."

"I'm good. Thanks for that, though. I needed a laugh."

"Well, as with most things in my life, I wasn't even really trying to be funny, but I'll take credit if you want to give it."

We pull into the parking lot of a large redbrick building— obviously the high school—and come to a stop in one of the spots near the front doors. There is a group of students hanging out there, looking matchy-matchy in their uniforms.

I move to unbuckle my seat belt.

"Where are you going?" he asks.

I glance up. "I'm going to get in the back seat so your sister can sit up here."

"That's very nice of you, but if you think I'd rather have my sister up here than a pretty girl, you are sadly mistaken."

"We've known each other for thirty minutes and you're already breaking out compliments about my looks?" Talking to him like this—light and silly—feels comfortable and right.

"I would have said something right off the bat but all I could manage was hello." There's that wink again. What a flirt! I laugh because none of it is serious. None of it is weird or skeevy. He's just being nice. No threat at all. Obviously, he's better at the charm thing than his father.

Is that how *my* father did it? Charm them until they didn't see the danger they were in? I shake the thought off.

"All right," I allow, leaving my seat belt alone. "If it offends your sensibilities to have your sister sit up front, I'll stay where I'm at. I'd hate for people to make the wrong assumptions. After all, I know how you Southerners sometimes like to keep it in the family." I hold my breath.

"Fuck," he says, looking at me. Slowly, a big grin spreads across his face, and he starts laughing. I let out my breath and laugh along with him. After the last couple of days—hell, after the last few years—it feels good to just be foolish and not worry about it. What's Luke going to do? Tell Neal I'm weird? Whisper about me at school?

We're still chuckling when I spot a small group of girls leave through the main doors. I pick Darcy out immediately. She's the tallest of the group, with the same dark hair and eyes as Luke.

"Seriously, did your parents feed you two growth hormones or something?"

Luke laughs. "Dad is the shortest of his family. We get it from his side."

If Agent Logan is the shortest, I do not want to meet the giants that make up the rest of his family. Ever.

One of the girls flips her hair as she looks toward the vehicle. I'm fairly certain that's for Luke's benefit. She says something to the others and they glance over.

At me.

Shit.

Darcy says something to them, then obviously says goodbye and starts toward the vehicle. She jumps in behind her brother and immediately thrusts her upper body between our seats.

"Hi, I'm Darcy. You're Scarlet, right? Dad said you were coming. I totally lied and told Nichelle you were Luke's new girlfriend from college."

Luke and I both gape at her. "Why would you do that?" her brother demands.

She grins at him, revealing perfect teeth. "Because her sister is friends with she-who-shall-not-be-named and that cow will know all about it by tonight. I hope she loses her fucking mind."

Luke shakes his head, but he doesn't give her a hard time. I smile. "I have no objection to being used for such a good cause."

Darcy turns that grin of hers on me. "I knew we'd get along. Okay, let's go to the park. I want to have the skunk smell off me by the time we get home."

Is it weird that I feel at ease with these strangers? Probably. Or maybe not. They know who I am, and they don't really seem to care. I guess growing up with an FBI agent for a father, you get used to this kind of stuff. I'm nothing special. Just one more offspring of a nutjob. It's kind of comforting, actually.

We end up at what I would call a hiking trail more than a park. It's obvious the siblings have a spot in mind because we park in a particular section and Luke sets off toward a marked trail. It's a pretty place, and the sun is still fairly warm, even though it's starting to sink.

The walk is maybe five or ten minutes—seems longer than it is because it's unfamiliar to me. They could be taking me out here to kill me, or set me up, but I don't think so. That's the way my mother thinks. The way she's always wanted me to think, but I figured out a long time ago it was not a way I wanted to live my life. I'm not going to let who my father is make me less trusting now. I'm just not. I have instincts and I have faith in them. For the most part.

We veer off the main trail to one that curves into the woods. A few moments later we turn onto another that isn't marked by blazed trees. It ends in a small, circular clearing with several large boulders sticking out of the ground. There are four other people there—two guys and two girls.

"Hey," they chorus, looking at me with curiosity.

"Hey," Luke replies, and he shakes hands with one of the guys. I watch Darcy hug them all.

"Who's your friend?" one of the guys asks. He's tall with dark skin, close-cropped hair, and pale green eyes. I know the look in his eye. It's nice to have someone find me attractive, but that's a predatory gleam if I ever saw one. This guy's a player. Probably a good one.

"This is our friend Scarlet from up north," Luke replies. "Scarlet, this is Rhett, our resident ladies' man. Or at least he thinks he is."

Rhett laughs and sketches a bow. "I prefer to be called a charmer, but ladies' man will do. Nice to meet you, Scarlet." His eyes widen. "Hey, Rhett and Scarlet. We're like *Gone With the Wind*."

Darcy rolls her eyes. "What are you, like eighty or something? That movie's ancient."

I don't mention that it was a book first. I just smile at Rhett. "It's nice to meet you too."

The rest of them step forward. They're all really attractive, but in an almost careless way, as if they don't care. The other guy is Ramon. He's quiet but has a nice smile. The girls are Jessica and Mazy. Jessica is pale with hair the color of wheat and Mazy is dark with long braids, some of which have colorful pieces woven in.

"We've all known each other for most of our lives," Darcy explains to me. "Grew up on the same street. We meet here once a week to catch up."

So they're between my age and Luke's. Agent Logan said he was nineteen, right? In his first year of college.

Mazy, who's sitting lotus-style on one of the rocks, takes rolling papers and a bag of weed out of her purse. "You guys have never mentioned a friend named Scarlet before."

"We haven't seen each other in a long time," I say before I can stop myself. I catch Luke's gaze. He smiles conspiratorially.

We share a couple of joints between the seven of us—nothing crazy. I get the feeling that for them it's more to relax than get high. They all seem to be overachievers—honors students on the ambition fast track.

And then there's me, plunked in the middle of them. The one who wants to tell stories with film. I don't mind, though. I don't say much, just sit there, smoke, and listen to the rest of them talk about how much pressure they're putting on themselves so they can have the lives they want. Part of me wants to tell them that life doesn't care what they want, but why bother? Maybe they'll get thrown a curveball, maybe they won't. Maybe each of them will get exactly what they want.

Or maybe one will find out everything they thought they were is a lie. Maybe they'll find out that their father didn't abandon them, but instead is a monster in a maximum-security prison. Whatever, I'm high enough that it doesn't matter. I just have to deal. I can't worry about it. It won't change anything.

It's almost dusk when we leave. We file out of the woods together and down the path—a quicker walk this time—and into the parking lot.

Darcy lets me have the front seat. "Nice cover out there," she tells me. "How many years has it been since we've seen each other?"

"Ten," I respond. "Easy to remember."

"Mm," Luke agrees. "Maybe you should be a lawyer."

I laugh, even though it's an echo of what Lake said. My mouth is dry and bitter, but I feel loose and at ease. Luke offers me a piece of gum, and I take it while Darcy spritzes us with a little bottle of Febreze she takes from her bag. I make a face and roll down my window. "What the fuck?"

"It helps with the smell," she explains.

Coughing, I shake my head. "Yeah, because no one will think you've been doing something you shouldn't if you come into the house smelling like a laundromat."

Luke laughs and starts the engine. "She's right, Darce." He puts the windows down. "Let's see how much we can diffuse before we get home."

By the time we get back to their house, it's getting dark. All the homes along the street look warm and inviting. Inside, the Logan house smells delicious. There's gravy somewhere, I know it. My stomach growls, but Luke's is louder, and we laugh. I'm going to eat *so* much.

When we enter the kitchen, Mom's standing at the counter wiping her eyes. She's been crying. Instantly, my good mood disappears. I go to her, not caring if she'll smell the pot—or the damn Febreze.

"What happened?" I demand. "Are you okay?"

Sniffling, she looks up at me with a smile. "Oh, honey. Everything is wonderful. You're going to meet your grandparents tomorrow. Andy's arranged it."

My grandparents. Wonder blossoms inside my chest. Family. All my life it's been me and Mom and now . . .

I'm not even embarrassed when I start to cry too. These emotions—they're too much. I can't even explain them. I have family.

Mom and I don't have to be alone anymore.

Chapter Ten

In the morning, I wake with a mix of excitement and dread. Last night I couldn't get to sleep, so I spent the night running scenes from my favorite movies in my head, except the way I would have shot them. Eventually, I must have passed out, but the faint purple smudges under my eyes highlight how tired I am.

Obviously, I'm thrilled I get to meet my family, but before that, I have to see Lake. Agent Logan figured it would be for the best, so it wouldn't be hanging over our heads when we go to my grandparents'. That way we can spend as much time as we want with them.

Not going to lie, as I sit at the breakfast table in the Logans' nice house, the sun shining through the windows, what I really want to do is pop one of my anxiety pills or smoke a joint. Either would take the edge off, but I'm not going to take a pill unless I have to.

Mom has always said that my anxiety is no different from

having asthma or some other condition I'd have to take drugs to treat, and I know she's right. I mean, she's the one with the degree in what pharmaceuticals do to the human body. I just don't want to depend on pills or pot to get me through life unless it's medically necessary.

Mrs. Logan—Moira—has made a huge breakfast. I've never had anything like it outside a restaurant.

"Oh, my lord," Mom drawls. "You beautiful woman, you made grits." She immediately drops a ladle of the stuff on my plate. I stare at it. WTF? The smell of coffee and fried things teases my nose, and my stomach grumbles. Is that sausage? Oh, she made waffles too.

Luke saunters into the room, rubbing a hand through his already-mussed hair. He's wearing sweats and a T-shirt that pulls across his chest and arms. Seriously, the boy is built. He's almost too much with that bedhead going on.

"Good morning," he says to all of us. His smile lands on me last. "You ever have grits before?"

I shake my head. "Looks kinda gross if you ask me."

He chuckles. "Dump some syrup on them. Trust me." He pulls out the chair next to me and drops into it. Suddenly, the table doesn't seem nearly big enough anymore.

Maybe it's pathetic to be so aware of a guy I just met, but I've decided to enjoy it. He's hot and nice and I don't care why he's being friendly to me, I'm just glad for it. When he offers me the plate of sausage and bacon, I take a bit of each, then watch as he makes a small pile of each on his plate.

"Seriously?" I ask.

"I'm going for a long run later."

"Of course you are. God, no wonder you're single."

Every head in the room turns to look at me. Darcy starts

laughing even before her brother does. I flush, face filling with terrible, shameful heat.

"Scarlet!" Mom looks mortified.

But Luke laughs like I've said the most hilarious thing.

"I'm sorry," I say. "I didn't mean—"

Smiling, Moira sets a mug of coffee in front of me. "Don't you fret, sweetheart. We've been telling him the same thing for years. He spends so much time on school and sports and then wonders why girls get fed up with him."

"That and he's attracted to girls who are *drama*," Darcy chimes in, before taking a drink from her orange juice.

"Hey," Luke says, holding up his hands. "What is this? Attack Luke Day? I'm just trying to feed myself, man."

"Sorry," I murmur.

He turns to me, frowning. "For what? You didn't say anything wrong. You're absolutely right." Taking the maple syrup bottle in hand, he takes the liberty of pouring a swamp of it over my waffles, grits, and sausage. "If you want to make me feel better, you have to clean your plate."

"That might be impossible."

He winks. "I guess you'll have to make it up to me another way."

And now I'm warm for an entirely different reason. Fabulous.

After breakfast, Agent Logan, Mom, and I get into his SUV. "You don't have to come," I tell Mom for the second time as she buckles her seat belt.

"I'm not letting you do this alone."

"But—"

She turns her head. "No." And I know better than to argue when she uses that tone.

"Fine. But it can't be fun hanging out in a prison hospital

while the man who destroyed your life plays head games with your kid."

She pales even more. "It's not, but I'll do it." She turns to face the front, and I settle back, feeling like an ass. I watch her through my sunglasses.

Has she lost more weight? I don't like seeing her so thin. She ate more than I did at breakfast, so hopefully she'll put some pounds on. She's starting to look almost as gaunt as Lake.

My breakfast roils in my gut. If Mom were sick, would she tell me? What if I never found out about her family and she got sick and died? Where would I go? What would I do without her?

Oh, yeah. There comes my old friend, panic. I dig through my purse for my pills and dry-swallow two. Mom glances back at me with a frown. "You okay, bug?"

She hasn't called me that in years. I nod. "Just feeling it."

She hands me a bottle of water from her purse. She always seems to have exactly what I need in there, like it's some kind of magical portal. I twist the cap off and take a deep swallow. The pills that had stuck to the sides of my throat slide down to my stomach with ease. I lean my head back and wait for them to kick in.

"Everything good?" I hear Agent Logan ask Mom. She murmurs something I can't make out, but a few seconds later we back down the drive and onto the street, so I know she didn't pull the plug on today's visit. Honestly, I was almost hoping she would.

By the time I reach the door of Lake's prison hospital room, I feel more centered and chill. I can do this. He's just a man. A monster, but still a man.

Lake glances up when we walk in. He looks better today. His bed is raised so he's sitting up. They must have given him a bath and washed his hair, because it smells like cheap soap and shampoo instead of sickness. The bag hanging off the bottom of his bed has only a little bit of liquid in it, and his johnny shirt looks freshly pressed.

He smiles, stopping me in my tracks. It's not a smug smile. Not even a predatory one. I think maybe he's genuinely happy to see me. I'm not prepared for that.

"Darlin'!" he exclaims. "Don't you look fresh as a daisy this morning."

I think he might be trying to be polite? "Thanks. You look good too."

He preens as if I've given him the greatest compliment. "I used to look a lot better than this. Cancer has a way of destroying a man's ego as well as his body. But I don't want to talk about that, come sit."

There's a chair a couple of feet away from his bed. I guess it's for me to sit on so we can be eye level with each other. I'm not sure I want to be at his level, but standing feels awkward, so I sit.

"Sorry, Logan," Lake says with absolutely zero sincerity. "I don't have seating for you."

Agent Logan smirks. "That's okay, Jeff. I'm not staying. You've got an hour."

Lake's face descends into a frown. "That's it? I haven't seen my baby girl in years and you're giving me an hour with her?"

"Your doctor doesn't want you to overdo it," Agent Logan replies. "But don't worry. If you keep your agreement, Scarlet can come back another time."

Another time. I suppose I hadn't given it much thought, though I knew this wouldn't be a one-and-done kind of thing.

Not exactly realistic to think a master manipulator like Lake would accept me looking at him for a few minutes and then hand me a list of names.

Lake is processing what he's been told; I can practically see the information turning around in his head as he looks for how to best use it to his advantage. He turns that unnerving gaze of his—not as bright and manic today—on me.

"Do you want to come back again, *Scarlet*?" he asks.

"I guess it depends how this visit goes," I reply. It's the closest I can get to the truth without admitting that I'd rather poke my own eyes out.

His lips curl a little. "You mean if I give you what the FBI wants."

"I mean whether you treat me with respect or if you're an asshole."

He brightens at that. Chuckles. I have nothing to lose talking to him like this, but he likes it when I show backbone. He thinks I get it from him, so I might as well let him think about it. Anything to make this go as easily and quickly as possible. I do not want to give this man any more of my life than I have to.

"Girl, you are a delight," he tells me. Then to Agent Logan, "All right, you can get now. If all we have is an hour, I don't want to spend it with you hovering like a vulture."

Agent Logan merely inclines his head before putting a hand on my shoulder. "I'll be right outside, Scarlet."

Again, I see Lake's reaction to him taking an almost fatherly tone with me. He hates it, and I believe Agent Logan knows it. They're like teenage girls who both like the same guy. Ugh.

When the door clicks shut, Lake and I look at one another, holding each other's gaze in appraising silence.

"What do you know about me, child?" Lake asks.

"Only what I've seen in the media," I reply. "I know you gave my mother a dead girl's necklace."

He shrugs. "Everybody knows that."

"Can I ask why?" Ashley is going to die when I tell her I asked this. Am I allowed to tell her?

"What does the *media* say?" he asks with a disdainful sniff.

"That you got off on it. But that makes it sound like a sex thing, and it wasn't. Was it?"

He watches me for a moment. I've held my head that exact same way before. Looked at someone with that same gaze as I tried to figure out if they were sincere or not.

"No," he says. "It was never about the sex. Not really. I mean, that's part of it, but it's not *the* part."

"They say it's because it gave you power, which might be closer to the truth, but I'd like to hear it from you."

"You writing a paper or something?"

"You're my father, whether I like it or not. I'm never going to feel anything but revulsion for you if I don't try to understand you."

His gaze narrows as he leans toward me. Even if he lashed out, he wouldn't be able to reach me, so I don't move. Don't show fear.

"I wish I knew if you were sincere or just saying what Logan's told you to say. I don't know whether to be pissed or impressed that you can hide it this well."

I shrug. There is some pride in knowing I've thrown him, and that's a dangerous path, I think. "What does it matter? You and I only have a finite amount of time, right? We can waste it wondering about motives, but there's not much point. You know I'm here because the FBI asked me to come. And you only asked to see me because you're dying and figured you'd play whatever cards you have left. Maybe I'm curious about you as my father and maybe you're curious about me, but we don't need to play games with one another. I'm not really interested in doing that, to be honest."

"Yes." He drawls the word out. "I can see that. I suppose you're right. It doesn't matter what brought us to this moment, only that we're here."

I nod. "So, we can talk some if you want, or you can just give me a name and I can leave. It's up to you." I don't know if this bravado gives me the upper hand or not, but I feel in control, and that's good enough.

"You believe I'm just going to hand my girls over to you, huh?"

"You said you would," I remind him. "If you're not a man of your word, there's no need for me to be here. I can be content with only knowing you as well as Wikipedia."

He frowns. "You've got some of your mother in you, I see."

I shrug. "You're the one who married her, so don't blame me."

He chuckles. "I did. I thought for a while she might save me. My darker self went to sleep for a while after we got together. I thought she chased him away." His tone is so wistful I can't help but feel for him, as much as I don't want to.

"But she didn't."

Lake shakes his head. His scalp is visible through his thinning hair. It's so hard to see him as a handsome predator the way he is now. "No. She didn't." He clears his throat. "You asked why I gave her that necklace."

I nod.

His gaze narrows as his fingers pleat and unpleat the sheets covering him. "Do you really want to know? You may not like it."

"I don't expect to."

"I gave it to her because it was pretty. I gave it to her because looking at it reminded me of what I had done, and I liked remembering. And I gave it to her because she enjoyed when I gave her gifts. It made me feel like she was in on that part of my life, even though I knew she'd leave me if she ever found out the truth."

That was a much more complicated and chilling explanation than I thought I'd get. I could handle how he liked remembering—that's something all serial killers seem to enjoy—but that it made him feel like Mom supported him . . . well, that puts a sour taste in the back of my throat.

"You were right. She did leave."

He nods. "Took her a while, God love her." He laughs. "Not that God's got anything to do with anything, yeah? Poor Allie. She tried to believe in me. She wanted to believe in me, and that damn necklace is what finally showed her the truth. It didn't matter how much I lied anymore. She was done believing."

"Did you lie a lot?"

"You have to, darlin', when you're someone like me. If you want to have any semblance of a normal life, you must lie."

"Did you want a normal life?"

"I thought so. Once. But I started to realize that I didn't think like other folks. My brain's wired different. I didn't feel the things I was supposed to feel. Felt things I wasn't supposed to. I fought it for a long time and then . . ." He grins at me. "Well, you know what happened."

I try very hard to hide the shudder that ripples across my back. That smile is not a smile of a man who has any regrets. He's not capable of them. I *have* to remember that.

"They say you killed fourteen girls, but it's more than that, isn't it?"

He nods, never breaking eye contact.

I swallow. "How many more?"

"That's getting ahead of ourselves," he says in that smooth tone. Like a blade so sharp you don't even realize you've cut yourself until you see blood. "You were right when you said we only have so much time, but I'm taking as much as I can. After sixteen years of being denied my paternal rights, I'm entitled to as much of your time as I can take."

"Entitled?" I echo, with a scowl. "What, like you own me or something?"

"You're mine," he says emphatically. "No denying that."

"You gave up any right to me before I was even born. You lost that when you decided to murder."

His lips curve slightly. "Don't change that my blood is in your veins. You're part of me, child. Always have been. Always will be. If that don't make me own you, nothing does."

My eyebrows rise with my temper. "You're a dick," I tell him. "And I don't need to be here." I stand.

"You leave now, you'll never get those names."

"Don't care," I lie. "I don't think you are ever going to give them to me. You just want to grab what pathetic little control you can before you die. I don't want any part of it." I turn and walk to the door.

"Michelle Gordon!" he cries out.

I stop, heart kicking against my ribs. I turn. "Who?" The name is familiar. Didn't Agent Logan have a sheet about her?

"Michelle Gordon," he repeats. "Pretty little runaway from South Carolina. She was eighteen. Sweet. July fourteenth, 1994, is when I picked her up on the side of the road and gave her a ride. I took my time with her. She's buried in a hole in the woods not far from the middle school in Darlington."

I swallow, my throat dry and sticky. Agent Logan did have a sheet on her in his file. She's one of the girls he suspected of being Lake's victims. How many more will he be right about?

Lake's narrow gaze locks with mine. "I like you, Scarlet. I really do, but don't fuck with me, girl. I said I'd give you names, and I am a man of my word. Now, I don't feel like talking anymore, so you run back to Logan and give him that name. I'll let you know when I want to see you again, and you will come when I ask, or I will take those sweet girls to the grave with me, and you can live with that on your conscience for the rest of your hopefully very long life. I don't think you want that, do you? You strike me as an honorable person."

I stare at him.

He smiles. "That's what I thought. You run along, darlin'. I'll see you real soon. Love you. Logan!"

The door opens and there's Agent Logan to my rescue. It takes all my willpower not to run to him, but I refuse to let Lake see how freaked out I am. How terrified I am of him. Agent Logan takes me by the arm and escorts me from the room.

Mom is suddenly there, and the second her arms close around me I start crying. Not hard, not loudly. I don't want Lake to hear. It's not that he scared me that badly, or even that I'm horrified by the things he told me. I'm crying because he's got me trapped. He knows me so much better than I'll ever know him. I got into a pissing contest with a skunk, and I lost.

I don't want to live with the loss of those girls on my conscience. I can't. The next time Jeff Lake asks to see me, I'll have no choice.

I'll be there whenever he wants.

BatesNoTellMotel.tv

Early Warning Signs of a Serial Killer: How to Protect Yourself and Loved Ones Before It's Too Late

Serial killers are notoriously good at blending in with society. So good that when they are outed as monsters, their loved ones are often the most surprised. Luckily for us, experts say there are some common behaviors that show up in a psychopath's background.

1. Unemployment: Despite effectively hiding in plain sight, most serial killers have a hard time maintaining steady employment. This may be because of antisocial leanings, or because their urges are so overpowering that keeping to a regular schedule is impossible.

2. They're Smart: It's a popular misconception that serial killers are evil geniuses. This isn't necessarily so. Many have average IQs. However, they are incredibly intelligent when it comes to topics that aid them in fulfilling their dark fantasies. But those with high IQs tend to evade capture longer. Ed Kemper was only a few points below genius level.

3. They Like to Watch: Many serial killers start off as "Peeping Toms" like Ted Bundy. He liked to watch the girls in his neighborhood get undressed in their rooms. Another reason to keep your curtains closed.

4. Addiction Issues: In addition to being addicted to killing, many have substance abuse problems. Perhaps to numb the pain of their affliction, or to make it easier to give in to their urges. Regardless, if anyone close to you is abusing drugs or alcohol, intervention is a good idea. Just don't make it a solitary effort.

5. Terrible Childhoods: Often their formative years were filled with abuse and neglect. This kind of tragedy suggests the creation of a rage that may become impossible to control.

6. All in the Family: Many come from families with psychiatric issues or criminal connections. This social disconnect blends with the emotional and psychological to make it easier to view others as prey rather than see the world with empathy.

7. They Start Young: The preoccupation with cruelty and murder may start in childhood, either with animals or other children. Many serial killers (as many as 70 percent by some studies) have a history of animal cruelty and hone their skills on creatures such as cats or dogs.

8. Fire Starter: Many have a history of arson, as it is believed that fire is power, and power and control are driving factors for most serial murderers. Long before he became the Son of Sam, Berkowitz was known as "Pyro" and was rumored to have been responsible for more than 1,000 fires.

9. Loners: Antisocial behavior is a huge factor in the psychopathy of serial killers. Often the abuses they experience as children cause them to retreat into themselves, such as in the case of Jeffrey Dahmer, who became reclusive after apparently being molested. If an outgoing child suddenly becomes shy and withdrawn, seek professional assistance right away.

Chapter Eleven

One name. That's all I got, but it feels like *something*. Maybe it was just a bone, tossed to keep me at Lake's feet, but I can't look at it that way. Agent Logan was so happy with that little scrap of information, he hugged me for it. Told me I'd done good—that there were seasoned agents who hadn't held up as well against someone like Lake. I don't know if he was telling the truth or not, but it was nice to hear.

We went back to the Logan house after. Mom thought we should have some downtime before going to see her parents, and Agent Logan wanted to look into Michelle Gordon. I suppose he'll need to get a search team out to where Lake said he left her.

I need a shower. I had one earlier, but I need another one. This visit with Lake sticks to me like oil and dust. I need to scrub myself free of him.

When I come out of my room, dressed in clean jeans and a light sweater, I run into Luke coming out of his room across the hall. He doesn't look the least bit surprised to see me. Had he been waiting for me to come out?

"Hey," he says, softly.

"Hey." The corridor seems a whole lot smaller with him in it.

"How did it go?"

I shrug. "He gave me a name, so your dad's happy."

"What about you?"

I look away. Those dark eyes of his see too much somehow. "I'm okay."

"Meaning you don't want to talk about it."

"Not right now, no." I force myself to look up. "Thanks, though."

He nods. "A few of us are hanging out tonight if you want to come with. No big deal, but you're welcome to join."

"Thanks. Um, I appreciate you and your sister including me. You don't have to."

"I know."

I really wish he'd stop looking at me like he's trying to peer inside my soul. "I don't know how long we're going to be at my grandparents'."

He smiles. "Yeah. I suppose spending time with them takes priority."

"Kinda," I reply with a grin. "You know, especially since I have no previous memory of them. I might be kind of an emotional mess by the time we get back."

He holds out his hand. "Let me give you my number just in case."

I unlock my phone and open my contacts before passing it over. His thumbs tap over the screen quickly before he gives it back. "There. Text me if you want to join and I'm not around."

"I will. Thanks." A moment of awkward silence. I really suck at talking to hot guys. The only person I seem to talk freely with is Lake, and that's not something I want to think about too much. "I should probably go find my mom."

"Right. I have a game to get to anyway."

We walk downstairs together and into the kitchen, where our mothers sit together at the counter drinking tea, talking. From the looks on their faces when I walk in, I know who the subject was.

"I'm okay," I say, giving Mom a pointed look.

The arch of her brow strikes me as defensive, but all she says is, "I know you are. You all set?"

I nod. "How are we getting there?"

"Moira's lending me her car." Mom jangles keys. "I thought maybe we'd do a little tour first."

"If it's Emmaline Beatty's house, I've already seen it."

Luke laughs. "Right." He flashes me a grin before giving his mother a kiss on the cheek. "I'll be home after the game."

Once Mom has her purse and phone, we head out. It's another sunny day—cool, but certainly not as cold as it would be in Connecticut. I'm going to miss this weather when we get home tomorrow. I wonder when Lake will snap his fingers and expect the FBI to bring me back. Maybe he won't.

Moira's car is a cute little blue Mazda. Mom has to push the driver's seat back.

"So," she begins once we've backed out onto the street. "You and Luke seem pretty friendly."

I roll my eyes. "He's okay. At least you don't have to do a background check on him and Darcy."

She smiles. "No worries there." A quick glance out of the corner of her eye. "Luke's pretty cute."

"Cute"? That's like saying a redwood is a big stick. Like

calling a tsunami a "big wave." Way to undersell it, Mom.

"Mm."

"That's all you're going to say?" She shakes her head. "When I was your age, I would have been all over that."

"The hell?" She never talks like this, not to me. My entire life, men and boys were to be avoided. Dangerous.

She laughs. "I suppose I've shocked you." Her laughter fades. "Before Jeff, I was a normal girl, you know. I had lots of boyfriends. He ruined that."

"He ruined a lot of things," I remind her. "At least he'll be dead soon."

"Yeah. Being back here . . ." She sighs. "It's reminded me of everything I lost or gave up. I don't know how to feel. I'm happy, but I'm sad, and I wish to hell you didn't have to see him."

"Not going to lie, he's fucking scary. But if the information he gave me is real, it will be worth it. Like a bonus point with the universe, you know?"

"Yeah," she allows with a quick glance in my direction. "I know. I feel like I could use a few bonus points myself—especially with you."

"We're good." At least we are for now. "You excited to see your family?"

"Yes. And terrified. They're going to love you, though. Be prepared to be smothered with love."

"I'm totally okay with that."

As we drive, she points out landmarks to me—places she used to go or hang out, or something of historical interest. I've never seen her so animated. She's happy to be back here, I realize. Despite the situation, she's happier than I've ever seen her. Maybe some of it is not having to keep her secret from me anymore, but I don't think that's all of it. She's missed this place. She only left it for me.

My grandparents live in a quiet neighborhood about twenty minutes from the Logans' house. It's a large, white house with black shutters and a perfectly manicured lawn. There are three cars in the driveway. No huge welcome wagon. Good.

"It's just Mom and Dad and your uncle Garret today. We didn't want to call attention or overwhelm you."

"I have an uncle?"

"My baby brother." Her eyes are already a little wet. What's she going to be like once we get inside?

"It must have been so hard for you not to talk about them."

"It was." She grips my hand and squeezes. "But we can talk about them now. We can know them if you want. If we're careful."

Part of me doesn't care if people find out, but I understand where she's coming from. I only know some of what she went through when Lake was arrested, and that's bad enough.

We get out of the car and approach the house. I follow Mom around to the back door. It opens as soon as her foot hits the steps.

I don't know what I expected, but my grandmother isn't it. Trudi Michaels is little and curvy with bright blue eyes and dark hair cut in a shaggy bob. She looks younger than she is. She takes one look at us and starts crying.

Mom loses it right then. The two of them embrace on the porch, leaving me standing awkwardly to the side. My throat is tight, but the moment doesn't hit me like it hits Mom. I've never known this woman, so I've never been able to miss her.

But . . . when she releases my mother and turns to me, her mascara starting to run, something inside me breaks.

"My sweet girl," my grandmother whispers, reaching up to touch my face with trembling, reverent fingers. "Oh, my sweet, sweet girl."

Tears, hot and scalding, run down my face. I thought Lake drained my reserves earlier, but these are different. These are happy tears—something I'll never have for him.

"Hi," I whisper.

She pulls me close, into an embrace that smells of sugar and cinnamon with a hint of jasmine. My arms wrap around her ribs, holding her as tight as I dare.

I'm ugly-crying and I really don't care. All I've ever wanted is family. People who are mine and love me unconditionally. Someone to belong to other than my mother and the imaginary father who abandoned me.

"Oh, look at this," comes a gentle male voice. "Come inside, my lovelies, before you cause a flood."

I pull back. My grandmother doesn't let me go right away. When she does, I wipe at my eyes and turn toward that voice. The man in the doorway smiles, but his eyes are wet too. My grandfather Peter. He's tall and lean. Mom gets her build from him, but her features from her mother—mostly.

"Hi, Dad," Mom manages, voice breaking on a sob as he puts his arm around her and leads her into the house. My grandmother clings to me as we follow. I don't mind.

The house is warm, and the smell that I caught on my grandmother is stronger here. She's been baking. My mouth waters almost as badly as my eyes.

"Sunny," comes a voice. It's Mom's brother, I guess. Garret. He looks like a taller, male version of her. They hug and then everyone's hugging everyone and I have no idea what's going on as I'm enveloped in almost more love than I can possibly stand.

Finally, we're done. I wipe my eyes on the tissue Mom gives me and pull myself together. We sit at the kitchen table with warm cookies and glasses of sweet tea. My grandmother sits beside Mom, gripping her hand. My grandfather sits beside me.

The cookies are amazing. So's the tea. The only thing that dampens my enjoyment is the fact that I don't really look like these people. I have the same coloring as my grandmother and uncle, but my face isn't reflected in theirs. I wish it were.

"Tell me everything about you," my grandmother says to me. "Everything I've missed and need to know."

I glance helplessly at Mom. "I . . ."

"I've told you most of it," my mother says, coming to the rescue. "I sent you her school photo, right?"

"How?" I ask.

"VPN," she replies. "It's a wonderful thing. I use a USB drive at the library—look, I could be a spy."

We all laugh.

"It's just so good to have both of you here." Trudi blinks back more tears. "Where you belong."

"I suppose we need to discuss what you can call us," my grandfather says, smiling at me. He has a cookie crumb on his bottom lip. "Do you prefer Gumpy or Pops?"

"You don't look like a Gumpy."

"Pops it is." His grin is triumphant.

"He's always wanted to be a Pops," Uncle Garret explains to me. "He heard it on a TV show once."

"If you gave me grandchildren, they could call me whatever they want," Pops replies good-naturedly. "Didn't I give Scarlet a choice?"

"Well, I want to be called Nan," my grandmother adds. "Nothing pretentious about that."

Nan and Pops. I can handle that.

"I have no special request," my uncle says. "Garret will suffice."

"*Uncle* Garret," Mom corrects.

He rolls his eyes at her. I smile.

It's a lot to take in. Like, a *lot*. But it's amazing to see where Mom grew up. She takes me upstairs and shows me her old room. Pops shows us old home movies that he had transferred from VHS to DVD. I get to see my mother when she was my age.

"You look like a vampire," I remark. Pale, with dark lips.

She shrugs. "I was going through a goth phase. I wanted to look like I belonged in a Concrete Blonde video."

I laugh at some of the images of her. The goth phase didn't seem to last too long. There are snippets of birthdays and Christmases. All moments from her life long before me.

"Oh. We don't need to watch this," Pops says when a new clip comes up.

"Wait," I say. Then to Mom, when the screen pauses, "Can we watch it?"

She nods, lips thin. "It's okay, Dad. She should see it."

It's a Christmas video. Younger versions of these people gathered around me are seated in this very room—with different furniture, of course. A huge, beautifully decorated tree sits in the corner, piles of presents stacked beneath and around it. My mother's wearing a red minidress, and her dark hair hangs almost to her waist. A guy stands beside her, his arm around her waist. He has a drink in his hand—eggnog, maybe. He's wearing dress pants and a crisp shirt with a tie. The tie has the Grinch on it. He's blond and tanned, with intense blue eyes. He's good-looking and they make a beautiful couple. He looks at her like she's his entire world.

The woman he thinks can save him from the monster inside him.

It's not the Lake that I've met. This is Jeff Lake in his

prime. It's December 2000. He's already become a master of his craft. Britney Mitchell has been dead for years. That familiar shiver snakes down my spine.

"We were living in New York then," Mom explains. "Jeff wanted to make sure we came home for Christmas. He said it was important to be with family. He proposed later that night. In front of everyone."

Regret weighs heavy in her voice.

"He asked for my blessing," Pops adds, a touch of confusion in his tone. If he hasn't made sense of this—if Mom hasn't—how can I ever hope to reconcile who my father was? Is?

"Didn't he wrap the ring in a huge box?" Uncle Garret asks.

Mom actually laughs. "It was like those Russian dolls. I'd open one box only to find another inside. One of them had a potato in it!"

"Your father got up and went to make a fresh pot of coffee. When he came back, you were still unwrapping." Nan smiles.

"And then I got to the ring box." Mom shakes her head as if to fight off the memory.

"It was a good Christmas," Pops laments. I watch as his smile gives way to something that looks a lot like guilt.

I look at them—each lost in the memory of a happier time before they knew what Jeff Lake was, back when they thought he was someone good. Someone worth my mother's heart. There's nothing but regret and confusion in this memory. I know without asking that each of them wonders if there was anything they could have done differently. Anything that might have stopped my father from becoming the monster he was.

"You can fast-forward now," I tell my grandfather. "It's okay."

He does, but the damage has been done. I just wanted to

see my parents together. I never thought of the pain it might cause my family.

"I'm sorry," I say to Mom.

She shakes her head. "No, it was good for you to see. You don't have anything to be sorry for, bug. You're the only innocent here. The rest of us have to live with our choices, but you—you weren't given any. And for that, I'm so very sorry." She glances at the TV. "Dad, play that one."

The picture slows and begins to play. A close-up of a toddler with cake all over her face.

"Is that me?" I ask, squinting.

Mom chuckles. "Your second birthday."

Nan laughs too. "Oh, look at how much cake you had in your hair!"

They comment on how cute I was, and we watch as I smear cake and ice cream all over myself and run around a house I don't recognize, ripping open gifts and jabbering only semi-coherently.

No one mentions the man who's missing. They're much happier they don't have to look at him. In August 2006, Jeff Lake was in prison, awaiting trial. I didn't know what my father had done, and my mother still believed he was innocent. I shared a name with a dead girl, who had been found buried in the woods along with thirteen others.

My mother laughs at something I do on-screen and flashes me a bright smile. I force myself to smile back. She hasn't noticed what I have. When I look at her on the television, I see it.

She's wearing that dead girl's necklace.

I didn't say anything to Mom about the necklace. Putting my thoughts into words didn't seem possible. They were all so sharp but jumbled. I didn't know how I felt—I still don't.

It's late when we finally leave. I text Luke and tell him I'm not going to be able to hang out with him and Darcy. Once we get back to the house, I go straight to my room, leaving Mom downstairs with Moira and Agent Logan. Our flight leaves fairly early tomorrow morning, so I get everything ready for the trip. I even lay out the clothes I'm going to wear.

I just want to go. This weekend has been too much, and we only got here yesterday. I want to go back to Connecticut and my normal life and pretend that this part doesn't exist for as long as I can.

Maybe Lake will simply drop dead and I won't have to see him again. It'll suck for the families of those missing girls, and for Agent Logan, but at least Mom and I will be free.

I'm so selfish. I tell myself most people would be in this situation. I tell myself I can't be held responsible for horrible things that happened long before I was even born. I almost believe it.

Almost.

I flop onto the bed. Seeing Mom in that necklace, knowing who it belonged to . . . It's one thing to be told she believed Lake, but it's another to see it with my own eyes. At the time of my second birthday, she still believed he was innocent, despite fourteen bodies having been found on his property. Despite *everything*.

She loved him. I thought I understood that, but I'm having a hard time with it, to be honest. How could she? And how could she watch that birthday video and not think about it? She'd laughed and smiled the same as my uncle and grandparents through the entire thing. None of them mentioned Lake, even though he might as well have been with us in person.

The shock of my past is lifting, and I'm starting to feel things. Think things. And the first thing I always think about and can't seem to forget—maybe forgive—is how my mother married a killer and believed him innocent right up until she couldn't anymore.

It makes me question what kind of person she was then. I know she's not that person now. No one as paranoid as her would ever make that mistake again.

I unlock my phone and do a video search on "women who love killers." After a brief glance at the list, I see an interview with Ted Bundy's onetime fiancée, Elizabeth Kloepfer, and click on it. I need to understand, because I know myself. This agitation I'm feeling will make me say something stupid or mean, and I'll hurt Mom or start a fight. I don't want that.

I just want to go home.

In the interview, Kloepfer talks frankly about her relationship with Bundy and how she wanted to believe in him, but she also talks about how she eventually became suspicious. Despite that, she stayed with him. And even after his arrest, she would accept his phone calls. His letters. He wrote to her right up until his execution, even though he married another woman.

What the fuck?

I set my phone down on the mattress, facedown. If Mom hadn't left when she did, would she be getting monthly letters from prison? Would she be giving interviews talking about how much she believed in him, and the guilt she carries because of it? Would people pity her like I do this poor woman?

I have more sympathy for Kloepfer somehow. Back in the 1970s, we didn't know about serial killers like we do now. Monsters like that were incomprehensible. Mom knew better. Or she should have. Right?

Someone knocks on my door.

"Come in."

Mom slips into the room. She's had a couple of drinks. I can smell wine and her cheeks are flushed. Funny, she looks good. This trip has been like opening a window and letting in fresh air for her.

"I just wanted to check in before going to bed," she says in a soft voice. "You okay?"

I could tell her—confess how I feel. Ask her to explain it to me. "Yeah." I clear my throat. "I'm good."

She smiles. "Your grandparents didn't overwhelm you?"

My smile is genuine. "They were awesome. It's a lot to take in, but yeah. They were great. Thanks for letting me meet them."

The happiness drains from her face. "Scarlet . . . sweetie. I'm sorry. I know I made a mess of a lot of things for you, but I need you to know I did what I thought was best. I only wanted to protect you from my mistakes."

"And you were ashamed."

Mom nods slowly. "So ashamed. I still struggle with that. Moira says there may be times when you struggle with my shame as well. I want you to know we can talk about it whenever you want. I'll be completely honest with you, even if I don't want to be."

"Okay." Just not right now. "How would Moira know?"

"Oh, she's a psychologist. That's how she and Andy met— she worked for the bureau for a time."

Hm. Maybe I should talk to Moira. Or maybe Moira should mind her own fucking business. I sigh. I'm getting angry again, I really need to go to sleep. "I'm good, Mom. If I need to talk, I'll let you know."

She doesn't completely believe me—I see it in her gaze. I

think maybe she understands me better than I want her to. Way better than I understand her, at any rate.

"Okay." She nods. "Well, I'll let you get to sleep, then. Love you."

"I love you too." I mean it, but how can I love someone I don't really know? So much of her has been a lie.

She hesitates, then comes close enough to bend down and kiss me on the forehead. "Please don't hate me," she whispers. "I can stand the hate of anyone else. I can't bear it from you."

She's gone before I can reply, the door closing with a sharp click behind her. I wipe the damp of her spilled tears from my face with desperate fingers, wanting to erase every trace of her sadness. It's not because I despise her for crying.

I'm angry at myself, because I don't have any tears of my own for her, and I know what that means. I do hate her.

Just a little.

Chapter Twelve

TMZ News

JEFF LAKE
Daddy's Girl: Baby Britney Comes Out of Hiding to Visit Ailing Father in Prison

2/14/2022

After almost sixteen years of successfully avoiding the limelight, "Baby Britney Lake," aka Scarlet Murphy, has surfaced, along with her mother, Allison Michaels, aka Gina Murphy.

The following photos show the two leaving Central Prison in North Carolina on Saturday, February 12, after visiting with Lake, who has been incarcerated at the facility since his arrest in 2006.

According to Lake's current wife, Everly Evans, this is the first time he has seen his daughter since being apprehended for the murders of 14 women. Britney and her mother disappeared during Lake's trial in 2007 and have managed to avoid media attention until now.

Allegedly, he was diagnosed with pancreatic cancer, and his dying wish was to see his daughter. Evans went on to say Lake is "hopeful" that he and Britney will be able to forge a relationship in the short time he has left, and that he wants to die knowing he's "made peace with his past." The families of his victims may have something to say about that.

Of course, this also raises the question of any unnamed and potentially undiscovered victims out there. It's been speculated that Lake's actual victim count vastly outnumbers what law enforcement can prove, and the Federal Bureau of Investigation would like very much to get ahold of any other names before Lake's demise. When asked about other victims, Evans replied that her husband is "a man with many regrets, who wants nothing more than to earn the forgiveness of his daughter and the Lord." Apparently, he knows better than to hope for the forgiveness of his victims' families.

Now that Britney and Michaels are back in Lake's life, what does this mean for Evans? Will Michaels finally admit what she knew about her ex-husband's crimes? Will Britney hold up the family tradition of supporting her father? Is there a mother-daughter book in the works? That all remains to be seen, but Evans maintains that this father-daughter visit was not a onetime event, and that Lake is hopeful Britney will return to see him soon. "He doesn't know how much time he has left," Evans said, "and he wants to spend as much of it as he can with his family." She went on to say that she has not met Britney yet, but she hopes to soon.

So, where have Britney and Michaels been hiding all these years? A small town in Connecticut called Watertown, where Britney attends an elite school and Michaels works as a pharmacist—a job related to the Ph.D. she obtained while married to Lake. There have been those who speculated she might have given Lake drugs to sedate his victims, but it's never been proven.

As for Baby Britney, it's always been maintained that she is innocent of her father's crimes, but now that she's reunited with Lake, is it only a matter of time before she's tainted by association as well? And what of the families of Lake's victims? How will they react to his being able to see his daughter after he so horribly took away their own?

"What the hell is this?" Ashley shoves her phone in my face.

It's Monday—Valentine's Day. I'm alone eating lunch and I have no idea what the hell she's talking about. I glance down.

Oh.

Oh, fuck.

There's a photo of Mom and me leaving the prison staring back at me. It's not a good picture. We look tense and upset, holding each other's hands so tight you can see the tendons in our arms.

"*You're* Baby Britney?"

I lift my head. Meet her gaze. She's pissed. "Don't call me that."

"It's your name, isn't it?"

"No. It's not." I push her phone away. "My name is Scarlet Murphy, and it has been for a long time. What site is this from?"

"TMZ."

Double fuck.

"Do you know how stupid I feel finding out like this?"

"Yeah," Sofie chimes in, at Ash's elbow. "Pretty fucking stupid, Scar."

I don't like feeling ganged up on. I don't care how upset they are. "Well, I found out when the FBI showed up at my house last week, so get in line. And while you're at it, back off. My life is not all about you."

Sofie opens her mouth to say something, but Ashley stops her and slides into the chair across the table from me. "Last week? Seriously? You didn't know before that?"

I shake my head. "Mom never told me. I still wouldn't know if Lake wasn't dying."

"Fuuuuuck." Resting her forearms on the table, Ashley leans forward. "Is that why you were asking me those questions about him?"

"Yeah. Congrats, Ash. You know more about my father than I ever have."

She looks stunned. Had she really thought I'd kept this

from her ever since we met? I'm not that good a liar. It would have come out at some point—I know myself well enough to know that. Mom had been right not to tell me if she wanted to keep it a secret.

"I can't believe you're Bab—" I give her a sharp look. "Her. Did you really meet him?"

"Yeah." I push away my tray. I'm not hungry anymore. Mom is going to lose her mind. *TMZ of all places*. I thought we'd have more time.

Taylor shows up and takes the seat next to me. "Did you show her?" she asks.

Ash nods.

"She's *explaining*," Sofie adds, full of bite.

I look at her, eyes narrowed. "What's your problem?"

"You, the daughter of a monster. That's my problem."

That hurts. "Then go sit somewhere else," I tell her.

She looks surprised. "No."

"Then shut the fuck up." I turn back to Ashley, tap my finger against her phone case. "How did they find out? Does it say?"

"No, but they mention talking to Everly Evans."

I know that name. "Lake's wife?" At her nod, it falls into place. Asshole. "He played us. This was his plan all along."

"Swan song," Ashley comments, clearly following me. "He wants another fifteen minutes of fame before he dies."

I meet her gaze. "And he wants revenge on my mother."

Sofie snorts.

I ignore her. Honestly, I don't even know why I'm friends with her lately. When I don't speak, she gets up and leaves the table. Good riddance.

"Why did you meet him?" Ashley asks. "Because he's dying?"

"No. He said he'd give the FBI the names and locations of his remaining victims if I did."

Her jaw drops. "Scar, that's like an episode of *Criminal Minds* or some shit."

"Right?" I drop my head into my hands. "This is so messed up."

"I want to ask you so many questions right now."

I look up with a half smile. "Please don't. Later though, I promise."

"Sof's flapping her gums," Taylor says in a low voice.

I follow her gaze. Of course Sofie went to the table where Neal and Mark sit with their friends. They're looking over at me.

"Why does she hate me all of a sudden?" I ask Ashley. "I haven't done anything to her."

"Neal," my friend explains as if it's obvious. "She's had a thing for him since middle school."

She made out with him at a party when we were fourteen. I haven't heard her talk about him since. Pretty obvious he's not that into me if he's over there and not here, so . . . *Have at him, bitch.*

Ashley fidgets in her chair. "What was he like?"

"Ash . . ." Taylor's voice holds a note of warning.

"He was a monster," I tell her. "And he took great delight in telling me how he took his time with one of his victims. Is that what you want to hear?"

Her light eyes widen. "He talked to you about unknown victims? Who was she?"

I push my chair back so hard the screech echoes throughout the cafeteria. "I'm going home." I grab my bag and start for the exit.

"Scarlet, wait! I'm sorry."

I keep walking. My phone pings when I reach the hall. No one seems to notice me as I stomp toward the nearest exit, and I'm grateful.

The text is from Luke. You okay? I just saw it.

A sound between a laugh and a groan rasps up from my throat. A guy I've only known for a handful of days has just shown me more consideration than my closest friends and the guy I almost slept with last weekend combined. Seriously? Neal couldn't even come say hi?

I slam my palms into the door so hard, it hits the wall. Another door and then I'm out in the snow. Cold air hits me like a slap. I forgot my coat. Motherfucker. I stand on the walkway, shivering, debating my options.

"Scar!" Footsteps come from behind me. I turn to see Taylor running toward me, her feet slipping on the ice, my coat in her hands.

I grab the coat—and her—before she falls. Keep her upright with a hand on her elbow.

"Thanks," she chirps. "You really skipping?"

"Yes." I shove my bag between my knees so I can pull my coat on. "Want to come with? You left your vape at my house."

"Hells, yeah." She links her arm through mine, and together we continue down the walkway and across the parking lot to the street exit. As we reach the sidewalk, a car marked as belonging to a local newspaper pulls in.

My house isn't that far from the school—maybe a twenty-minute walk. The snow and icy bits make us a little slower. Not everyone has made sure the sidewalks in front of their houses are clear from the snow that fell last night.

"It's going to be okay," Taylor tells me. "You know that, right?"

"Sofie sold me out because she's jealous, and Ashley sits

me as a source of primary research for her future thesis. But, sure! It's all going to be Gucci."

"Well, I still love you."

I stop long enough to hug her, sniffling to keep my nose from running all over us both. "I love you too. Thanks." I refuse to cry out here on the street, so we keep on walking.

When we reach my street, I realize something's wrong.

There are news vans outside my house. More cars than normal parked along our street. Strangers standing in our drive and on our snowy lawn. They line the sidewalk in front. Voices rise, echoing as they drift toward me on the chilled air.

"Oh, my God," Taylor says.

They're here for Mom. They're here for *me*. Why? Not because they're concerned, but because they want to know about *him*. If I wanted fifteen minutes of fame, now would be the time to seize it.

I want to run.

"There she is!" someone yells.

Like a horde of zombies in a movie, they turn their heads in unison. I freeze.

"Britney!" someone yells.

"Scarlet!" cries another.

They move like zombies too—the hive mind driving them toward me in unison.

"Fuck," Taylor whispers. She grabs my hand, pulling me backward. "Run, Scar."

Where the hell am I going to run to? I have no idea, but the animal part of my brain has no trouble doing as she commands. Pivoting on my heel, I sprint down the street, Taylor at my back. I hear the crowd fast behind me, their voices and footfalls on the pavement.

"Britney!" they yell, disjointed.

I want to scream that my name's not Britney, but I don't. I need to run, and I'm already breathing heavily. I should have tried harder in gym class. Should have taken up some kind of sport.

The blast of a car horn sounds from behind. I glance over my shoulder. A familiar car speeds toward us, slamming on the brakes as it reaches us. We don't wait for an invitation, but yank open the doors of Ashley's car and dive in. Taylor's in the front. I'm in the back. The locks click into place.

"Drive!" I yell as hands slap against the window. Someone tries to open the door.

Ashley floors it and we lunge into motion. I almost fall on the floor. My cheek smashes into the back of Taylor's seat. I don't even care.

"Are you okay?" Ashley asks, with a quick glance. "I would have gotten here sooner, but Neal tried to stop me."

I don't ask her what he wanted. If he was interested in me, he would have texted or called before this. I don't play hard to get, and I'm not interested in a guy who does. Sure, I could have approached him today, but I texted him last night to let him know I was back. I'm not throwing myself at him.

Leaning back against the seat, I fasten my seat belt and close my eyes. My heart pounds like a jackhammer against my ribs.

"What the hell was that?" Taylor wonders out loud. "Reporters?"

"And probably some Lake aficionados," Ashley joins in. "A few whack jobs too—you know, wanting to pray for your soul, or tell you how you're going to hell."

"Fabulous," I mutter. I have to go home sometime. How many of them will still be there? More? Less?

I text Mom and warn her. I'd call, but I don't want Ashley

to overhear. It's not that I don't trust Ash, but she's already expressed interest in Lake, and I don't want to feed that curiosity.

"Thanks for showing up," I say as I type. "Our only other choice would have been to circle back and hide in the house."

Ash glances at me in the rearview. "You and your mom might want to stay in a hotel for a couple of days. They're not going away anytime soon."

I grit my teeth. This is exactly what Mom was afraid of. She's going to beat herself up over this, if she hasn't already started. We never discussed what might happen if Lake leaked our visit to the press. To be honest, it never occurred to me that my father would hurt me like that.

I should have remembered that he's not a good father. He doesn't care about me. How can he? I'm a means to an end.

And his end can't come soon enough. How long does pancreatic cancer take to kill someone? And is there any way to speed it up? If he thinks I'm going back to visit him now . . .

My phone rings. It's Mom. Crap.

"Hello?" I say.

"Where are you?"

"In Ash's car with her and Taylor."

"Good. Go to one of their houses, and stay with them until I can get you. I've already called Andy to see if he can give us any kind of protection."

Protection? "Do you think we're going to need that?"

A heartbeat of silence. "We might. Jeff is both worshipped and despised by people whose mental stability is questionable, who might be driven to extremes."

Ashley's aforementioned "whack jobs."

"We're going to Taylor's," I decide, shooting a glance at Ash in the mirror in case she planned to head to her place. "Call me before you leave work."

"I'll pick you up there. Under no circumstances do you go to the house, okay? Not without me."

"Okay." I say goodbye and hang up.

Ashley turns left onto the next street, heading toward Taylor's house. "Your mom?" she asks.

"Yeah. Tay, do you mind if I hide out at your place until she comes to get me?"

"Of course not. Stay the night if you want." She turns her head to look at Ashley. "You're not going to tell anyone where she is, got it?"

Ash looks offended. "I wouldn't do that."

"Maybe not on purpose, but you might mention it to Sof and she's being just bitchy enough to tell someone else who'd have no problem selling Scar out to reporters."

"I won't say anything." Our gazes meet in the mirror once more. "I promise."

I nod. "I know. You just freaked me out earlier asking about him."

"I couldn't help myself. I know it wasn't cool. I'm sorry."

I believe her. To be honest, if she'd told me she'd met a director or found out Guillermo del Toro was her father, I'd ask questions too. It's just . . . well, that we know of, del Toro hasn't killed anyone.

Taylor's parents aren't home when we approach the house. Ashley drives right on by it, however.

"Uh, Ash? Where are we going?" Taylor asks.

"I'm paranoid," Ashley replies. "I want to make sure we're not being followed."

I never would have even thought of that. "Thanks."

"Of course." We circle the block before pulling up in front of Taylor's house. "I'm just going to drop you off—in case they got my license plate or something."

"You really are paranoid," I comment with a smile.

She smiles back. "I'd never forgive myself if I did something that got you hurt, Scar. Seriously, call me if you need anything."

I give her shoulder a squeeze before getting out of the car. Taylor already has her keys out and we hurry to the back door.

"That was good of her to pick us up," I say once we're inside.

Taylor shrugs. "I suppose being the friend of a serial killer's daughter will look good on her Abnormal Psych application."

Harsh, but Taylor's just looking out for me like she always does.

The first thing we do is smoke on the back deck. I'm well aware of how much medicating I've been doing lately—medically and self. I don't even care. I'm freaked out, and I need to not be. The pot is just enough to take the edge off.

I remember that I hadn't finished lunch, so Taylor finds some frozen waffles in the freezer and we toast the entire box. Not like there're that many in it. I could eat the entire thing by myself.

"I've never seen anything like that," she comments, wiping maple syrup from the side of her mouth with the back of her hand. She licks her knuckles. "It was like something out of a movie."

"My whole life has felt like that lately," I admit. "I mean, this time last week the only thing I had to worry about was whether or not Neal liked me."

"Yeah. Beginning to think maybe he's not such a great catch."

I laugh. "You think?" I cram half a waffle in my mouth, chew and swallow. "Did I tell you about Luke?"

"No. Have you been holding out on me?"

"He's Agent Logan's son. I met him in Raleigh." I search

for a photo on my phone. I had to take at least one of him when he wasn't aware. I find one of him and Darcy.

"Oh. My. God," Taylor says when she sees him. "He's got a superhero name *and* face."

"And body. He's, like, built like Chris Evans. Ugh."

She passes my phone back. "He's reason to go back to North Carolina if nothing else."

"I do have to go back," I confide. "I don't want to, but I can't let Lake ruin our lives again for nothing."

"You want to get the rest of the names?"

"As many as I can, yeah. It's the right thing to do. I mean, it is, isn't it?"

"You're awesome," she tells me, giving a dopey smile. "I love how awesome you are. Even though it would be easy to say 'fuck it,' you're going to do the right thing."

"You'd do it too." Why am I getting defensive about doing what's right?

"After that scene on your lawn, I'd be ready to move into a bomb shelter and never come out! Hell, I never would have met the guy to begin with. You're a rock star, Scar. Oh, that rhymes."

I snort. "There aren't enough waffles. What else you got?"

"You know where all the food is."

The doorbell rings right as I'm getting up. "I'll get it," I say, spying the mail truck through the window above the sink.

I open the door off the kitchen entrance, expecting to see the postal guy, but he's already back in his truck and leaving. Instead, there's another man on the doorstep, holding a package. I recognize his car as the one that pulled into the school lot as we were leaving. It belongs to a local paper.

"Hi, Scarlet," he says. "Got a minute?"

My heart jumps into my throat. "Who are you?"

"Ralph Autumn. I'm a reporter. I'd like to talk to you about your father."

"I don't think so," I reply. "Could you give me that package, please?"

He pulls it away as I reach for it. "How about you answer my questions first?"

"No." I start to pull the door shut but he grabs it, shoves his body between it and the frame.

I jump back as he comes into the house. He offers me the package. "Come on, just a few questions."

I take the parcel. His fingers latch around my wrist, holding me tight. "What was it like to meet your father? How sick is he? Did he give you any information about other victims? Did he say anything about the part your mother played in his crimes?"

I can't believe this. "Let me go."

"Just give me something."

Panic seizes my chest. "Let me go!" I scream. I kick him in the balls. He doubles over, letting go of my wrist, and I shove him out onto the steps. I barely manage to slam the door and lock it before he starts pounding on it. I'm shaking so hard I can barely move.

Suddenly, Taylor is there. I guess she heard me scream. She's got her phone to her ear. "Yeah, my friend and I are alone at my house, and this guy just tried to force his way in. . . . He's still outside. . . . Yeah, I'll stay on the line." She crouches beside me. When did I slide to the floor? When will the cops get here?

And more importantly, how did that guy find me?

Chapter Thirteen

The reporter's gone by the time the police show up. I'm completely useless, but thankfully Taylor got a photo of the guy and the car. She recorded some of the altercation as well and gives all of this to the female officer who questions her.

"You okay?" a male officer asks me as he hands me a glass of water. My hands shake. Holding the glass helps.

I nod. "I think so." My teeth chatter.

"Could you get a blanket?" I hear him ask.

Next thing I know, Taylor hands him one of the throws from the living room. It's soft and plush and oh so warm as the officer wraps it around my shoulders.

"Scarlet, can you tell me what happened?" he asks.

I look up, clutching my water in one hand and the ends of the throw in the other. "Didn't T-Taylor tell you?"

His expression and gaze are perfectly patient. "I'd like to hear it from you."

I tell him as much as I can remember. My voice sounds like an old recording—jumpy and warped.

"Why did the reporter want to talk to you?"

I stare at him. He doesn't know. This makes me laugh. "Because I'm Baby Britney," I tell him. His expression doesn't change. "You know Jeff Lake, the serial killer?"

When he nods, I set the glass of water on the table. Some of it sloshes over the side. "He's my father."

He recovers quickly, but there's no hiding that first flash of surprise—and revulsion.

"Yeah," I say. "That's how I felt when I found out too."

"We need to have some adults present," the female officer suggests. "These girls are under eighteen. And this warrants some discretion."

"Britney—" the male officer begins.

"Scarlet," Taylor corrects. "Her name is Scarlet now. I can give you her mother's phone number."

Taylor takes care of everything as I sink deeper into my warm cocoon. The conversation around me fades into something that sounds like the adults in a Charlie Brown cartoon. In my head, I keep seeing the reporter's face. Feel his grip on my arm. Feel the impact of my shin and his balls. I've never been so scared in my life.

Is that what my father's victims felt right before he killed them? They say he drugged them, but they must have felt something. No amount of drugs can totally erase that desire to run for your life completely, can it?

This is what he wanted to happen. When he told me not to fuck with him, he meant it. This is what I get for being stupid enough to think I could possibly stand up to him.

Never get in a pissing contest with a skunk. Lesson learned, I guess. I can imagine how smug he'll be the next time I see him.

I can't go back there. I can't. There's no way I can stand in that room and not let him see how much he scares me. How much I hate him.

But I can't *not* go back. I don't think my conscience will allow that either. What will be worse—facing Lake, or living with all those unknown dead girls?

I think of Mom and how tired and frail she looks sometimes. How different she is from the girl she once was. That's what those ghosts have done to her. I don't want to be my mother. I don't want to be haunted and alone.

Taylor's parents arrive first. Mr. and Mrs. Li sit at the table with me and Taylor while she tells them and the police everything that happened. The officers don't talk to me until Mom arrives. She comes in like a storm cloud, smelling of perfume and cold air.

"You need to call Agent Andrew Logan of the Raleigh FBI," she tells them. "He can apprise you of the particulars."

Her face appears before mine. She's on her knees in front of me, hands clasping mine. Her fingers are warm. Her eyeliner is smudged. Normally her makeup is perfect.

"Hi," I say.

She smiles. "Hi, baby. Are you okay?"

I nod. "He just scared me."

"I know. I'm so sorry that happened. I'm going to talk to the police and Taylor for a few minutes and then we'll go home, okay?"

"We can't go home," I whisper, but she's already on her feet and talking to the others. I hear her asking what happened after we left with Ash. Taylor fills her in.

And then it's the police's turn. I have my head down, but my ears are suddenly wide open as I listen to them question my mother.

"So, your real name is Allison Michaels?"

"That's my birth name. Gina Murphy is my legal name."

"And you are Jeff Lake's wife?"

"I was. We're divorced."

"Weren't you implicated in his crimes?"

Mom's lips thin, the only sign of her exasperation. "I was cleared. Look, I'm not the one who broke the law here. This reporter tried to force his way in here to harass my daughter. What are you going to do about that?"

"Yes," Mrs. Li joins in, her tone like steel. "I would like to know what you are going to do about the man who trespassed on our property and frightened our daughter."

"We're going to do everything we can, Mrs. Li," the female officer placates. "Your daughter has photographs, plus his credentials, so he ought to be easy to find. If you wish to press charges, that is within your discretion."

"I want to press charges as well," Mom says. "He assaulted Scarlet."

"Sounds like she gave better than she got," the male officer replies.

I lift my head. "So, I deserved it, is that it?" I ask, my voice suddenly strong and clear. "My father's a monster, so I deserved being grabbed and shoved around?"

The female cop gives him a look that clearly tells him to keep his mouth shut. "No one's saying that, Scarlet."

"But he thinks it." I jerk my chin toward her partner. "That's victim blaming, isn't it?"

"You want to talk victims?" he says, his expression turning ugly. "Let's talk about what your daddy did to those girls."

"Out," his partner commands. "Now. I've got this."

He gives her a sullen look, but leaves, his cheeks flushed. Mom looks resigned, and even more tired than before. This is why she lied to me. She knew there would be people—

strangers—who would treat me like I had something to do with what Lake did. I'm guilty by association, just like her.

"I would like to apologize for my partner," the woman says. "I'll make sure his behavior is reported to our superiors."

Sure you will, I think. I won't hold my breath.

"Scarlet," she says. "I'd like to hear your side of the story, if you don't mind repeating it one more time."

"Yeah," I mutter, pulling my blanket tighter around my shoulders. "Where would you like me to start?"

She smiles. "Wherever you want."

I'm sure she thinks she's doing me a favor, letting me believe that what I want matters, but we both know it doesn't. What I want doesn't fucking matter at all.

Taylor's parents don't want us hanging out for a while. They're freaked out that a guy forced his way into their house and we had to call the cops. They're freaked out by discovering that Mom and I aren't who they thought. They're just plain freaked out.

"We have to think of our daughter," Mr. Li says. "Scarlet, I want you to know we think the world of you, but if being around you puts Taylor in danger, we cannot allow it." He looks at Mom. "I'm very sorry."

"That's not fair!" Taylor exclaims.

I stop her. "He's right. I don't want to put you in danger either. I'd never forgive myself if I got you hurt."

"I'm not going to stop being your friend," she declares, emphatically. "I don't care what happens. If you need me, I'm here for you."

She's going to make me cry. "I know."

We leave shortly after that. Neither Mom nor I want to

impose any further, and really, I need to be somewhere else. I can't stand my best friend's parents staring at us with a mix of pity and wariness, and I keep waiting for someone else to come pounding on the door. No one does, though.

Will the Hernandezes be next? I wonder. Will Ashley's parents want to keep her away from me as well?

Mom drives us to a hotel—a nice one—a few towns over and parks. "We're going to stay here for tonight at least," she says, opening her door. "Let's get settled and order some food. You look exhausted."

Grabbing my bag, I get out of the car. "What about clothes?"

She opens the trunk and hands me a stuffed weekender that I've never seen before.

"Is that a freaking go bag?"

She nods and slings the strap of another over her shoulder. "I put them together last week, in case."

She's like a spy or something. How much of our comfortable lives has been because of her planning and staying one step ahead? "Mom, how—?"

"We'll talk inside. Come on."

I follow her through the sliding doors. The girl at the front desk looks up at us with a smile—no hint of recognition, thankfully. Mom checks in with a name I've never heard before and hands the girl a credit card. I'm not even surprised, that's how messed up my life is.

"Have a nice stay," the girl chirps, flashing those straight, white teeth in my direction as well. I manage a small smile in return.

We ride the elevator to the fourth floor in silence. Mom leads me to a room near the end of the long corridor, presses the key card against the lock, and opens the door.

The room is warm—maybe too much, but it's hard to tell because I'm so cold. We remove our boots before going any farther. It's a large room with two beds and a huge bathroom off to one side.

"This should do until we get this sorted," she announces. "No school tomorrow."

"Why not?" Not like I mind.

"You told the police you noticed that reporter's car pulling into the school parking lot when you were leaving. I assume someone there—not a teacher or administrator—told him where to find you."

My heart sinks. Not Sofie, I hope. She can't hate me that much, can she? Everyone in the cafeteria saw me leave with Taylor. It could have been anyone who knows where either of us lives. Still, that someone would just give that information to a stranger . . . I shudder. No friend would do that.

"Did he hurt you?" she asks.

I shake my head, but I'm not 100 percent certain. "He creeped me out."

Her arms wrap around me, the heavy fabric of our winter coats mashing between us. "He wants to unsettle you."

If this is how people react more than fifteen years after the murders, how did they act then? What did she have to deal with? And why the fuck do I have to deal with it now?

I pull free of the embrace. "I don't know how to feel." Tossing my bags on the sofa, I turn so I don't have to look at her. "I'm angry and scared and confused."

"I know."

I force myself to meet her gaze. "I'm angry at you."

There's a change in her expression—enough that I know she's hurt. "I know that too."

"I don't know why. I know you went through worse than this. I know it must have been horrible, but I want to blame you for everything."

"You can, if you want."

"Don't tell me that! Tell me to blame him! He's who I should blame, not you!"

"Yes, but I didn't fool him like he fooled me, and I think that's what bothers you the most. After years of me treating you like I know everything that's best for you, you find out I'm as naive and gullible as anyone else. More so. It has to be maddening."

Now I'm mad at her for understanding me better than I do, but I don't say it, because as mad as I am, there's something so much stronger clawing its way to the surface. It's something I've never been good at dealing with.

"And scary," I admit, sitting down on end of the nearest bed. "Really scary."

"Do you need one of your pills?"

"No." I don't want it. "I want to go back to last week and not agree to see him."

Mom smiles weakly. "You wouldn't do that. You're too good a person."

I think maybe she's wrong, but I don't say that either. I just sit there, slumped, while she turns on the TV. The local news has started.

"Really?" I ask.

"We need to know what we're up against." She sets the remote on the dresser and stands in the middle of the carpet, hands on her hips, attention fixed on the screen.

It only takes a few minutes before video of our house appears. There Taylor and I are, two bright spots of color against the snow and gray pavement.

"It's her!" someone on-screen exclaims. It's weird seeing

myself from this angle, feeling their excitement at the sight of me. I watch myself turn and run and get the rush of chasing myself as the cameraperson starts running. It's like playing a video game.

Mom wraps her arms around herself.

I watch as on-screen me jumps into Ash's car, like it's happening to someone else. The cameraperson gets a glimpse of me sprawled in the back seat—a great shot of the fear on my face when someone tries the handle.

We speed away—groans of disappointment follow.

"Vultures," Mom says, voice dark and bitter.

Ash was right to drop us off. There's a clear shot of her license plate. God, I hope they haven't gone to her house.

"I'll call Ashley's parents in the morning," Mom says, as if reading my mind. "Apologize for getting them involved. Hopefully they won't talk." She rubs a hand over her forehead.

"What did Agent Logan say?"

"For us to lie low. He's going to see about getting a police detail for the house, so we can at least hunker down in our own space. Local police in Darlington found remains where Jeff said they would be. They're testing them to see if they belong to the Gordon girl."

"It has to be."

She rubs her hand over her forehead. "When I think of how many more there might be . . ." She pulls her shoulders back. "Andy wants us to come back to Raleigh."

Of course he does. The name panned out. Now they want more. I'm only a little bitter about it. If I were Agent Logan, I'd want me to come back too. "Won't it be worse there?"

"Maybe. Maybe not, but he'll be able to control it better. I think he feels like he has to protect us."

"He does. We wouldn't be dealing with this if not for him."

She looks over at me. "No. We're here because of Jeff. Don't ever forget that. Everyone else has just been trying to clean up after him."

"You didn't." It comes out sharper than I intend, but there's no taking it back.

She turns toward me fully, her posture rigid. "I hired someone to dig up our backyard to see if there were bodies there. I gave them the names and addresses of every place we ever vacationed. Every gift he ever gave me I turned over to the police, no matter how personal. I told them intimate details of our sex life, Scarlet."

I look away. Shame burns the back of my throat.

"Nobody has tried to atone for what Jeff—my husband and your father—did more than me. If I could have given my life for one of those girls, I would have done it gladly."

"But you couldn't."

"No, so I gave it to you."

Her words hit like a slap and chase away my shame. I stand up. "You want me to say thanks? You've never let me do anything. You've embarrassed me and freaked out my friends because you're so paranoid. You've never allowed me to make decisions for myself. I've never even had a real boyfriend because you chased them all away! People think I'm weird, Mom."

"I was trying to protect you."

"Well, you did a shit job of it!"

We stare at each other, the words hanging between us like frost. I want to take them back. I want to apologize. I don't.

Suddenly, my mother—my rigid, seemingly unmovable mother—dissolves into tears. I don't mean silent trickles running down her cheeks, but huge, gasping, ugly sobs that drop her to the floor. She draws her knees up to her chest and buries her face in them, making noises I've never heard from another human.

This is what someone breaking looks like. And it's *my* fault. If I were a better person I'd cry too, maybe. But I can only stand there like an idiot and watch her. Listen to her. Finally, the sound is what forces me to my knees beside her. My heart can't take it anymore.

"Mom," I whisper.

No response.

"*Mom.*" I put my arms around her, pull her against my shoulder. "It's okay. Mom, it's all right. Just . . . just breathe." *Just stop, please.* I don't know how much more of this I can witness before I break. We can't be broken at the same time. Who will pick up our pieces?

My touch seems to help. Stiffness eases from her muscles as she leans into me. Maybe if I hold her tighter it will help.

"It's okay," I whisper, in case she didn't hear me the first time. "We're okay. You didn't do a shit job. I'm the one who's shit. I'm sorry."

Her arms wrap around my waist, so tight I can barely breathe, but I don't care. All that matters is holding the two of us together, and that hold is tenuous at best.

Chapter Fourteen

I have a hard time settling down later that evening. Mom soaked in the tub after her meltdown and I ordered room service. Wine for her. Dessert for both of us. After, we got into her bed and watched a movie. We didn't talk much, but we didn't need to. I'd already apologized, and we had talked. There was nothing more to say, and after talking so much to the police earlier, it was nice to be quiet.

Mom fell asleep before the movie ended. Getting so emotional had to be exhausting. I should be tired too, but I'm not. As the credits roll, I pick up my phone. So many messages— text and voice. I ignore most of them.

Me
U there?

I count silently in my head. If he doesn't respond in one minute, I'll go to bed. I'll take a pill to sleep if I have to.

Luke

Yeah. How are you? Stupid question?

> Me
>
> LOL. I'm . . . I have no idea
> what I am. It's surreal.

Luke

Can't imagine. FYI, Dad was making
calls all day to see what he can do to
help.

> Me
>
> Yeah, Mom talked to him, I
> guess.

Luke

Anything I can do?

> Me
>
> Can I call you?

There's a pause.

Luke

Yeah. Give me two minutes.

Relief washes over me. I give him three minutes instead. I
leave the TV on as I slip out of bed and make my way to the
bathroom. There's a dim light coming from somewhere over
the vanity, so I close the door and sink to the floor beside the
tub. I tap my phone screen to dial his number.

"Hey," he says, picking up on the first ring.

"Is it too late?" I ask, voice low.

"No. I was up reading for class. I'm outside now so I don't disturb anyone."

"Thanks for saying yes. Not many people would want to talk to a freaking-out stranger."

"We're not strangers. We've been friends since we were kids, remember? Ten years."

I smile at his tone. "Yeah. We know each other's secrets." It occurs to me that he probably knew the truth about me before I did. Weird.

"And apparently you are my new girlfriend, so I should be here if you need me."

Even though he's joking, my stomach trills a little bit at that. "True. I don't need to thank you for just doing your duty."

"So . . . rough day?"

"Ugh. People looked at me like I was a killer. One of my best friends went into total bitch mode. Another kept asking questions. The guy I thought liked me didn't even speak to me, and reporters were waiting outside my house. They chased me and my friend."

"I saw that online. Your friend should be ashamed of herself. As for that guy . . . well, his loss."

"Says the guy who *likes* girls who are drama."

Luke laughs. "Darcy said that, not me. Hey, this might sound trite, but it's going to be okay. The media will move on, eventually."

"That's the key word. 'Eventually.' Until then, my life is going to be a freaking circus."

"I'm sorry."

His words bring tears to my eyes. I believe him. He didn't offer solutions or advice. All he did was say he was sorry, and

I hadn't realized how much I needed plain, sincere sympathy with no "but"s attached.

"Thanks. What were you reading for class?"

"An article on Hammurabi and law in ancient Babylon."

"Who?"

I hear a smile in his voice. "You want me to tell you about it? It'll probably put you to sleep."

I laugh. "Yeah. Tell me all about it then."

So, he does. More than I ever could have possibly wanted to know about Hammurabi and his code, but now I understand where "an eye for an eye" came from.

Luke's voice—especially with that slight accent of his—lulls me into a state of relaxation I've only ever achieved with pills or pot. I actually yawn when he's done talking.

"It's almost one," he says. "You should probably go to bed."

"You too," I add. "Thanks for this. I really appreciate it."

"Anytime. Good night, Scarlet."

"Good night." I hang up with another yawn and pull myself to my feet. In the main room, Mom snores softly. I turn off the TV and crawl into bed. I thought it would take me a while to fall asleep, but Luke's voice drifts across my thoughts, dragging me down into sleep.

The smell of bread and coffee is what wakes me the next morning. It's after nine, and Mom is already up and has ordered breakfast.

"I got you French toast," she says. "And some fruit."

"Bacon?" I ask, throwing back the covers. "I want to eat all the things."

She chuckles. "Oh, sweetie. I got us all the things. Let's stress eat together."

And we do. It's so good! She really did get a little of everything. I smother my French toast in butter and syrup, add some sausage and bacon to my plate. I eat the melon and grapes and strawberries that came with it. There are hash browns and pastries. At least she only ordered one serving of everything. We don't finish, but we give it a great try.

"Oh, I am so full," she says afterward.

"You should gain some weight," I tell her. "I feel like you haven't been eating as much during all of this."

She raises an eyebrow but doesn't argue. "I got a text from Logan. He's arranged a protection detail for us at the house."

"Does he still want us to go down there?"

She nods. "I told him it depends."

"On what?"

"On if you want to go."

I raise a brow. "I don't really have a choice."

"Yes, you do. It's just not one you want to make, because you're a good person."

I snort softly. "Not that good. I'd rather be almost anywhere other than here right now. Even Raleigh." Sighing, I pick at the discarded leaves of a strawberry. "What do you think Lake wants us to do?"

"I imagine he wants to see us looking frightened and harassed."

"He'll love that clip of me cowering in Ash's car."

"I don't imagine he'll see that. He's not really allowed access to the news."

"His wife will, though. And he has access to her."

Mom sighs. "That's true. He probably wants to force you to come back. He likes being in charge."

I let this churn in my brain a bit. "So, if we went back before he asked—but not too quickly—he wouldn't expect that?"

"I have no idea what he expects, honey. In all honesty, I've never really known."

"Yeah, I guess it's kind of impossible." I sigh. "I'm going back to school tomorrow."

"Are you sure that's a good idea?"

"No, but it's one of those bandages that needs to be ripped off, as Agent Logan would say."

That makes her smile. "You know . . . going to Raleigh would mean a mini vacation for you—at least from class. It's a valid reason to go."

"You're probably right." My lips curl up. I hadn't thought of that. I could run away and not look like a coward!

"I'll call Mr. Schott today and arrange a meeting with him and your teachers," she decides. "We can get any important assignments from them so you don't fall behind."

I try not to let my disappointment show. Of course she'd want me to continue the work even if I'm not there. Ugh.

"You want to go back, don't you?" I ask. "To Raleigh." I heard the hopefulness in her tone.

"Yes," she admits without hesitation. "My family is there, and even though this will be hard on them, I want to see them again. I want their support. I ran from it before, thinking I was protecting them, but it didn't change anything. I want my friends, my family. I don't want Jeff to have control of my life anymore."

"And you want to be there when he dies."

She looks surprised that I think that—or maybe that I said it out loud.

"I want to be there when he finally sets me free, yes."

"Me too," I admit, though I just realized it. "And I want to get those names from him, if I can."

"He'll make you work for them. It won't be easy."

I shrug, feeling brave now that the shock of yesterday has worn off. "It's kind of my legacy, isn't it? You and I can spend the rest of our lives feeling guilt that isn't ours, or we can do something to fight it."

Reaching across the room-service cart, she takes my hand and squeezes it. "When did you get so smart and grown-up?"

"Since life kicked me in the butt," I reply with a half smile. "It's amazing what finding out your father is a psychopath will do for your perspective."

That makes her laugh—both of us, actually. When she sobers, however, her gaze locks with mine. "Okay, let's go back to where everything started and finish it, regardless of how it plays out. No more running. No more hiding."

I nod. "The next time I see reporters I'm going to talk to them. So are you. I don't want him hearing about us running away. I'm more ashamed of that than I am of being his kid."

"No more running," she whispers. "I'm so proud of you right now."

"Of course you are," I quip. "I'm clearly awesome." And talking out my ass, but who cares? If I tell myself something enough, I can make myself believe it. It's a simple case of fake-it-till-you-make-it. So, until I make it, I have to fake being brave and thinking I know what I'm doing. I may not have any control over the situation that brought me here, but I can control what I do next. I can't change Jeff Lake being my father. I have no choice but to be his daughter.

I don't have to be his puppet.

Are Serial Killers Born or Made?
by Ashley Hernandez for Mrs. Zenelli, AP Psychology

Since humanity first became aware of itself, there has been the growing concern of Nature vs. Nurture. In the 1800s, there were people who believed that you could determine a person's penchant for criminality by mapping out the bumps and structure of their cranium, a practice known as phrenology.

Today, we know that phrenology is not any kind of real science, but the interest and the intent to learn what made some people tend toward darkness while others did not prevailed. During the Victorian Era, which gave us Jack the Ripper, Lizzie Borden and H. H. Holmes, both the medical world and the authorities discovered new ways to determine a person's predilection toward violent crime. Some of these discoveries were the result of botched lobotomies. Walter Freeman, a lobotomist, called these "fortunate mistakes" (1). These accidental injuries to the brain allowed him to witness the subsequent results, such as damage to the frontal lobe turning a previously gentle man violent.

Today, we know that many serial killers have reduced gray matter in the limbic system of their brains—the part that controls emotional response. As with an injury, this reduction can also result in a lack of empathy, backing up the theory that psychopaths are quite simply unable to feel for their victims, and that also, they have a higher tendency toward violence and impulsive behavior.

That is the nature aspect of the equation, but with serial killers, it's not always as simple as having been "born that way." These killers are largely an American phenomenon, which begs the question, what are we as a country doing wrong? Almost 70 percent of serial killers are American, and just as high a percentage of them experienced some sort of abuse in their childhood. This leads many researchers to conclude that there is, indeed, a *learned* aspect of being a serial killer.

Can a tendency to violence and lack of empathy be reversed? Obviously, not everyone with antisocial personality disorder becomes a serial killer, not even all of those who have the disorder and who have been abused go on to kill, so what is it that causes the tipping point? And if we're able to detect it, will we someday be able to treat it?

For this paper I will be using two American killers as examples upon which to test my theories. Of course, without actual test subjects, this is all subjective. The first killer is Aileen Wuornos, acknowledged to be one of the few female serial killers on record. The second is Jeffrey Robert Lake, one of America's most prolific serial killers, who also still happens to be alive. . . .

Neal

So, you weren't with another guy
last weekend? You were visiting your
father in jail?

Me

Yeah. Who told you I was with
a guy?

Neal
Sofie.

> **Me**
>
> And you believed her?

Neal

Didn't think she'd lie.

> **Me**
>
> Well, now you know.

I toss my phone on my bed and continue packing my suitcases. If Neal's that stupid, it's just as well things didn't go any further between us. I have bigger things to worry about anyway. Funny, after months of wishing he'd pay attention to me, it's so easy to walk away.

We weren't a couple, and I never thought we were, but Luke checked in on me before Neal when it really mattered. Neal isn't into me, and now that I have a better idea of the real him, I'm not into him either.

I don't bother telling him I'm going away. I can't risk anyone talking to reporters again.

Mom and I spent last night at the hotel and returned to a house guarded by cops. The press is still here, but we managed to get by them, and there aren't as many. The police presence made it easier. They kept the reporters from getting too close so we could get inside.

Agent Logan acted fast once Mom let him know we wanted to come back to North Carolina, and told her there was housing already available for us—with security. He and Mom decided it would probably be safer for us to drive down and avoid airport altercations and the potential for being seen.

I really don't want to be trapped on a plane with someone who has figured out who we are.

I pack my favorite oversized sweater, fresh from the laundry, and the jeans I wear most often. We don't know how long we're going to be gone—a few weeks, at least—so I want to have all my important stuff.

I glance at my phone again as I fold a pair of leggings. I still can't believe Neal believed Sofie. Or . . . maybe I can. Sofie can tell a pretty convincing story, and most guys don't realize when they're being lied to.

Most girls don't either, I guess, because I thought Sof was my friend. If it weren't for all the other crap going on, I'd be so hurt right now. Instead, I'm mad. Did she tell that reporter how to find me? I really don't want to think she'd be that spiteful over a guy. He's not worth ruining a friendship, but maybe she thinks he is. Heaving a sigh, I shake off my thoughts.

I check my camera bag and make sure my gear is there. It's not a huge kit, but it's all I need for now. I've been saving up for better equipment when I go to college. I've done some short films with Ashley, Taylor, and Sof, but most of my work is more like documentaries. Script writing isn't really my thing, and my friends aren't great at acting—we just end up laughing. Once I'm sure I have everything I need, I burrow into my fuzzy, heated blanket and let the warmth lull me to sleep.

My alarm goes off at midnight. Mom's already up and has a pot of coffee made for the drive. I take our luggage out to the garage and put most of it in the back of the Subaru. My camera and our laptop bags go in the back seat. While I'm doing this, Mom makes us sandwiches and chucks any perishables. I guess we really will be gone awhile.

"All set?" she asks once she has our travel mugs filled and the coffeepot cleaned.

I zip up my favorite boots—they're motorcycle style, with straps and buckles. They're also a rich, vibrant wine color that matches my hair dye. I don't wear them in the winter because I don't want salt to damage them, but they don't usually have that problem in North Carolina. I take my victories where I can.

"I'm good," I say. "You called work, right?"

She sighs. "After the circus yesterday, they'll be glad to have me gone for a bit." Apparently, she'd had some reporters—and even some customers—come to the pharmacy to ask her about Lake. She didn't tell me, though. I had to overhear her tell Agent Logan on the phone. No one was overly aggressive, thankfully, but the staff was upset by the whole thing. It was a disruption for everyone.

"Isn't it going to be worse for us in Raleigh?" I ask—probably too late. The plan has been made. "I mean, they chased us out before."

"I expect it there," she replies, handing me a mug. "And we have backup in Raleigh. Here? We have no one."

It stings, but she's right. I don't even have Taylor anymore, at least not in the same way. I might have Ash, but there's no way she'd be able to keep herself from asking me questions. "Maybe Darcy and Luke will take pity on me and hang out." It takes a couple of seconds for me to realize I said this out loud.

Mom clears her throat. "There is something I wanted to talk to you about."

Shit. "What?"

"Your aunt Catrina contacted Andy. She wants to see us."

I blink. My brain is still trying to wake up. "My aunt?"

She nods. "Jeff's sister."

"Oh." I let that sink in. I try to remember who played her

in the movie, and I can't think of the actor's name. "Do we want to see her?"

"I always liked Cat. She gave up on your father before I did. I haven't spoken to her in years, but I would like to see her again."

"So, you don't think she wants to spy on us or anything?"

Mom chuckles. "I doubt it. She has a daughter your age. Maybe the two of you will hit it off."

And that is what pity from your mother looks like. *Hey, maybe your murderous father's family will accept you as one of their own since everyone else has rejected you.* I know that's not what she's saying, but . . . it's what she's saying.

"We can talk about it on the drive," I hedge. "We should get going." It's a ten-hour drive without traffic and stops. She wants to drive straight through, and there's no way she'll let me do any of the driving. We'll have to stop a few times for bathroom breaks and to stretch our legs. It'll take even longer if she gets tired and needs to nap or get something to eat. We'll have a few hours' head start on the media, at least, but the more daylight stopping we do, the better chance we have of being seen.

We pull out of the garage at a quarter to one. It's dark and completely quiet on our street. The cops would have chased away any lingering reporters a couple of hours ago. Our neighborhood is pretty strict about nuisance and noise.

Mom stops at the end of the drive and rolls down her window when the uniformed officer there approaches.

"I did a sweep around the area," he informs us. "No sign of anyone, but here's my card, just in case. Call me if you think you're being followed."

Mom thanks him and we pull out onto the dark street.

It feels weird to be out this late on a school night—with my mother. I obsessively check my side-view mirror every few minutes until we hit the New York state line. Only then do I relax, like reporters aren't allowed to cross or something.

Mom finds a radio station that plays a lot of stuff from the nineties. It's the only music we can usually agree on.

Somewhere in New Jersey we stop for a bathroom break. Mom comes out of the gas station with a bag full of junk food. She hands me a package of red licorice. "Open this for me, will you?"

I raise a brow. "Going on a sugar bender?"

"Road trip food," she informs me with a smile. "I'll share."

We eat licorice and chips and drink Diet Dr Pepper until I think I might puke. Mom doesn't seem the least bit bothered. In fact, she's wired in a way I've never seen her before. Not jumpy, just upbeat and alert. This mess has set her free, and I'm seeing the real her for the first time.

I fall asleep right outside Baltimore. I can't help it. I wake up when we stop to pee again—no idea where we are. I don't even ask. I'm asleep again as soon as we get back in the car and I don't wake up until Mom nudges me.

I open my eyes. We're in a parking lot and it's bright and sunny. Still morning, but it's been a while since sunrise. "Where are we?"

"Virginia." She grabs her purse. "I'm hungry. Let's get breakfast."

I stumble out of the car, bleary-eyed, and my bladder full. "Waffle House?"

She grins. "I haven't been to one of these in years."

"What if someone sees us?"

"No one's going to pay any attention to us here. C'mon."

There's that accent—the one she rarely ever shows in Connecticut but seems to come out whenever she's south of Maryland.

She's right. No one pays any attention to us as we eat.

"You're going to go into diabetic shock," I warn as she drowns her waffles in syrup.

"Hush." It's like she's making up for lost meals or something.

When we return to the car, I get out my camera and film some of the scenery the closer we get to North Carolina. I film Mom too, singing along with the radio—laughing self-consciously when she messes up Courtney Love's lyrics.

"What were you like before him?" I ask, still filming.

Her expression sobers. "Fun—I think. Hopeful. I was one of those young women who liked to see the best in people. The press called me naive."

"What did your friends call you?"

"Sweet, I suppose. Bubbly. That was when I had friends, though. Most of them disappeared when the trial started." From her expression, she's thinking of me and my friends now.

"None of them stuck by you?"

"One did. My friend Kim. She went to court with me, babysat you when I needed someone. She would come over and just be there for me."

"I want to meet her," I announce. "And I want to meet my aunt too. I want to meet everyone who knew you then."

She smiles. "Okay."

I want to tell her I'll stick by her. That I won't ever leave her, no matter what, but I don't. She'll cry and I'll cry and neither of us wants that. I offer her a piece of licorice instead and take one for myself.

"What about diabetic shock?" she teases.

I shrug. "We'll do it together."

Something flickers in her gaze. Something soft and warm. She knows I'm not talking about sugar or diabetes.

"Together," she echoes.

Chapter Fifteen

"You came back." That's what Lake says when I see him next.

I'm glad Mom made me wait a couple of days to visit. Aside from forcing Lake to wait, it's given me time to settle into our temporary house and get comfortable with being in North Carolina.

It's an FBI safe house, so there's a lot of security. I feel safe there, and while it's not home, it's still pretty comfortable. Mom went shopping and got us some fresh sheets for the beds, so they'd feel like ours, and some towels. Agent and Mrs. Logan made sure the fridge and cupboards were stocked with groceries before we got there. I put my clothes in the closet and dresser in my room. Tacked up a couple of posters and pictures. I feel steadier than I did the first time.

I lean back in the chair near the hospital bed. "That's what you wanted, isn't it? You demanded it. Really, you engineered it. Or, your wife did."

His eyes narrow. He doesn't look any different from the last time I saw him, but it hasn't even been a week. "I am not entirely certain I like your tone."

"I don't like being a publicity stunt, so I guess we both had better get used to disappointment, huh?"

"I suppose that's fair." He doesn't offer an apology and I don't expect it. "Were the photos my darlin' Everly took of you not flattering?"

"They were pretty shit, but that was the point, right? Have a little chuckle at making me and Mom look bad?" I smile. "Does that take the sting out of looking in the mirror?"

"Ouch," he winces mockingly. "Why, there is more than a little Lake in you indeed. I am sorry your ego got bruised, baby girl, but a dying man is a desperate one. Come to think of it, dying women can be incredibly needy as well."

I can't stop the shiver that runs down my spine. He chuckles softly. "Ah, I'm just playing with you." He adjusts his blankets. "Truth be told, I am pleased to see you. Seems I have more familiar feelings toward you than I initially thought. Bit of a surprise that realization was."

Okay, so all my research indicates that he's not capable of those kinds of feelings, so either he's lying, or equates feeling some kind of ownership as a tender emotion.

"I can't say the same," I confess.

"No. I can only imagine what your mother has told you about me."

"My mother never told me shit about you. Ever. The media, however, has told me more than enough."

"She never talked about me? Ever?" When I shake my head, he looks genuinely hurt. "What did you think happened to your daddy?"

"That he left when I was a baby and we were better off without him."

He inclines his head. "Well, I suppose that isn't far from the truth. I was locked up before your second birthday and growing up with my . . . *notoriety* hanging over your head would not have made it easy for a little girl to thrive."

"That's an understatement."

A soft, almost affectionate smile curves his lips. "Well, you're here now. I don't care if it is only to get information out of me. Seeing you is like turning on the sun when it's been night for far too long."

I don't buy it, but I don't antagonize him. "Thanks. What do you want to talk about today?"

His expression turns almost coy. "Don't you mean *who*?"

I shrug. "You've made it clear you'll only give me names when you feel like it. Me coming across as overly anxious won't change that, will it?"

"Your mother used to have trouble with anxiety when she was younger. Tell me, do you? It's so hard to fight those scary voices in your head, isn't it?"

As if on cue, that familiar weight pinches my chest, making it feel as though I can't draw a deep enough breath. "Yes," I confess. "Sometimes."

I expect mockery. That smirking smile. Instead, he tilts his head. "I know what it's like to fight yourself. It's like trying to wrestle a greased pig, as my granddaddy was fond of saying. Sometimes it seems futile. In my case, it was."

I stare at him. Is he really trying to compare my panic attacks with his compulsion to kill women? "Are you saying you couldn't help yourself?"

"I got tired of fighting it. The voices got too strong, and when I gave in . . ." He smiles self-deprecatingly. It's chilling.

"Well, you know what I did. You probably understand it better than I do. They've tried explaining my *antisocial-behavior disorder* to me. I'm not a dumb man by any stretch, but they can explain why I'm like this all they want, doesn't change anything, does it? They can't make it go away."

"No."

"So, you explain it to me. If you were going to tell someone why your daddy did the things he's done, what would be the simplest answer you could give?"

He wants me to call him a monster, I can feel it. He's desperate for it. "Because you're brain-damaged," I say.

Lake looks as though I hit him. Before I can enjoy the victory, he starts laughing. "Oh, my lord! Child, you are more vicious than I ever could have hoped! That was mean, girl!" He's still laughing.

Cold washes over me. He wants me to be like him. Likes it when I'm nasty, especially when I'm quick with it.

He wipes his eyes with the back of his long, thin hand. The one not manacled to the side of the bed. The one with the IV in it. "I thought you'd say I was a monster or something like that—something that sounds mean but isn't really to a man like me. But brain-damaged?" He laughs some more. "Well, that stings, even if it is true. Undeveloped frontal lobe and all that. You know what I should have been born?"

I shake my head. I don't dare speak, because I want to tell him that I don't think he ever should have been born at all.

"A barn cat. Big, strapping tom. Eat what I want. Fuck what I want. Kill what I want. I never should have been born human. Humanity doesn't have respect for apex predators anymore."

My mouth is dry. It's the matter-of-fact way he tells me all of this that is the most unsettling. "So, killing is just like scratching an itch for you?"

His humor fades. "I don't think you've really been listening, else you're not as intelligent as I first hoped. It's more than an itch. It's my calling. My *raison d'être*. You know what that means?"

"Your reason for being," I answer. "I take French."

"Do you? I always wanted to go to Paris. Never made it, though. Your mother and I were planning to go for our tenth anniversary." He sighs, lost in thought for a moment. When he looks at me again, I know his brain has switched gears. "If I never got caught, do you think you'd be sad to see me dying like this?"

"If you never got caught, would you have been the kind of father who deserved sadness?"

"Don't know. That Rader fella did all right, didn't he?"

"Who?"

"Dennis Rader."

I shake my head.

"BTK—Bind. Torture. Kill. He was like me. Didn't get caught for a long time. Seriously, you've never heard of him?"

"I didn't know his real name." Ash would know, though. God, if only she were here. She'd know what to ask.

"Well, he had a daughter. I think he was pretty good to her."

"So long as she didn't get in the way when the itch started," I comment before I can stop myself.

"Yes." He frowns. "Your mother probably would have divorced me by now. Or maybe something else would have got me. Hard to say. To be completely honest, I never gave much thought beyond whatever day it was. Mine was not a lifestyle that lent itself to longevity."

"Lifestyle?" I echo. "You're going to lump murder and necrophilia in with piercings and body mods?"

Lake sighs. "I was wondering when we'd get to that. Frankly,

I thought it would take longer. Didn't think you'd have the spine to bring it up. Looks like we both underestimated each other."

I don't say anything. I concentrate on holding his gaze. His eyes are too bright. It's like they have spotlights behind them, lighting them up.

He turns his palms up, the chain on the right jangling against the bed frame. "What? You want me to explain it in a way you'll understand? How are you ever going to understand that your daddy likes to fuck dead girls? Sweet little thing like you isn't capable of understanding."

He makes it sound like a compliment, but it's not. Not to him. More than anything else, I think what he really wants is for me to *try* to understand him. That's his win. That and shocking me. Upsetting me. He likes that too.

"You're right. I don't understand. I mean, I get that it's about having complete control over your victims—that you didn't have to worry about consent or a struggle. What I don't get is how you could do the violence you did and then . . ." I stop. I can't even finish the thought.

"If I hadn't been with your mama, I probably would have gotten myself one of those fancy sex dolls. You know what I'm talking about? The ones that look real?"

I nod. I refuse to let him see how much this bothers me.

"Maybe if I'd had one of those, I could have kept my fantasies to myself. Kept them private and no one would have had to get hurt." He shrugs. That's the extent of his remorse—a shrug. I don't buy it.

"But where's the fun in that?" I ask bitterly. He merely inclines his head, regarding me with interest. My stomach turns in tandem. I swallow. "Can I ask you a question?" *And change the subject?*

"Of course, darlin'. This is the most I've talked to another human being in years. Certainly the most honest conversation I've had in a long damn time."

"Why did you want to name me Britney?"

His face darkens. I don't fool myself into thinking it's shame, because I highly doubt that. Maybe it's anger at the mention of her, or maybe he thinks I should already know the answer. Or maybe he's a little excited, but I'm not going there.

"You asking for you, or for your mama?"

"For me. I don't think Mom cares anymore. She gave me a new name and that was that."

He licks his lips. They're chapped, I notice. It must be hard for him—a man who used to rely so heavily on his appearance, his charm—to look like he does. Wasted. Gross. Like his teeth are too big for his mouth.

"What do you want, girl? Honesty or the soft sell?"

"Let's go for honesty," I suggest.

"You might regret it."

"We'll add it to the list."

He chuckles. "Fair enough." Shifting against the pillows, he gets comfortable before he continues. "Britney Mitchell was the first girl I ever wanted to possess. This was before I knew what I was, so I mistook it for love in the beginning. You know, that feeling of infatuation when you think someone is special? It's usually destroyed by finding out what they really are."

I can't help but think of Neal, but I don't say anything. I nod.

Lake snorts. "Oh, sweetheart. You're just getting started. Anyway, Britney was the first girl I felt more than lust for. I suppose I adored her. Course, the more she got to know me, the more she realized I wasn't what she originally thought either. Broke my heart, she did. As much as it could be broken."

"So, you killed her in revenge?"

His chin snaps up, gaze locking with mine. "Revenge? Nothin' so pedestrian. No, I did it so I could keep her with me. Always. At least, that's the theory the doctors came up with, and it's the one that feels the most authentic to me, if I'm being completely honest, which is difficult sometimes. Could you scoot that cup of water closer, darlin'?"

I start, confused for a moment. Water, right. I inch the paper cup with the paper straw toward the edge of the nightstand so he can reach it.

Suddenly, long, almost skeletal fingers clamp around my wrist, hauling me closer. I jerk back, but he's strong—way stronger than a man so frail ought to be. It's like he's been saving up all his strength for this moment.

I freeze like a rabbit, heart hammering in my throat as he leans up on his elbow, brings his face within inches of mine. He smells of toothpaste and disease.

"I'm not going to hurt you. I just want to make sure you're listening," he says in a strangely soothing tone. My heart hurts, it's beating so hard. "People will say I named you Britney to make you some kind of living trophy. That I wanted you to be a reminder of my first kill, and I will not deny that's true, in part. But what you need to know most of all is that I named you Britney as a reminder of how special that girl was to me. How special you were to me. Giving you that name was a message to the darkness inside me that you were off-limits. I didn't ever want to hurt you like I hurt her. You were my trophy. You were also my penance. How ironic is it that a man like me be given a daughter to raise up? And let me tell you, sweetheart, if I had been there to watch you grow, you would have known how to spot a man like me at twenty paces. You would not have grown up prey."

He releases me. Blood rushes to my fingers in sparking pinpricks of sensation. My wrist aches from the relief. I hesitate only for a split second before jumping off the chair. I want to bolt.

Only prey runs, whispers a voice in my head. My heart slows—not much but enough. Lake watches me with interest, waiting to see what I do. Waiting to judge.

Slowly, legs shaking, I force myself back into the chair. I'm not sure I could make it to the door anyway. I'd probably fall flat on my face. Lake looks past me over my shoulder. Agent Logan is probably watching. Waiting for a sign to rescue me. The room is wired, after all—someone can hear everything we say.

"Mom taught me to be cautious," I inform him. My voice is thin and reedy, but I force the words out. "She taught me not to be a victim."

He makes a scoffing sound. "No disrespect, darlin', but your mama is the last person who should be giving you advice. It took figuring out I gave her a dead girl's necklace to finally show her what I really am."

"That means she wanted to believe in you. Not that she was weak."

"She saw what she wanted to see. You need to see what actually *is*."

I lick my dry lips with a tongue that feels like sandpaper. "What I see is a dying man desperate for one last shot at relevance." I'm not proud of it. Every time I make a dig, I feel like it makes me more like him, that I please him.

He nods, his little smirk back in place. "That's exactly what I am. Sixteen years I've been in a cage, reduced to made-for-TV movies and clickbait. I want to die with the world watching. I want them chanting outside the prison like they did for Bundy. I want T-shirts and celebrations of my villainous demise. I want everyone to know my name and what I did. Call me vain, I don't mind a bit."

Vain. Monstrous. Evil.

Pathetic.

"Will you cry for me, baby girl?"

"No," I reply, my voice stronger. "I hope not."

He nods. "But you might. Your mama will, but they'll be tears of relief rather than grief. The only person who's going to miss me will be my dear Everly, but only because she's too dumb to know better."

"You're an asshole, you know that?"

His sparkling gaze locks with mine. "Yes, I do. I love your spirit, girl—honest Injun."

I scowl, shaking my head. "Can you lay off the 'aw-shucks-racist-Southerner' routine? It's old, and not all that honest, is it?"

"You're right. Pussy's pussy, no matter the color." Then, he grins, revealing those big teeth.

I sigh. "Okay. I'm done."

He arches a brow. "Leaving without a name?"

I stand. "I've jumped through enough hoops for one day. I don't care if you give me a name or not." I turn toward the door.

"You lasted longer than I thought you would," Lake allows. "I reckon that deserves a reward. Jackie Ford."

I stop, turn and face him. I swallow. "Jackie Ford."

"Little cutie from Waynesboro, Virginia. She was walking home from a party the night of August first, 1996, when I stopped and offered her a lift. I'd been watching the party—it was a big one—so she thought I'd been there when I mentioned it. Guess that made her think I was trustworthy. She was wearing these tiny little low-rider jean shorts and a red crop top. Real sexy. Brown hair and sparkling green eyes." Lake closes his eyes as if lost in the memory. Another chill engulfs my spine. I'm getting used to them. I don't even shudder that much.

"She cried a lot. I had to kill her before I wanted to. I kept her a couple of days, though. I pretended to be hiking the Appalachian Trail and had her in my tent. I knew better than to linger too long, so I cleaned her up, burned her clothes and the tent, and buried her in the woods. If Agent Logan would be so good as to bring me a map, I can show him where. Your mother and I camped not far from there once."

He says he wanted to protect me from himself, and then he does this. I don't think he understands what he's doing any more than I do. His moods shift faster than the moods of anyone else I've ever known, but the one thing I'm learning to trust is that malicious gleam in his eye. When he recounts details about his victims, he's not lying. He needs me to hear them, and I don't know if it's because he wants to hurt me, or if he wants me to understand, or if he just wants to jerk off to the power trip when I leave.

"No description of how she fought?" I ask. "No details about how desperate and *needy* she was as she begged for her life?"

He shakes his head, that little bemused smile twisting his lips. It doesn't matter. I have another name. One more family Agent Logan can hopefully bring peace to.

"Thanks," I say, without any inflection, before knocking on the door to be let out.

"When are you coming back?" Lake asks.

The door opens, revealing Agent Logan and Mom, and the sight of them immediately strengthens me. I glance over my shoulder at the withering monster tethered to his bed.

"When the joy of watching you die outweighs my revulsion," I reply honestly, and leave the room.

"You all right?" Agent Logan asks as the door clicks shut, locks slipping into place, sealing Lake in his tomb once more.

I glance up at him. "When you find her, I want to know about Jackie Ford. And I'd like to know about Michelle Gordon too, please."

He frowns. "Okay. Sure."

I walk over to Mom and give her a hug, letting her take away the film of shame and disgust that seems to hang over these visits. I'm getting better at this, and I don't know how to feel about that.

But I do know that my father's victims deserve better than being called needy. That they weren't stupid just because they didn't know a predator when he bared his teeth. I need to know them. I need to make sure they don't just belong to him.

They belong to me now too.

Chapter Sixteen

CBSNews.com

April 9, 2018

The One Who Got Away: The Woman Who Escaped Serial Killer Jeff Lake

[VIDEO LINK]

[HOST]: Serial killer Jeffrey Robert Lake was known as a Southern "gentleman," but for several years he lived in New York with his former wife, Allison Michaels. In fact, authorities believe he may have additional victims based there. And now a woman has come forward as believing she narrowly escaped being one of Lake's victims. Lauren Robinson was 22 and dancing at a gentlemen's club in Manhattan at the time. On this particular night, the club was visited by a large group of businessmen in town for a convention. But there was another man there who demanded her attention.

[LAUREN]: There was this guy watching me. He was quiet compared to the convention guys. He bought me a drink and asked if I was okay when one of them got handsy. He was really nice. I hate to say it now, but he was a real gentleman.

[HOST]: At this point, Lake had been carefully covering his tracks and was well beneath the FBI's radar with the spate of missing women from his native North Carolina. Women like Lauren fit his profile of young, vulnerable women who worked at night and didn't have a large circle of friends and family who would be concerned immediately if they went missing.

[LAUREN]: When I finished my shift that night, my car wouldn't start. Before I could go back inside, the guy who had been so nice to me comes over and asks if I need help. I didn't get weird vibes off him at all. He offered to drive me to the nearest garage or wait with me if I had someone I wanted to call. I should have called someone, but that money I'd just made was for tuition and groceries and he seemed so nice. . . . [SIGHS] Stupid. I was so stupid.

He walked me to his car, opened the door and then grabbed me by the hair and slammed my face into the doorframe. He broke my nose. I could feel blood running down my throat.

I thought he was going to rape me. I started screaming. One of the bouncers who had been leaving heard and started running toward us. That's when the guy jumped in his car and took off.

[HOST]: Lauren chose not to call the police, since her parents didn't know she was dancing to help pay her tuition. When she sought medical attention for her broken nose, she told the hospital staff that she'd tripped and fallen.

[LAUREN]: I was lucky. You can't tell me I wasn't. I've thanked God every day since. When Jeff Lake got arrested a few years later and I saw him on TV, chills ran down my spine. It was him.

My aunt Catrina doesn't live far from the Logans. Turns out my cousin Maxine and Darcy attend the same high school. Small world, I guess. That's how my aunt was able to get in touch so fast—she caught up with Moira at a PTA meeting or something.

I take my cues from Mom. She's not nervous about seeing this woman, so I won't be either. She's looking forward to it, which does a lot to soothe my anxiety. Maybe not everything connected to Jeff Lake is going to suck major ass. Meeting Mom's family was awesome, and the more I know about where I come from, the less of me I feel belongs to Lake.

We drive over late Monday afternoon, after my cousin and aunt get home. The house we pull up to is more modern than the Logans', but still has that old-fashioned look. It's dark redbrick with a cream portico and trim. Surrounded by full, leafy trees, it looks like something off a TV show.

"Cat's a few years younger than me," Mom says. "Jeff was nine when she was born. They're half siblings, not full."

"Right." I frown. "Is it true his father was a rapist?"

Mom rolls her eyes. "According to his mother, it was a boy she dated who took off when he found out she was pregnant. She was assaulted at a party, however, and he likes to say that was how he was conceived. Makes for more drama."

"Douche," I mutter.

Mom smiles. We get out of the car and approach the front door. "I think you'll like Cat. You've always reminded me a bit of her. And I mean that as a compliment, just FYI."

I see why when she opens the door. My jaw drops—and so does my aunt's. If my hair were short and blond, you'd swear she was just an older version of me. Like, it's a little unsettling how much we look alike, especially since she's Lake's sister.

"Oh my God," Catrina whispers, still staring at me. "I had that hair once." Then, blinking back tears, she opens her arms to Mom. "Sweetie, it is so good to see you."

I glance over my shoulder at the street to see if we're being watched. We are. There's a guy with a camera sitting in a car across the road. He's not even trying to hide what he's doing. Like it's his right to invade our lives. I used to love this kind of tabloid stuff when it was focused on celebrities, but now that it's on me . . . well, let's just say I've changed my mind.

"We should go inside," I say, tempted to give him the finger. The only thing that stops me is that Lake would probably find it hilarious.

"Oh, is that vulture still there?" Catrina asks, craning her neck to look around me. "He's been there since this morning. I almost flashed him my tits, but he doesn't deserve the thrill."

I choke on laughter and she gives me an affectionate smile. Maybe being like her isn't a bad thing after all.

She ushers us into the house. It's nice. Not too neat, but not totally chaotic. She's got a lot of stuff—a lot of color and art on the walls. I like it. It feels welcoming and lived-in. Warm.

A girl about my age sits curled up in an overstuffed armchair in the living room, texting on her phone. She looks up when we walk in. Wow. She and I are definitely related. She's blond, obviously, but looks a lot like her mother.

"Maxi, this is your aunt Al . . . Gina and your cousin Scarlet. Sorry, Gee."

Mom shakes her head. "Please. I can only imagine how strange this is for you. Hello, Maxine. It's good to see you. You were a baby last time I saw you."

My cousin gives us an assessing look. "Did you see the reporter out front?"

I stiffen, but let it go. I'd be pissed too if I were her. She's had to live with this shit her whole life, and now it's raised its head again. I don't like it, but I should acknowledge it. Right?

"Yeah. Don't worry, I stopped your mom from flashing him," I tell her in a dry tone. "Sorry if you feel like we've messed up your life."

She stands up and walks toward us. We're even close in height. She might be an inch shorter than me, if that. "I'm used to it, and I'm pretty sure you didn't start it." There's nothing but resignation in her voice. "You want a coke?"

"Coke," I've learned, doesn't necessarily mean a Coca-Cola. "Whatcha got?"

She inclines her head toward the kitchen, and I take the cue to follow her. Mom and Catrina disappear into the living room.

"So, it's Scarlet, right?" she asks as she opens the refrigerator. "I prefer Maxi, or Max. You like diet or non? We've got some Dr Pepper made with cane sugar."

"Dr Pepper's good." Taylor makes fun of me for liking it. She says it tastes like cough syrup.

She hands me a bottle. It's nice and cold in my hand. "Wanna sit out here, or in there with them?"

"I don't know," I reply honestly. "I really am sorry for whatever hassle this has caused."

"Ain't your fault," she says, leaning against the counter. "We know where to put the blame. He's *loving* the attention." She takes a deep drink from her soda and stifles a belch. "You seen him?"

I nod. "Three times now."

She shudders. "We don't visit him. Don't even talk about him much unless my—our—grandmother's around."

I'm surprised. "She's still alive?"

"If you can call it that. She had a stroke a couple of years ago. Mom and her other brothers—Will and Mike—they put her in a home. She kinda just sits there and blinks."

"Fuck," I whisper.

My cousin arches a brow. "Yeah. But better than listening to her blame herself for how Jeff turned out. You'd swear to God all that blood was on her hands instead of his." She pales slightly. "Sorry. That was inconsiderate."

I shake my head. "Please. He's nothing to me. I wouldn't have bothered to meet him if the FBI hadn't asked."

"And now you're neck-deep in the shit circus." She smiles. "They will back off—just so you know. Every once in a while, something will happen and they show up, but they always go away. Kinda like herpes."

I snort soda out my nose. "Oh, shit! Fuck." I feel like an idiot.

Laughing, my cousin hands me a wad of paper towels. "Sorry 'bout that."

She's not really sorry. It's okay, though. Other than the burning in my sinus cavities, I'm good. I like her. I like her mother. There's no BS, only honesty. Even though we just met, I feel like I've known her my entire life. More than at my grandparents' house even, I feel accepted here. I feel . . . like we're family. I'm not sure I could ever articulate how that feels after seventeen years of thinking it was just me and Mom. To have it happen twice in only a couple of weeks is overwhelming.

I blink back tears, cover them up by blowing my nose in the paper towel Max gave me. Sniffing, face tingling, I throw the crumpled mass in the garbage can.

"You okay?" Maxi asks, giving me a concerned look.

I nod. "It's just weird, y'know? I've spent my whole life thinking it was only me and Mom and now I have all this family . . ."

"It's got to be a lot," she allows. "Don't go getting all emotional, though. Give us a bit and we'll be more pain in the ass than anything else." She grins and I smile back, feeling better.

I meet my other cousin, Joey, and my uncle Steve when he comes home from work. They're both stocky with dark hair and big grins. Joey is twelve and it's obvious he wants nothing to do with his sister, or me.

We stay for dinner—pizza delivery—and well into the evening. Before we leave, Aunt Catrina gives me a banker's box. It's heavy.

"I talked to your mom and she said it was okay to give you this."

"What is it?" I ask as the weight of it pulls on my shoulders. I heft it onto my forearms.

"It's my box of Jeff," she replies with a shrug. "I'm not sure what else to call it. I thought it might help you understand what he did—and what it did to us. It's not all bad. There are some things from when I was a kid . . . well, take what you want from it, if anything. I don't want it back. I made it for you."

I'm not sure what to say. I'm both touched and filled with a morbid sense of dread. "Thanks."

"I'll text you tomorrow about the party," Max says. "I can pick you up if you want."

I nod. "Great." I figure Mom will veto that as soon as we're outside.

As we leave the house, I notice the reporter—or whatever he was—is gone. There might be someone else watching, but I don't see anyone suspicious. We put the box in the back seat. I'm tempted to buckle it in, like whatever's inside it is volatile.

"You and Maxi seem to hit it off."

I open the passenger door and get in. "I really like her."

"Cat said she was anxious to meet you." Mom sighs and shakes her head, settling behind the wheel. "My God, it was good to see her. Scarlet, I . . . I feel like a weight has been lifted off my chest. Isn't that ridiculous? Our lives have been turned upside down and I actually feel better than I have in years. Do you hate me for it?"

"No. Not at all. It has to be a relief. I mean, for me these people are all new, but for you . . . they're family. They love you."

"They love you too. And I want nothing more than for you to love them. I've had so much guilt not just for denying you them, but for denying them you. I'm so happy they're getting to see what a fabulous kid you are."

My throat tightens. "Thanks." I swallow, collect myself. "Would Aunt Cat really have flashed that guy?" I ask as we back out onto the street.

Mom laughs. "She really wanted to, but she knew it would just stir things up. She settled for giving him the finger."

I smile.

Chapter Seventeen

Our school assigns every student an email so we can keep in touch with our teachers and classmates. It's how I'm supposed to get copies of notes, lectures, and assignments so I don't fall behind while we're in North Carolina, which is great. What's not so great is that when I check in on Monday, my inbox has blown up with messages from "friends" wanting to know how I'm doing. There's even one from Neal. Like he lost my phone number or something.

It's so tempting to delete them all. Instead, I copy the addresses into one message:

Hi, it's Scarlet. Thanks so much for thinking of me. I'm doing great. See you soon!

I hit send before I can think better of it. Screw them. Sofie hasn't reached out at all, and I kinda respect her for it. At least she's not pretending. I don't owe these people anything. I say as much to Taylor and Ashley when I FaceTime with them that night.

"It's crazy," Taylor confides. "So many people have asked me about you. I just tell them you're not allowed to talk about it."

"I tell them to fuck off," Ashley adds, frowning. "I hope you don't think I'm like them, Scar."

"No. You were my friend first, morbidly curious second." Plus, she rescued me and Taylor from the press that day, and I'll always love her for it.

She laughs, thankfully. "Not gonna lie, I have *so* many questions."

"And someday I'll tell you everything I can," I promise. "It's just that right now it's too much. *He's* too much. I should probably be asking you stuff about him."

"How's that going?" Taylor asks. "Have you seen him?"

I tell them about the last visit and that I'm scheduled to see him tomorrow. "I don't know how long this is going to take, but at this rate, it's going to take a while."

"Is that okay?" Ash asks.

I shrug. "Aside from the fact that he'll probably die on me first? It's going to have an effect on me, right? I mean, how can it not? I'm trying to keep his sick from sinking in. Every time he says my name, he makes it sound like he's mocking me."

"Your name is your name," she insists. "He's just trying to play head games. He's probably mad that your mother changed it."

"Oh, he is. It's not bad enough that he killed Britney Mitchell, he took her name too. It's like he wanted to own her completely."

There's a moment of silence between the three of us. I can

practically hear Ash's brain working. She wants to say something, but she's holding back. Finally, she says, "Maybe you could give Britney her name back."

My brows pull together. "How?"

She looks at me like it ought to be obvious. "Scar, you're where it started. Where she was killed and buried. You've got your camera with you. Go turn this shit into something positive and beneficial. Film it."

Taylor's jaw drops, and she looks into the camera like she wishes she'd thought of it. "Ohmigod. That's perfect. It would be like therapy, only more productive."

Ash continues, "Also, it will make one hell of a project for film school."

Not going to lie, that assessment sends chills down my spine. They're right. Not only am I sitting on something I can use to my advantage, but I can do something good with it too. I can take control of the situation—as much as possible. And it would be like giving a huge finger to my father.

"Not just Britney," I say. "Maybe all the victims. I can honor their memories." As quickly as my excitement came, it evaporates. "Wait, no one's going to want to talk to me. I'm his fucking kid. They'll hate me."

Ash shakes her head. "I don't think they will. Not if you're sincere in wanting to remember their daughters."

"You could do a web series," Taylor suggests. "Use this attention for good. Get his victims out there so people talk about them instead of him."

Shit. She's right. This could be huge, but more than that, it would make me feel like I'm doing something meaningful. I'm not just listening to Lake verbally masturbate about his victims but making sure they're honored.

"I love the idea of giving Britney back her name," Ash

comments. "She was first. You need to start with her. Your mom knew her, yeah?"

I nod, my brain still trying to process and put the pieces of how this might work together. "I need to make a plan."

We spend the next half hour talking about the things I could do. I write them down, scribbling in the notebook at my desk. I need to be careful how I do it, but I think Mom will appear on camera for me. Agent Logan probably would too. And maybe he could reach out to Britney's family for me?

No. That needs to be me. If I'm going to do this, I can't take any easy paths. The point isn't to make it easy. It's supposed to be hard. I need it to be hard. I'm not doing this to profit from my father's crimes. In fact, I need to leave him out of the project as much as possible. It's the victims. Only the victims. That includes everyone Lake hurt.

I guess that includes me too, huh? I'm not sure I can talk about it on camera, but if I can't do it myself, how can I expect anyone else to trust me with their stories?

Okay, this is making me way too anxious. Or maybe that's excitement. It's hard to tell sometimes.

After we hang up, I go out to the living room of our temporary home to talk to Mom. She has to be okay with this before I can do it.

She looks up from the TV when I walk in and immediately presses pause on the remote. "What is it?" Her voice is a shard of concern, slicing into my skin.

"Nothing bad," I assure her. "At least . . . I don't think so. I have something I want to talk to you about. Got a minute?"

"Of course." She turns the TV off and pats the space beside her on the couch. "Come sit."

I do, taking a moment to gather my thoughts. "What would you say if I told you I want to make a documentary about

Lake's . . ." No, wait. If I'm going to do this, I can't continue to distance myself. I have to own this. I swallow. ". . . about my father's victims?" Calling him that feels so wrong, but it's the truth. I can't run from the truth. I'm not responsible for him, but I am responsible for how I handle this.

Mom pales. It's like I see the blood drain from her face. "A documentary?"

I nod. "Most people don't remember the victims. They're just interested in him. I want to make sure people know about the women he hurt. That includes you—if you'll help me."

She looks away, stares at the blank TV screen.

"I'm going to do this," I affirm—to myself as much as her. "I need to do this. It's the right thing to do, and I'm not going to live the rest of my life in his shadow. You shouldn't either. It's time to change the narrative."

A tiny smile curves her lips as she turns her face toward mine. "Change the narrative. I like that. He's been in charge of the story for far too long. If you want to do this, I'm okay with it, but it's not going to be easy. There will be people who accuse you of trying to cash in."

I nod. "I'm going to mention him as little as possible. Do you think I could meet some of the families?"

"Oh, honey . . ." She wants to stop me, I can feel it. She wants to wrap me up in the cocoon she's had me in for the past sixteen years, ever since she ran away. I see the moment she realizes she can't do it. There's no going back, for either of us.

"Maybe," she says. "I don't know. Andy would be better to talk to about that. You can ask him when we go to dinner tomorrow night."

Right. I'd forgotten that we were invited to the Logans' for dinner. Moira wants to make it at least a weekly thing while Mom and I are in Raleigh. I'm looking forward to seeing

Darcy again. And Luke. Yeah. Now that Neal has revealed himself to be clueless, I can rid myself of the disappointment by flirting with someone who at least thinks enough of me to ask how I'm doing.

"I will," I say, and vow to keep that promise. No chickening out. I'm taking charge of the narrative. I just hope I can give the plot a happy ending.

"I want to tell you a story," my father says when I sit down next to his bed the following afternoon.

Immediately, I stiffen. The expression on his face is full of far too much anticipation for this to be good. "About?"

"About my favorite victim."

I try to look relaxed, but I'm sure he can see the twitch in my left eyelid. "Why?"

He smooths his free hand over the blankets covering his lap. "Because I think it will help you understand me better." He gazes up at me through lowered lashes. "Don't you want to understand me better?"

"I don't want to understand you at all."

"Sure you do. Everybody wants to know about their parents. I grew up without my father—my real father—and I've tried to find out everything I can about him, even though he was a rapist."

"I heard your father was your mother's ex-boyfriend. Not a rapist."

"You heard wrong."

I shrug in the face of his darkening expression. If he wants to cling to that story, what the fuck do I care? Maybe it makes him feel better. He's a monster because his father was one. Maybe he thinks that makes him sympathetic.

"Is it Britney?" I ask. It would be one hell of a coincidence if it was. Last night I decided to learn more about her and now he's going to hand information to me?

"No. Someone else." He shifts against the pillows. He looks terrible. "Do you want to know more about Britney?"

"You named me after her. She must have meant a lot to you."

"She did. Once. And then she just pissed me off." He shakes his head. "But this isn't about her. She was my first, but not my favorite. My favorite is someone I got to play with for a while."

Swallowing, I force myself to hold his glittering gaze. "Are you doing this because you want to upset me?"

He opens his hands, chain jangling against the side bar of the bed. "Of course not. I want to explain it to you. I want to make you understand, if I can, what it's like to be me."

His tone is so patently false that I hesitate. I don't know if this is going to be even remotely helpful to Agent Logan's agenda, but I can't walk out if this girl is a victim he doesn't know about. My father—inwardly I cringe—knows this.

"I have done some research on serial killers," I tell him. "I know the science." Sort of.

He makes a face. "Pfft. That's all theories and nonsense from folks who have no idea what it's really like to be one of us. I won't insult you with that stuff you can get from doing an internet search or watching *Criminal Minds* reruns."

"It's mostly streaming now. Hardly anyone says 'rerun' anymore."

He doesn't like being corrected, but the dark look he gives me isn't a surprise, so I don't freeze up like a rabbit. "You know what the experts have to say, but the men who have been like me—predators—we're all different. They try to paint us with the same brush, but ain't a one of us who completely fits in their mold."

"Like snowflakes," I drawl. "You know, there have been female serial killers too."

"It's not the same."

"All right." I'm not going to argue with him about it, because I really don't care what he thinks. His arrogance is just so tedious. "So, tell me your story."

"You got somewhere you need to be?"

"The nurse said you have radiation today." Though, to be honest, I'm not sure why they're bothering.

"Right. Well, I will endeavor to be less verbose than usual, then." When I don't say anything, he begins, "She was the prettiest thing I'd ever seen—prettier even than Britney."

I focus on the spot between his eyes rather than his gaze. It makes it easier to pretend I'm listening to a podcast or something and not a real person confessing their darkest deeds.

"I knew right then and there, I had to have her. I needed to spend as much time with her as I could before finally giving in to my dark urges. And that's what they are, you know. Urges. It's like being presented with a glass of water after being thirsty for days. Gulp it all down and you'll regret it. You gotta take sips, even though it feels like you'll never get enough."

His eyebrows are a little uneven. The hairs long and sticking up. I study them. "It's public knowledge that you liked to keep your victims around for a bit—before and after you killed them."

"Ah. I suppose that must be a little disturbing for you. But there is something so completely delicious about flesh that yields under one's touch."

My gaze slips, locks with his. "Unresponsive, you mean."

His gaze brightens. "Precisely. I could try to explain it, but I don't think you'd ever comprehend."

Is that supposed to be an insult? Because it's really not. "No. I don't think I would. But you were going to tell me about a specific person, not generalizations."

"I'm glad to see whatever education your mother secured has afforded you a reasonable vocabulary. There's been a shocking dumbing down of this country in the last fifty years."

I do not roll my eyes. I sit and watch him expectantly. He seems to find it amusing. He finds *me* amusing. It makes me want to press a pillow over his face until he stops squirming. The thought sits heavy in my stomach. It doesn't make me like him. It doesn't.

Does it?

"Right, so my favorite girl. She came along long before you, of course. I mean, you're my true favorite, you know that, right?"

"You don't have to flatter me," I reply. "I don't have any delusions about your fatherly feelings toward me."

He clucks his tongue against those big teeth of his. "Ouch, baby girl. That stung. Well played. All right, where was I? Right, as soon as I saw this girl, I had to have her. It was ridiculous how infatuated—*captivated*—I was by her. The smell of her shampoo made me dizzy. The idea of touching her made my hands tremble. Tremble! I kid you not."

I don't think I've ever met anyone as in love with the sound of their own voice as my father. Forget the death sentence, they could just put him in a room with a bunch of other monsters and let him talk them to death.

"Okay, so she was pretty awesome." I don't add, *And then you killed her.*

"Yes. 'Awesome' is a perfect descriptor for her. Long, brown hair, mesmerizing gaze. She looked at me like I was the most amazing man she'd ever met. People gave us such a hard time for being so into each other. I was smitten. Well, as smitten as a man like me could be with anyone other than myself." He gives me a charming grin. It looks more like a grimace, pulling the skin of his cheeks back over those sharp cheekbones.

Unease slithers down my spine as he keeps going.

"I wanted to spend every waking moment with her, and when I wasn't with her, I fantasized about what it would be like to finally kill her. For a while, I didn't go out looking for other girls at all. She was everything I needed. Sometimes, when I asked her to, she'd pretend to be asleep or unconscious when we had sex. She'd let me do whatever I wanted. She was my muse, feeding my fantasies. I'd practice on her what I'd do to my other girls, and when she told me she was pregnant—"

Realization hits me like a physical slap. He's not talking about someone he killed.

I jump up from the chair. "You sick fucking bastard. Shut the fuck up."

He smiles. He laughs. "Took you long enough! I was starting to wonder if I'd have to spell it out for you. Not as smart as you think you are, huh?"

I'm shaking. "You're an asshole." I glance over my shoulder at the door. "I'm done!" I yell.

The door opens. I expect to see Agent Logan, but it's Mom who walks in like some kind of movie badass. All she's missing is a gun, or a sword. Agent Logan is a few steps behind her.

"Allie." Her name is a whisper. A trembling breath. But his smile. Oh, there's no denying the delight Jeff takes in seeing her. If he were anyone else, I'd say he loved her, but he doesn't know how to do that. She's just his crowning achievement. His favorite.

Mom hesitates a second before walking to his side. I watch as her fingers gather one of the IV lines feeding into his arm and begin to pinch and twist the tube.

My father looks concerned. "What are you doing?"

"The only thing that makes your pain bearable is the morphine they steadily supply," Mom says, her voice so cold I can almost see frost in the air. "That pain you've caused others, Jeff—it's so much. All I have to do is clamp this line and you get to feel what you deserve."

No one—not the nurse or the guard, or even Agent Logan, tries to stop her. No one cares if Jeff Lake experiences a few moments of pain. In fact, we all want to witness it. There's probably too much morphine in his system for it to amount to much, but it's more the show of power. My mother is finally putting her ex-husband in his place.

He doesn't ask for help—he knows better. He doesn't look anywhere but at her. She doesn't flinch, just stares at him, her face a composed mask of cold hatred. It's only when panic starts to show in his expression, when his discomfort becomes obvious, that my mother shows any other emotion. It's only a flicker, but her satisfaction is palpable.

"Does it hurt yet?" Her voice is a low rasp. "All that cancer eating you alive. It must be so horrible. You fantasized about killing me? Well, guess what, *darlin'*? I've fantasized about killing you too, and I have to tell you, the reality of this is so much better."

"Allie . . ."

She presses a finger to his mouth. How can she even stand to touch him? "Let me enjoy this, sweetheart. It's been a while, hasn't it? You know, I used to hope you'd go to hell—if there is one—but lately . . . lately I've started hoping there's a heaven. That's where I want you to go, Jeff. I want you to be greeted at the pearly gates by all the women you hurt, and then I want the angels to turn their backs so those women can do whatever they want to you for all eternity. I want you to suffer like no other soul has ever suffered. But you know that, don't you? It's what you want. You like knowing you've made me this hard and cruel."

"My girl," my father says with a gasp of pain as his left hand—clawlike and thin—reaches for her. "My . . . best girl."

Mom releases the med line and my father collapses against his pillows, sweating and gasping for breath. He never did manage to touch her.

"Come, Scarlet," Mom says, holding out her hand. "You're done for the day."

"But . . ." I want to tell her that he didn't give me a name, but I stop myself, because he did. And it's a reminder neither of us needs.

It's what you want. I will remember her saying that until the day I die.

Not all of my father's victims are dead.

Chapter Eighteen

We don't talk about it. Not when we leave, or when we're in the car. We don't talk about it at the Logans' when we arrive for dinner later. I don't know if Mom and I will ever talk about it, or if it even needs to be discussed.

I don't think Mom would have actually killed my father, no matter how much she might want to. I do know that, if given the time, she would have stood there and held that line until he begged her for relief. She would have made him suffer with no remorse. I'm not going to judge her for that.

To be honest, it gives me a new respect for her. It also made me realize how much he fucked her up. If he'd never been caught—if she had stayed with him—what kind of damage would it have done to her? What would she have become?

And what about me? How twisted would he have made me? Judging from the games he's played the few times I've seen him recently, probably very.

So, yeah. I don't think we're going to talk about it. At least not anytime soon.

Agent Logan hands Mom a glass of wine as soon as we enter the kitchen. She gives him a grateful smile. I'm going to end up driving back to the safe house tonight, I know it.

He offers me a "coke," which I accept with thanks as Darcy breezes into the room. "Scarlet!" she exclaims. "Hey. I'm just finishing some homework, want to come up?"

She grabs another can of what I'm drinking, and I follow her upstairs to her room. There's a pile of laundry that needs to be put away on the trunk at the foot of her bed, and her laptop is open on the desk. Taylor Swift's new album plays softly. The room smells like vanilla and sugar.

"I'm actually done. Just need to save it. I didn't want it hanging over my head while you were here. How are you?" She says it all in one breath.

I smile at her energy. "Okay. Saw my father today and he was his usual charming self."

She makes a face. "I'm sorry. Do you want to talk about it?"

I shake my head. "I'll save it for future therapy. Tell me something good. What's been going on with you?"

"Ugh. School. Nothing exciting. Oh, but I saw Maxi today, and she mentioned you met."

"I didn't know you were friends."

"We're not, really. I mean, we know each other and we're friendly, but we don't hang out. I see her at parties sometimes 'cause we have mutuals, but that's about it. I should probably hang out with her more. She's cool." There's a soft pink in her cheeks as she says this, like it embarrasses her.

"I like her," I say, as if my recommendation carries any weight. "I mean, we just met, but I liked you as soon as I met you too."

She smiles as she closes her computer. "Well, obviously you're an excellent judge of character!"

I want to ask about Luke, but I don't. I haven't really heard from him since the night I called him.

"Maxi invited me to a party this weekend."

Darcy brightens. "The bonfire?"

I shrug. "I don't know. She said it was at something called 'the pit.' "

"Yes!" Her squeal pierces my eardrums. "I'm going too! This will be so cool."

"Is Luke going too?" I keep my tone casual. "Or did he get back with the ex?"

"No, not for her lack of trying, though. Ugh." She rolls her eyes. "Some girls are just desperate, y'know?"

An image of Sofie swims in my head. "I just lost a friend because of a guy. Why do we give them so much power over us?"

She gives me a lopsided smile. "No idea, but we give it to anyone we like."

Something in the way she says it makes me inwardly smack myself. I'd made assumptions about her. "You're queer?"

Darcy nods. "Bi, to put a point on it. So, it's not only guys we act stupidly over. I've made a fool of myself over a couple of girls." She shakes her head.

I don't care who she dates, but I like her enough that I want her to find someone who treats her like she deserves. I take a sip of soda. "I'm glad you're going to the party. It will be nice knowing at least two people there."

"Luke will be there too! Sorry, you asked that, didn't you? So, you'll know three people. I'll tell you who to stay away from." She claps her hands excitedly. "Oh, this will be so much fun!"

"No one's going to care that I'm a serial killer's daughter?"

Some of her good humor drains away and I feel guilty.

"They're going to know who you are, but they know Maxi is his niece too. I mean, it will make you stand out, I guess, but no one's going to want to set you on fire or anything."

I laugh. "That's comforting."

"And look, you don't have to talk about him if anyone asks. People are nosy, but they don't have any right to know about you just because they want to know about him."

True enough. That's something I need to remember.

"So," I begin, changing the subject. "Is there going to be anyone you're interested in at the party?"

Darcy blushes. It takes me a second to figure out what that means. "Maxi?" I ask. That little blush a few minutes ago makes sense now.

"Oh, I feel like *such* an idiot." She throws herself across the bed, bouncing on the mattress. "I've known her for, like, ever, and never felt like this. It just hit me suddenly. Is that weird?"

I shake my head. "I don't think so."

"I don't even know if she likes girls."

"I don't either," I reply honestly. "I guess you can't just ask her."

"I could, but that might make it weird." She shrugs. "I'll just play it coy and see what happens." She looks at me. "Maybe we can find a hookup for you. You deserve some fun."

"I'm not interested in hooking up, thanks. The last time I did anything like that, he ended up being a loser. Not at all who I thought he was."

"I'm not talking long-term. Just have some fun. Not like you ever have to see anyone from here again if you don't want to."

She has a point. Weirdly, that makes me a little sad. I don't want this friendship to be temporary. "We'll see. Hey, what do you wear to these kinds of things? I don't want to look weird."

"Oh, just be casual. You'll be fine." She tells me what she's going to wear and that helps. It's not like I'm looking to impress, but the less I stand out, the better. Maybe no one will say anything about my father. Maybe someone will want to punch me in the face. I don't know, but being able to stick close to people I know makes the anxiety easier.

I tell her about the documentary I'm thinking of doing. "I might do it as a series of short films about each victim. Maybe upload it to YouTube."

"That sounds fab! Can I help?"

"Sure, if you want."

"I do. Not to make myself sound awesome, but most of the families of those girls know my father. It might help to know he's behind it. Wait, have you told him yet?"

"No. Mom figured I could talk to him tonight."

"Good idea. He could be a big help. Like, not only getting you access to the families, but with research and stuff." She frowns. "You sure you want to know what your dad did to them?"

"I already know a lot of it." I have no problem admitting that. "But I think I have to know. Does that make sense? Like, I realize I have no responsibility for what he did, but I feel like I do have a responsibility to the people he hurt."

She smiles at me. "You're a good person. A really good one, you know that?"

I squirm under the praise. "Thanks, but I think most people would feel the same way."

"You give humanity too much credit. No, you're a really good person, and if you want to hook up with my brother, you have my blessing."

I choke on a mouthful of soda, almost spitting it all over

both of us. Instead, some dribbles down my chin as I fight to keep it in.

Laughing, Darcy hands me a tissue from the box on the nightstand. "Sorry 'bout that," she says.

I hiccup and wipe my face. "Yeah, right." Like she sounds sorry. "Why would you even say that?"

"Oh, please. I've seen how you look at each other. How he wants to impress you by showing his vulnerable side." She makes a retching noise. "Still, I love him, and I really like you, so if you want him, go for it. Just don't leave me if it doesn't work out."

"First of all, you and me, we're friends now. You're stuck with me. Secondly, I do not want to hook up with your brother."

"Ouch," comes a familiar voice from the doorway.

I close my eyes in humiliation. Of course this would happen. Darcy starts laughing like it's the funniest thing ever and I want to crawl under the bed. I force myself to lift my head and meet his gaze. The corner of his mouth tilts up in amusement.

"Well, fuck," I say. "How far of a drop would it be if I jumped out the window?"

Luke laughs. "Too much, and I don't want to have to explain to the EMTs that it was my total lack of appeal that made you do it. Dinner's ready, by the way."

Darcy jumps off the bed. I follow a bit more slowly. "Please," I say, rolling my eyes. "You have mirrors in this house. You know how 'appealing' you are."

"Apparently not appealing enough," he comments as I start to brush past him in the doorway. His voice is low, for me alone.

I don't know what makes me do it. Normally I'd need the help of alcohol and maybe pot to have this kind of nerve, but

I pause, putting myself in the doorframe with him, so there's only inches between us. I lock my gaze with his. There's no denying what I see there, and I like it. My heart begins to beat a little faster.

I smile. It's flirtatious, kind of wild and dangerous. I could get hurt, but that's part of the fun, right? Or maybe some risks are just worth it.

I step closer. My legs brush his. He goes very, very still. Is he holding his breath? "Maybe you should try harder," I suggest.

And then I leave him standing there as I follow after his sister. I want to run, but I don't let myself. Every step is slow and deliberate, and I do not look back.

I feel Luke's gaze on me every step of the way.

It feels good.

Agent Logan takes me aside after dinner.

"Scarlet, would you help me get dessert?" he asks.

I glance at Mom, but she doesn't look concerned. "Uh, sure. Yeah." I push back my chair and follow him to the kitchen.

He gestures to a cupboard. "Get us some plates, will you, hon?"

I do as he asks.

"Thanks. There's no need for you to look nervous. I just wanted to make sure you were okay after what happened with your mom and Lake today."

I watch him cut a pecan pie into what look to be perfectly symmetrical pieces. "He deserved it."

"Mm, but the warden doesn't agree. He doesn't want Lake's wife suing, so he's decided your mother isn't allowed back in the prison."

My heart skips a beat. "What about me?"

"You're still allowed—especially now that we got the identification back on those remains in Darlington."

I meet his gaze as I hand him a plate. "Was it her?"

His mouth tightens into a line. "Searchers found a partial skeleton in a grave on the trail in Virginia as well. Should have dental records in a day or two."

"Jackie Ford." I frown. "Agent Logan—"

"Andy."

"Okay. Um, I've been thinking that I'd like to honor my father's victims."

He plops another piece of pie onto a plate and licks his thumb. "You already are. You're bringing them home."

"I want to make videos about them. Like, short films. Do you think that would be all right?"

"I can't see why not. How can I help? Information?"

"If you're allowed, yeah. I'd like to maybe interview you. Aside from their families, I don't think anyone cares about them as much as you do."

He smiles slightly. Sadly. "Maybe not. Tell you what, next time we go to Central, we'll take a little extra time and have a proper meeting. You write up what it is you'd like to do and I'll run it by my superiors. Meanwhile, you go ahead and start your research. But don't approach any of the families until I give you the okay."

I nod, glad that I hadn't acted on my first impulse to reach out myself. "I won't. I wouldn't know what to say."

"I'm sure you'd do fine. Now, why don't you take those plates into the dining room while I get coffee. Luke, come give her a hand."

I hadn't even noticed that Luke had entered the kitchen, I'd been too focused on Agent Logan and not screwing up.

I have two plates and Luke picks up the other four, his hands big enough to make carrying two in each look easy. He has nice hands. Long fingers. I wonder if he knows how to use them.

What a liar I am. I told his sister I wasn't interested in a hookup, but I'd hook up with him in a minute in any other situation. My cheeks burn just at the thought of the things I'd like to do with him. But it feels wrong to lust after him when there are so many other important things I need to do.

"You're quiet," he says as we head back to the dining room. "You didn't offend me, you know that, right?"

I don't pretend to not understand. "I'm glad. I didn't mean it the way it came out."

He smiles lopsidedly. "So I shouldn't completely give up hope then?"

My stomach drops and every pulse point shudders. He's only flirting, I tell myself. Still, I manage a coy smile in return. "You're welcome to try." Then, I walk past him to the table.

You're welcome to try? What the hell was that? Ugh. What a stupid thing to say. It doesn't even make sense as an answer to his question. I suck at flirting. Luke doesn't seem put off, though. Maybe he thinks awkward is hot.

When we get ready to leave later that evening, Agent Logan gives me a thick file folder. "Research for you," he says. "I'll let you know about the rest in a couple of days. I think it sounds like a wonderful project."

"Thanks," I say, trying to ignore how proud Mom looks. I'm not doing this to make myself look like a good person, but I appreciate his approval.

It's not until we're halfway back to our temporary home that Mom says anything. "So, about earlier . . ."

"You were a total badass," I tell her. "I'm happy to leave it at that."

She smiles. "All right. I'm fine with not talking about it. You know, I can give you the names of some places to film. We can visit them if you want."

I clear my throat. "Can we visit the cabin?"

It's dark, but a passing car illuminates the tightness of her jaw. "I'm not sure I want to go back there, Scarlet."

"Do the Lakes still own it?"

"They didn't want to sell it and have it become some kind of morbid tourist attraction, so yes. I'm not sure how much any of them use it, though."

"I think I should start there. Right? I mean, I should see it."

She's silent for a second. "If it were up to me, you'd never set foot on that property, but yes, I suppose you can't do a piece on the victims without seeing where they were found."

"You don't have to come with me. I can go by myself."

"No. Not by yourself. Take Luke and Darcy, or go with Cat and Max. Do not go up there alone, you hear me? God only knows what kind of freaks are stalking the place."

Her tone is one I know better than to argue with. "Fine. I won't go alone." I glance out the window. It's too dark to see anything but lights. "Did Agent Logan tell you they found bones in Virginia?"

"Mm. I'm not surprised. Jeff wants to be the big man. He's not going to lie yet. Once he's got the FBI running all over the place, then he'll start testing how much shit they'll put up with."

"Do you think he feels anything at all for me?" His opinion of me doesn't matter—or at least I don't think it does. He's my father. But it's got to matter more than I want it to. More than I'd ever admit.

"As much as he can, sweetheart. I'm afraid that's probably not much. I can tell you that when you were born, he looked at me and said that he wanted to be the father you deserved. I believe he meant it at the time. He just wasn't capable of making it happen."

"You sound almost sorry for him."

"I suppose in some ways I am. At other times, I'd cheerfully kill him—as you saw today."

"Would you really have done it?"

She doesn't look at me. "There's only one reason I wouldn't do it."

"What's that?"

Her expression tightens. "He'd love driving me to it."

Truecrimeconspiracies.tv

Did Jeff Lake Have an Accomplice in His Wife?

Carole Ann Boone is thought to have helped her lover, Ted Bundy, escape from trial in Colorado, and therefore acted as an accomplice in the assault and murder of members of Chi Omega sorority in Florida in 1978.

Karla Homolka assisted her husband, Paul Bernardo, with the rapes and murders of three minors in the early '90s, one of whom was her sister.

While many would have us believe that serial killing and violence is a mostly male-dominated sector, there can be no denying that there is often a woman, or several women, who somehow helped the killer carry out his horrifying agenda. This scenario is far more likely than one where the woman claims to have been completely in the dark about her husband's deeds.

In 2006, Jeffrey Robert Lake was arrested for the murders of 14 North Carolinian women, the bodies of whom were discovered at the family vacation home Lake shared with his wife, Allison Michaels. It was determined that he also gifted her several items taken from those same women. Michaels claimed to be ignorant of her husband's grisly obsession. In fact, there is an infamous clip of her collapsing in court when she realizes the necklace she treasured was ripped from the neck of a dying girl.

But how could Michaels not have known? In almost every instance of this type of violence, the woman behind the man has had suspicions. Ted Bundy's ex-girlfriend Liz Kendall even called the police because of her unease. Still, she continued to have a relationship with the killer despite her misgivings. A part of her knew what Bundy really was. How could Carole Ann Boone not have seen the same warnings? At least in the case of Lake's second wife, Everly Evans, we know that she's little more than a prison groupie, she knows full well what he did and—to some degree—doesn't mind. She got together with Lake once he was already in prison, and while she may not have a problem with what he has done, there was no way she could have assisted him.

Perhaps it's hindsight that makes us ask these things, but how could Michaels not have suspected her husband of *something*? By all accounts, she never even questioned his fidelity, though he would often come home late from work. She says she chalked it up to his being a busy lawyer. She never wondered about the gifts, some of which were obviously cheap when compared to what he was able to afford given his stellar career?

Maybe Michaels did suspect. Maybe Michaels *knew*. Maybe she was okay with it. Maybe she even helped, as in the case of Homolka. She served time for her involvement, why hasn't Michaels? Because she disappeared during Lake's trial and hasn't been seen since. The FBI claims they have no reason to suspect her involvement in the crimes, but perhaps that's because she sold Lake out in order to secure her own freedom. Michaels and her daughter—Lake's child, named after his first victim—are still out there, and I know I am not alone in wanting some answers.

Got a comment or theory? Post it below.

Chapter Nineteen

Maybe it's because I was named after her and have shame surrounding it, or maybe it's that she was his first victim, but I start my research with Britney Mitchell. It just feels right. She's at the center of everything and a huge part of my new life, even though she was dead long before I ever arrived.

I have to spend Wednesday working on a paper for history, but first thing Thursday morning, I look up Britney's senior yearbook online and screen-capture her grad photo. It's grainy, but it will do. I thought Google would give me more information than it did. I mean, there were a lot of hits, but most of them said the same stuff, the majority of it about my father, not Britney. What I did find had to do with her murder, not her life—even the interview with her poor parents focused on her death.

Mom knew her, and I'm going to talk to her, but I want to do some of this on my own first. Agent Logan gave me a bunch of stuff, and I have the box from Aunt Cat. She knew Britney too. Mom will give me information if I ask, and I know my father will. But I don't want their information just yet. I want to discover Britney Mitchell on my own. Before I look at her as my father's first victim, I want to see her as a person. Who was she?

The yearbook I found online is actually pretty helpful. Aside from her big-haired grad photo, there are lots of other photos of her. Britney was popular. She was in the drama club and on the prom committee. She was on the honor roll and tutored other students.

She was someone I would have sneered at. Someone I would be intimidated by. One of those girls who tried too hard and was into everything. The realization makes me feel more than a little guilty. Britney Mitchell should have gone on to be whatever she wanted to be. She should be a mother, maybe even a grandmother—if she wanted kids. My father took that choice away.

I look up the name of the high school online. When a photo pops up, I'm taken aback. That's Darcy's school. I knew Britney was local, but I didn't expect her to be *that* local. I text Darcy and ask if I can meet her after class, then log into my email to get my work for the day from my teachers. Half an hour later I get a text:

Hells, yeah!

I smile and then text Mom to see if she'll drop me off on her way to the hairdresser's later. Yeah, I could just go ask her, but I'm lazy.

I'm outside when the bell rings and students begin to file out. Darcy spots me before I see her. I guess this burgundy hair makes me easy to see. She's not alone—Max is with her. Is my cousin as into Darcy as Darcy is into her? That would be so freaking convenient—and a little unfair, I think bitterly. Why does it always seem easy for other people to find their person?

Right, because Luke hadn't basically told me he's mine for

the taking. I'm only leery because I actually *like* him as a person. It's not just his looks like it was with Neal.

"Hey!" Darcy says as she bounces up to me. "I met up with Max, so I invited her along. You mind?"

"Of course not." I hug them both. "I was doing some research today and I found out that Britney Mitchell used to go here."

Darcy frowns. "Why's that name familiar?"

"My uncle's first victim," Max replies before I can. "They used to have, like, a shrine or something to her here, but they took it out right before my freshman year."

"Really?"

She nods. "We didn't ask them to. I mean, it wouldn't have bothered me, but I guess the board thought it might. A few people have had things to say about it—like I set it on fire or something. It's still in the office, just tucked away where you can't see it."

"I'd like to see it."

Max glances at Darcy. "Want to come with, FBI man's daughter?"

Darcy chuckles. "Poor Emily is going to have a stroke if we all go in there." She looks at me. "That's the school secretary. She's, like, eighty."

A shrug from Max. "Let's go see."

Emily is not, as it turns out, anywhere near eighty. She's probably in her sixties, though. She's got that salt-and-pepper hair that looks really cool—like with the wide swath of white in the front. She's short, but in good shape, dressed entirely in black and wearing bright red lipstick. *Emily the Strange*, senior-citizen edition. Same name and everything.

"Maxine, Darcy," she says as a greeting when we walk in, but her gaze is fixed warily on me. "Who's your friend?"

She already knows, I realize. She's seen me on the news.

"Scarlet Murphy," I respond, offering my hand.

The older woman seems surprised, but she accepts the gesture with a firm one of her own. "Nice to meet you, Scarlet. What can I do for you?"

"We'd like to see the Britney Mitchell memorial," Darcy explains.

Poor Emily might not be old, but I'm not so sure about that stroke thing. She goes pale. "Why?"

"I want to make a documentary about my father's victims," I admit. There's no point in lying or pretending she doesn't know me. "They deserve to be known, and I want to know them. I'm starting with Britney. I won't touch anything. I just want to see her, and maybe film a bit, if that's okay." I might be on thin ice here, seeing as how Agent Logan hasn't really given me permission, but I'd rather have the footage and not be able to use it than not have it at all.

Emily thinks for a moment. I hold my breath.

"Come with me," she says.

We follow her through the reception area of the office to a closed door at the back of the room. She opens it and holds it for us to file in. Then, she joins us.

It's not a large room by any stretch, but it's bigger than a closet. We can move around fairly comfortably, even though there are a lot of things stored in here. I spot the memorial right away. It's in a glass cabinet on the back wall. The overhead light reflects in the glass, making it hard for me to make out much detail from where I stand.

I move toward it, heart stammering and skipping. I don't know what I think it's going to do to me, but I'm almost . . . afraid of it. Afraid to look.

Afraid to see her.

Yet, there she is. My reflection in the glass falls into place over her smiling grad photo. For a split second, we're one; then I move to the right so I can see better. The photo is but one item in the case. There's a collage of her with friends and teachers. A script for *Romeo and Juliet* with doodles and notes scribbled across it lies up front. A school jacket is pinned to the back wall, sleeves folded neatly, the name BRIT embroidered on a patch.

I swallow. The girl in these photos is my age. I mean, she was in the photos online, but these aren't scanned—they're actual photographs. It makes it all the more real.

"She was a good girl," Emily says from behind me. "A bright student. Popular. Lots of friends."

I catch Max watching me out of the corner of my eye. "You okay?"

I nod before pulling out my camera and switching it on. I record a slow pass of the case and the items inside before putting the camera away once more. I can't look at this anymore. I turn to Emily. "Thanks."

"I hear your father's dying," she responds.

"Cancer," I say.

She arches a thin brow. "He's going to hell, you know."

"I don't care where he goes, so long as I don't end up in the same place. Thanks again." I leave the room, Max and Darcy behind me.

Max has weed, so we drive to a convenience store and smoke up behind it. I'm paranoid about getting caught when the back door opens, but it's just the clerk, who sticks his hand out to Max. "Hey, girl. Give me a toot off that thing." It's obvious they know each other, so I will my heart out of my throat and back into my chest.

Comfortably buzzed, we stock up on chips, licorice, gummy bears, and soda before climbing onto the battered picnic table on the outskirts of the parking lot. I feel slightly numb and totally free. No anxiety, no itchy brain. That's what anxiety feels like to me—an itch in my head I have no hope of ever scratching.

"Weird place for a table," I comment, biting into a piece of licorice.

"There used to be a sandwich place here," Darcy explains, as if that makes me understand any better. And then, "Was it weird for you to see the pictures of her?"

I nod. Being high makes it easier to talk about it. "It made her real."

"Yeah. I take back what I said earlier," Max says. "I'm glad I don't have to look at her every day."

"She needs to be remembered, though," I say.

My cousin makes a face. "I don't have to remember her every damn day, though. Do I? Do you? I mean, we didn't do anything wrong. Your father killed her before we were even born." And then, "That's the most fucked-up thing I've ever said."

We all laugh. Yeah, it's probably wrong, but it feels good—like a release. She's right and I know it, so why have I taken on this shame? It's not like my father has any.

We hang out a little longer. I'm surprised Mom hasn't texted to see where I am. She's been more relaxed lately, but still . . .

"I should probably get home," I say, anxiety creeping in.

Max checks her phone. "Yeah. Me too. Give you a lift, Darcy?"

"Sure."

I get into the back seat, letting Darcy sit up front. Doesn't matter how much I like riding shotgun, that would just be a douche move when they're obviously checking each other out.

We drop Darcy off first. I try not to notice the longing in her gaze when she says goodbye to my cousin.

"So," Max begins as we head to my place. "You wanna drive up to the cabin this weekend and film there?"

My head whips around so fast my neck twangs. "Seriously?" Is she like, some kind of mind reader?

She grins. "Mom mentioned that you might be curious. There's not much to see up there anymore. Although, with you showing up and him dying, there will probably be a resurgence."

"A resurgence of what?"

She shrugs, eyes on the road. "Trespassers. People like to come looking for souvenirs. Someone stole one of the doorknobs once. Other people have broken in and taken things. We have an alarm now—and nothing of value is left up there anyway. Other people like to leave flowers and gifts where the bodies were found."

A shiver runs down my spine. It would make for some chilling footage. Emotional. "Your mom wouldn't mind if we went up?"

"If it's just you and me, she'll worry, but if we take some friends, say Darcy and Luke?" She flashes me a smile. "We should be good."

I can't help but grin back. "Are you trying to use our shared trauma to hook up with Darcy?"

" 'Hook up' sounds tawdry. I just want to spend more time with her. Besides, I don't even know if she feels the same way."

I shouldn't get involved, but how can I not? "Oh, I think you can assume she does."

"Has she said anything?"

"Only that she'd like to get to know you better too. As more than a friend. Other than that, I'm staying out of it. I don't know either of you well enough to play matchmaker."

"Too late." My cousin looks so pleased with herself. "Now I feel totally okay telling you that Luke wants to get to know you better too."

There's a tumbling sensation in my chest. "How would you know that?"

"Darcy told me. You've been a great conversation starter for us, if you must know. So, I owe you for that. Coffee? We can do a drive-through."

"Uh, yeah. Sure. Why were you talking about me and Luke, though?"

"Darcy was thinking of trying to get you two together, but she's worried it might mess up you and her being friends. I told her you can be her friend and still bone her brother."

I snort. "You did not say 'bone.' "

"I did." And we both start laughing like it's the funniest thing we've ever heard.

By the time Max drops me off in front of the safe house, I'm starting to straighten out. The coffee helps. I know it's not good for anxiety, but I like it too much to give it up.

"Is that an FBI agent?" she asks, nodding at the nondescript car parked close by.

"Cops, I think. Phelps and Marco. I met them the first morning we were here. They always let us know who's watching and when there is a shift change. The FBI has security all around the house, though. Cameras and an alarm system."

"It's got to be boring as shit sitting in a car for eight hours," Max comments, looking at them through the windshield. "So, hey, I'll pick you up around eight thirty Saturday night?"

"Sure. When do you want to go to the cabin?"

"Sunday?"

"I'll clear it with Mom and let you know." I open the door. "Thanks for the ride."

Max salutes me before driving off.

It's not until I reach the steps that I realize Agent Logan's car is parked behind the house. I frown. What's he doing here? Did Lake die already? Oh, God. Is Mom in trouble for what she did to him at the prison? Is he pressing charges?

I unlock the door and walk in. A woman with a sleek, dark bob sits in the living room. It's not until she lifts her head that I realize it's Mom. She's dyed her hair back to its natural color. I stand there, gaping at her. She looks so . . . different. Pretty

Except for that black eye and split lip.

"What the fuck happened?" I demand, dropping my bag and rushing toward her. I land on my knees on the hardwood floor and barely feel it.

"It's nothing," she says. "And don't swear."

"That's not fucking nothing." I turn to Agent Logan. "Who did this?"

He looks at Mom, not me. "Gina?"

She sighs, drawing me around to face her. "When I left the hairdresser's, I stopped by a bookstore. A woman there recognized me."

"And what? Hit you in the face with *War and Peace*?"

"Harry Potter, actually. Must have been one of the last ones, because it had some heft."

"How can you joke about this?"

She meets my gaze. "Because I've had two of your anxiety pills and a glass of wine. Given how you smell, I'd expect you to be slightly more chill."

My jaw eases open, like on a well-oiled hinge. I don't know

what to say. Behind me, Agent Logan chuckles. "At least tell me you hit her back," I mumble.

She shakes her head and lifts an ice pack to her eye. "That would have only made it worse. She hit me and then looked utterly horrified. Security grabbed her and escorted her out. The owner got me some ice and napkins. She gave me a gift card for free books before I left. I guess she felt sorry for me."

Okay, now I hear the slight slur to her voice. It's been more than one glass of wine. Or maybe more than two pills. "Are you okay?"

"I'm fine. It hurts like hell, but . . . I don't know. Now that it's happened, I'm not afraid of it happening anymore."

"Did she say anything? I mean, she didn't assault you just because she recognized you, did she?"

Mom looks at Logan. Clearly, she's wondering how much to tell me. Logan nods and Mom lowers the ice pack. "Sweetheart, she hit me because she knew one of Jeff's victims."

"And?"

She sighs. "And she thinks I helped kill her."

"You didn't, though."

"No." She looks so tired as she pauses. "But I was there when he buried her."

Chapter Twenty

WTF?

Mom doesn't let me wonder for long. "He said he wanted to get the cabin ready for Easter. We always spent Easter there with his family. You and I stayed behind because I had to work and Cat and I were going to take you and Maxi to have photos taken with the bunny at the mall."

I want to tell her to hurry up, but I don't. I sit and listen and don't want to miss a single word. This got her assaulted, so I need to hear it.

"Anyway." Mom clears her throat, rubs her palms on the tops of her thighs. "I decided to drive up with you on Sunday. It was a nice day and only an hour away. I thought he'd like the surprise. When I got there, he was covered in dirt. Filthy. I knew he'd been doing some landscaping and spring cleaning. . . . He got mad at me for showing up. He yelled—something he rarely did. I thought . . . for a second, I thought he might hit me."

"What happened?" I rasp when she falls silent, reliving the moment.

"You started crying in your car seat. It was like it flipped a switch inside him. All of a sudden, he was the man I married again. He hugged me. Told me he was sorry. Then, he got you out of the back of the car."

I think about him picking me up. Try to imagine him being that caring. "Why was he dirty?"

She gives me a sympathetic look. Looks at Agent Logan. It's not for permission, it's for something else. "He had gone on a spree and had three girls there. One of them was still alive—so I'm told."

Horror creeps over me, little prickles of disgust running over my back and arms. "He'd been . . . *visiting* one of them?"

She nods, unable to meet my gaze. I might puke. He hugged her. Held me, while the dirt of violating a corpse stained his skin and clothes.

"He might just have been burying her, I don't know. Regardless, he took you and me inside the cabin and told me to take a bath while he finished up. After, he'd hop in the shower. So, I did. I never questioned what he was doing out back. I heard him shoveling. I even saw him putting mulch around a new rosebush when I finished bathing. You were in the bathroom with me, still in your carrier. He came inside, showered, and made us dinner like nothing was wrong. Like I hadn't almost caught him with a dead girl."

I can't believe this. It's too much. Too horrible. I stare at her.

Mom lifts her chin. "They believe Lisa Peterson was in the shed behind the cabin that day. She was still alive, but Dina Wiley was in a shallow grave. I could have found either one if I only looked. If I'd been less trusting, I might have saved Lisa. That's why I deserve this." She gestures to her battered face.

"He would have killed you," Agent Logan says, and the edge to his voice tells me he's said this before. "Along with Lisa, and then Scarlet would have been raised by a psychopath."

She shakes her head. "I should have seen . . ."

His jaw is set. "Don't go down this road again. We both know where it ends."

I look between them. "Where? Where does it end?"

Mom is silent. Agent Logan's gaze stays focused on her. "A place your mother doesn't want to go back to."

She's the one who breaks their weird standoff. It's obvious neither is going to tell me what the hell they're talking about, and I'm not sure I want to know. Every time I find something out about my father, I wish I hadn't.

"Anyway," she says. "It was a friend of Lisa Peterson's who Pottered me."

She makes jokes to deflect, I realize. Her fingers tremble as they push back her glossy dark hair. Her fingernails have been bitten to the quick. One of her cuticles looks like it's been bleeding. She's a mess and just trying to hold herself together.

She's afraid.

I close the distance between us. Standing, I put my arms around her shoulders and hold her against my stomach. Her arms wrap around my hips and squeeze hard. I turn to Agent Logan.

"Should we press charges?" I ask. "Or would that make things worse?"

"Your mother doesn't want to file. I thought I might deliver that news to her assailant myself."

Neither one has called the woman by name. Is that for my benefit? Mom has to know I wouldn't have enough nerve to confront anyone by myself.

I nod. My buzz is completely gone, but I don't feel anxious. I feel angry.

"I want to see him tomorrow," I say. "Can you arrange it?"

"Of course." If he's surprised, he doesn't show it.

"Have they ID'd either of those bodies?"

"Michelle Gordon and Jackie Ford were both positively identified. Agents were notifying the families today. Our closest field offices in both states have press conferences planned for today." He checks his watch. "Probably as we speak."

Which means my father will get more new attention. The bodies will be secondary to his infamy. Ten bucks says they'll spend two seconds on the victims and five minutes rehashing his career as a serial killer.

"Did you ask anyone about my project?"

He nods. "I have a meeting about it tomorrow morning. We can talk about it more after your visit to Central if you want."

"I do. And so we're clear, if anyone hits me, I'm pressing fucking charges. I don't care who they were friends with."

To my surprise, Agent Logan smiles. "I wouldn't expect anything less." He rises to his feet. "I'm going to head out. I just wanted to stay with your mother until you got home. Don't forget to set the alarm after I leave, okay?"

I walk him to the door. As soon as it clicks shut behind him, I immediately set the alarm and turn the locks into place. Then I return to my mother, kneeling before her so I can get a better look at her face.

"Does it hurt?"

"It's not too bad." She tries to smile, but it turns into a wince as her lip pulls. She sighs. "I need more wine."

I'm the last person to criticize her for self-medicating, so I pour the glass myself. I pour one for myself too. Mom has never cared if I drink so long as I'm careful. I sit in the recliner beside hers and reach my hand across the distance that separates us. She glances at it in surprise before slipping her fingers through mine.

"You need a manicure," I tell her. "Maybe some acrylic tips you can't chew through."

"That would be nice. Maybe a pedicure too."

I smile. "Good idea. Next time some bitch takes a swing, you can claw her eyes out." Honestly I'm a little pissed she didn't fight back, even though it would have caused more trouble.

"I'll make appointments for us in the morning."

I raise my glass to her, and she does the same. And then we both take a sip.

I'm scared this situation is going to take us *both* someplace we don't want to go. Someplace there's no coming back from.

"Hey there, darlin'."

It's Friday. Just under a week has passed since the last time I saw my father, but he looks like it's been longer. He's faded and gaunt. There's not much left of him but a thin layer of aged parchment over a frame of bones. His sclera look almost turquoise in the yellowed whites of his eyes.

I would be horrified if he were anyone else. I'd want to do something to help him. Instead, I want to sit here and watch him die.

That's what he's done to me. What he's making me. The hate I feel when I look at him burns the back of my throat.

Is this what he wants?

"You not going to speak?" Amusement drips from his tone.

"I was just thinking," I reply.

"About how pretty I am?"

I pull a tight smile. "Yeah. Sure."

He coughs. "Doc says I don't have much time left. Looks like I will be takin' some of my girls with me after all."

That's why he looks so bright. Why he looks happy, even though he's being eaten alive by the disease inside him. He's going to win. It was never about giving up the names. It was about getting me here.

No. It was about *him*. I shouldn't be surprised by him pulling something like this. "Looks like," I say, keeping my tone flat. "Or you could give me all their names right now. And I can be on my way."

"Nah. I want my little girl with me until the end."

"Why do you hate me so much?"

His eyes widen. "I don't hate you. I don't feel much of anything for you, or anyone else to be honest."

"But you're not being honest. If you didn't feel something, you wouldn't take so much delight in messing with me. So, what is it?"

Lake purses his lips. "I suppose there's no harm in us being honest with each other. Not like I have the luxury of dragging out our reunion like I want. I don't like that you grew up not knowing about me."

"I knew about you. I just didn't know you were my father."

"That's what I mean. I lost out on years with you. Years I might have had if your mama hadn't bolted."

I arch a brow. "You think she would have brought me for Family Day? You're delusional."

"I've been told that before, by smarter people than you. Maybe I am. But I can at least leave this world with the satisfaction of having shown myself to you." He focuses his gaze on me. "I will leave a mark you'll never be able to lose."

I could tell him he's not that memorable, but we both know it would be a lie. I won't ever forget him, or this.

"What did you like about Britney?" I ask, changing the subject.

He blinks. I imagine the painkillers he's on make it hard to keep up. He must hate that. "Britney Mitchell?"

I nod.

"Why do you keep coming back to her?" His drawl is heavy today. He must be really medicated. "She's old news."

"You want me to understand you, right? Help me do that."

His bright and slightly unfocused gaze wavers as it meets mine. "It's because of your name, isn't it? You want to make this all about you instead of all about me."

For a man who puts so much vanity into his own intelligence, he really lacks an understanding of what makes people tick. "What did you like about Britney?"

"You mean, what made me kill her?"

"No. I mean, what did you like about her? I don't care why you killed her. I know why you killed her. I want to know about *her*."

It was the wrong thing to say. His eyes narrow. "What do you know, little girl? And why do you care? Because you think I regret doing her? Because me giving you her name means something more than making you a living trophy?"

I shake my head. Didn't he remember telling me about that already? "It's not about me, or you. You dated her for a few years. There must have been something about her that drew you to her, outside of seeing her as prey. Otherwise, you would have just killed her and been done. But you killed her after you broke up. I think because she actually hurt you. She made you feel something. I mean, she's kind of what made you."

He scoffs. "She didn't make me. She was smart. I liked that she could keep up whenever we had a conversation. And she was sweet." He shrugs. "She treated me like I was special to her. I liked that."

"Why did you break up?"

He's so quiet that, for a moment, I think he's fallen asleep. "Because she didn't think I was special after all. I tried to share myself with her and she got scared. She didn't want to see me anymore."

"Share yourself? You mean, you told her what you were?"

"No." He gives me a look of disgust—like I'm so beneath him intellectually. "I tried to show her what I liked. What I needed. She wouldn't give it to me."

There's no need for him to elaborate. I know what he means, and I don't want to know what he did to her, or what he tried to do. "She didn't understand you."

"Yeah. And I started obsessing over it. You ever obsess over anything?"

I know I'm looking at him now the same way he looked at me. "Uh, yeah. All the time."

He nods, smiling. I'm back in his good graces. "I began to obsess over her. She rejected me and I still wanted her. I know it wasn't love, but it was as close as I could get. When I saw that she'd moved on, well . . . it did something to me. I knew I'd never be free of her if I didn't do what I wanted to her. She was mine, after all."

I swallow. "So you killed her."

He shakes his head. "Killing her was an accident. I never meant to do that. I started out just wanting to drug and have sex with her. I wanted her to not respond. Not make any demands. I'd gotten that thought in my head, right? Couldn't stop thinking about what it would have been like if she hadn't gotten scared."

What the hell am I doing? Why did I ask for this? I want to run, but I grip the arms of the chair instead. I hold his gaze.

"I got carried away." He says it as if killing her was like eating an entire cake or going on a shopping spree. "It felt so good, I wanted to keep pushing it further and further, and then . . . there wasn't any further to take it—not at the moment."

I really wish I didn't understand what he means. Bile lingers on the back of my tongue. "How did you feel when you realized you'd killed her?"

"I was alarmed at first. But . . . there was this sense of elation that refused to go away, even when I felt shame for what I'd done. I knew it was wrong, but it felt so damn right." He laughs. "For that moment, I was a monster. And I liked it."

"You'll still be a monster," I remind him. "Dying won't absolve you of that."

"Nah." He waves a hand at me. "Don't try to butter me up. I'm nothing more than a rat in a cage. There's not a soul in the world that would be afraid of me these days. 'Cept maybe for your mother."

Our gazes lock. "You think she's *afraid* of you?" I thought she did a pretty good job of proving the opposite.

"Oh, you bet she's afraid. Not for herself, no. Afraid of what I might tell you. Afraid of how you might look at her after. Afraid of the doubts you might have. She's so afraid of that mark I'm going to leave on you."

"But that's not really the same as being afraid of *you*."

"Which one of us is the lawyer, child? Don't argue semantics with me, I will decimate you. And that's not why you're here, is it? You're here looking for another name, begging for scraps at my table to ease the blight on your soul."

"I feel like you must practice half of what you say to me," I tell him with a sigh. "It's not as impressive as you think."

He smiles—just a slight curve of those dry, thin lips. "You know what is impressive? How you try to stand up to me. How hard you struggle to hide your fear."

"Of *you*, a rat in a cage?" Maybe I shouldn't talk to him with such mockery in my tone, but it feels good.

He doesn't seem to notice. "Me? Oh, no. . . . Of how worried you are that you might be like me. Of how much of me is in you."

Moisture disappears from my throat, leaving me suddenly dry and parched. "You know, this taunting is getting really old."

He makes a *tsk*ing noise. "I love how you try to face me—as if we're equals."

"I don't want to be your equal. And while we're at it, I don't want to be anything like you. I'm not anything like you."

Another little smile. "You keep telling yourself that."

Asshole. "Tell me about Michelle Gordon."

"I already did."

"What was she like as a person?"

He looks at me with genuine surprise. "How the hell should I know?"

"You stalked her, didn't you? Watched her to make sure she fit your profile."

"My *profile* was nothing more than a certain appeal. They only had to remind me of Brit in some way. Only had to elicit a reminder of that first tingle of magic." He takes a sip of water from the cup beside the bed. "I wasn't looking to make a connection, child. I just needed the release of the kill."

A strange expression crosses his face. It's like wonder or surprise. "I've never admitted that to anyone but myself. Feels good to say it out loud."

"Are you feeling self-actualized?"

He laughs. "Your sarcasm is appreciated, baby girl. Any wit or quickness you got from my side of the family. Allie's family is a bunch of dolts. Wealthy, but dumb as a bag of rocks. Not sure how Allie got to be as smart as she is."

"Her name is Gina."

"Right. Gina Murphy. You know that was the last name of one of her exes? No? You should ask her about him."

"I don't think I'm going to do that." I try again: "How can you remember all their names but not know anything about them?"

My father sighs. "Just when I start to think you might be half-ass intelligent, you go and reveal your ignorance to me. It didn't matter who or what they were, okay? What mattered is what they became in my mind. What they became to *me*. You know what? You're boring me today. We're done."

I startle. "Done? But you haven't given me a name."

"That makes you panicky, doesn't it? No doubt they've found Michelle and Jackie by now. There's probably been a press conference. I've already had some reporters try to get in here to interview me. It's nice being relevant again. I could give you another name, keep the ball rolling, but it's better TV if I don't. We have to build the conflict and drama a bit, don't you agree?"

"You're an asshole," I say, voice low.

He laughs, but it quickly turns to a grimace of pain. Good. "When you leave, will you wonder if there was anything you could have done to entice me to give up one of my girls? How you could have tried harder? And instead, you just wanted to talk about old news?"

Oh, he is not putting this on me. I'm not taking responsibility for him being a psycho. "They're not old news to those who cared about them."

"You trying to sell yourself as a bastion of goodness, are you? Coming here because you see yourself as the hero of this story? This is *my* story, little one. I'm the protagonist. I'm the one who decides how the plot is going to go. Not you. My girls didn't matter to you before you found out who you are. Even now, you don't care about them, you just care about wiping my stain off you."

That cuts. It's way too close to the truth. "Your ego is astounding," I bite back. "You don't matter half as much as those women. You'd be *nothing* without them. That's why you hold on so tightly. They're why the media wants to cover you, why the feds give you what you want. It's not you. No one gives a flying fuck about *you*."

Oh, he hates me now. "I'll still be famous long after you're dead, kid. People will remember my name forever."

I shake my head. "Maybe. But it will always be because of those women, not because of you. You're not even going to leave a pretty corpse. Maybe they'll print photos of you after you're dead—like they did with Bundy. Everyone will remember you wasted and ugly. Even you would turn your nose up at the corpse you're going to leave behind."

That was too far. Something flashes in his eyes, and the bastard grins. "My girl."

I should have known he'd love seeing me so hateful. There's no way I can hurt him. I try to push the anger away, shove the ugly aside, and see him for what he really is.

"I almost feel sorry for you," I say. "You've ruined any love anyone might have had for you. Britney, Mom, me—even Everly. Or does she still see you as an 'apex predator'?" Throwing his words back at him gives me some satisfaction.

He shrugs. "I haven't seen her."

It bothers him more than he's letting on. Suddenly I'm exhausted. These visits steal a little bit of life from me every time. "Are you going to give me a name today?"

"No," he says. "I don't think I will."

Asshole. He's so smug, and I react without thinking. "Give me a name or I'm done with your shit."

He blinks. "Are you threatening me?"

"No. I'm telling you. I'm tired of this game and I'm tired of you. You said if I came to visit, you'd give me names. Either you're going to do that or you're a fucking liar, but I've put my life on hold to be here and let you make a mess of it. So, I'm *done*, Jeff. Give me a name and I'll stick this out. Don't give me one and kiss your legacy goodbye. No more me. No more press. Just dying alone."

He straightens up against his pillows. It takes effort, but he does it. "You're bluffing."

I might have laughed at his incredulous tone if I weren't so tired. "Am I? I'm your kid, as you love to remind me, so look into my eyes and tell me if you really want to press it." I force myself not to flinch as our gazes meet. Staring into those empty eyes of his makes my skin crawl, but I do it, and I hold his gaze as silence stretches between us. It's not about me and it's not about him. It's about his victims. That's why I'm here.

"Tami Klein," he blurts. His mouth opens as if he wants to give me every last horrible detail. He hesitates. "Tell Logan there's a bonus for him. And for you too."

I don't even frown at his cryptic words. "Thank you." I get up from the chair. "I'll see you soon."

"Tomorrow?"

There's a hopeful note in his voice that I want to squash.

I want to literally grind it beneath the heel of my boot. Prove just how much of his cruelty I have in me. I want to tell him to go fuck himself. But this isn't about me. It's not even about him.

"Sure," I say. "I'll see you tomorrow."

Chapter Twenty-One

I have this page in the back of my notebook.

REMEMBER THEIR NAMES:

Britney Mitchell
Kasey Charles
Julianne Hunt
Heather Eckford
Jennifer Stuart
Tracey Hart
Nicole Douglas
Kelly King
Wendy Davis
Tara Miller
Patricia Hall
Nina Love
Dina Wiley
Lisa Peterson

Michelle Gordon*
Jackie Ford*
Tami Klein *
Suzanne Wilson*

**Girls I helped bring home. Remember that when I
feel like giving up.*

Agent Logan was completely amped when we left my father. Apparently, Tami Klein's body had been found in a shallow grave in 1997, along with the body of another girl— Suzanne Wilson. Both were from South Carolina.

The FBI had suspected they were my father's victims— South Carolina had been an easy drive for him in '97—but hadn't been able to prove it.

Now I know why Lake said he'd given me a gift for Agent Logan. Two victims claimed.

I'm exhausted after the visit, like always. He takes so much of my energy I'm starting to wonder if that's what's keeping him alive. He's like a leech.

"He really doesn't want you to stop visiting him," Agent Logan tells me—needlessly—as he drives me home afterward. "He enjoys seeing you."

"Mm. Yay for me."

I feel him glance at me as I stare out the window at the now-familiar passing scenery. "You don't have to do this, you know. If it's too much, we'll figure something else out."

I would like that very much, but I'm already in. "I should finish what I've started." Not like my father's going to be around much longer anyway.

"And you have your own project now as well. I spoke to some colleagues. We would like it if we could help facilitate your meetings with the families. We'll give you access to certain information if you allow us to use anything you find in your research to help us find more victims."

"Well, yeah. I wouldn't want to stand in the way of that. But it's really about making sure I don't fuck anything up for you too, isn't it?"

His smile is rueful and reminds me of Luke. "Yeah, pretty much."

I nod, about to turn back to the window . . .

"The Mitchells want to meet you."

My focus whips back to him. "They do?" I didn't know he'd spoken to them.

He nods. "I took the liberty of asking when you first mentioned your project. They wanted to talk about it a bit, but yes. They'll meet you. Their only condition is that I be there."

I frown. "Are they afraid of me?" It seems ludicrous to even ask.

He doesn't look at me—his attention is on the road. " 'Wary' might be a better word. They don't want to hurt you, but they don't want to be hurt either. You're a smart girl, Scarlet. You must know that meeting the daughter of the man who killed theirs is cruelly ironic. The fact that he named you after her makes it even more painful."

"If it hurts so much, why did they agree?"

"They're hoping it will help them heal, same as you."

I'm silent. Is that what I hope this docuseries will do? Heal me? Yeah, I suppose so. Something needs to refill what my father has taken.

"Does next Wednesday work for you?" he asks.

"I'll check my calendar," I reply with a dry smile. "Yeah, that's great. Thanks."

He looks at me—once, then twice. "I'm glad you're going

to the party this weekend. Some time with people your age will do you good. Plus, your mother won't worry about you so much if Luke is there."

"Because he's a big, strong guy?" I can't keep the sarcasm out of my tone, so I smile to soften it.

He arches a brow. "You bet. I taught him myself how to take someone down."

Oh. The idea of Luke doing something like that is kinda hot. Not too far off from how those groupies feel about my father. My stomach twitches.

Agent Logan frowns. "Scarlet, I know you've seen nothing but people who want to harm you and your mother, but there are people out there who would want to be close to you for the same reason. Your father has a following. I don't need to tell you that."

"Yeah, I know. The cult of depravity. I've seen *Natural Born Killers.*"

"Good movie," he allows. "I saw it in the theater with Mo when it came out."

"The nineties had some great movies exploring the dark side of humanity," I comment. "One of my favorites is *Kalifornia.*"

"Brad Pitt was amazing in that," Agent Logan enthuses. "Nothing pretty about Early Grayce. Honestly, he's one of the most chilling depictions of antisocial disorder I've ever seen."

We talk about movies for the rest of the drive. The conversation replenishes a lot of the energy depleted by my father, and by the time I walk into the house I feel almost normal.

My phone pings with a text. I smile when I see from whom.

Luke

Hear you're coming to the party
tomorrow night.

Me

I am.

Luke

I'll have to make sure I shower.

Me

Only if you want to impress me.

Luke

Is that all it would take????

Me

What can I say? I'm a sucker
for good hygiene.

Luke

In that case, I'll even brush my teeth.

I chuckle.

Me

You're weird, you know that?

Luke

But do you like it?

I hesitate. He's being open with me. No games that I can
tell. How I respond to this determines how we go forward.

Me

I do.

Luke

:-) In that case, I'll even wear
deodorant.

"That you, babe?" Mom calls out from deeper in the house.
"Yep!"

Me

Gotta go. See you Sat.

I shove my phone in my pocket and kick off my shoes. I find Mom in the living room. She looks up when I walk in. One look at her bruised, swollen face and my shoulders sag.

She's going through the box of stuff my aunt Cat gave us. She tries to smile, but it's obvious the attempt hurts, so it's more of a wince than anything else.

"Hey, you." It's funny how much her voice has changed since we got here. Funny how I've gotten used to hearing her talk with a slight drawl. "I hope you don't mind." She gestures to the box.

"Find anything good?" I ask.

"Some old photos. Letters. Things that hurt even as they make me smile. Sometimes it's hard to remember I'm not supposed to love him."

Has she been drinking? I don't see a wineglass anywhere. "You can love who you thought he was," I say.

She shakes her head. "No, it's better if I don't, but he gave me you. I'll always be grateful for that."

I swallow, suddenly overwhelmed by the desire to cry. He wants me to doubt this, to doubt her. I can't let that happen.

Mom puts the lid on the box and gets up from her chair. She walks over and pulls me into a firm hug.

Sobs rack my body as tears stream from my eyes. I cling to her like she's the only thing keeping me from flying away.

"I just want him to die," I confess.

She rubs my back. "I know, baby. I know."

I don't return to the prison on Saturday. My father "isn't up for it." He must be feeling pretty shitty for him to give up the chance to torment me.

What if he dies today? I've only gotten four names. I'd like to think that would be the end of them, but I know it's not. Agent Logan has a list of potential victims, and that's only the ones they suspect. How many more are out there that might never be found?

I can't think about that, though. None of it is my responsibility. They wouldn't have gotten those four if I hadn't agreed to this. And I have to remember that for my sanity. I can't own this responsibility, no matter how much I think I should.

Since I don't have to go to the prison, I spend the afternoon figuring out what to wear to the party tonight. It's not like I have a huge wardrobe to choose from here, and not like I have anyone to impress.

Okay, so maybe I'd like to impress Luke, but he's seen me first thing in the morning, so the bar's set pretty low.

Aunt Cat comes over for coffee with Mom. She's so pissed off about the assault when she sees Mom's injuries.

"I could kill Jeff myself for what he's done to you."

"Nature's taking care of it, Cat," Mom says as she pours them each a cup of French roast. She's got coffee cake too. When have we ever had coffee cake? I hover like a vulture over roadkill, waiting for a chance to snag a slice.

My aunt grins at me. "For heaven's sake, girl, sit down and

have some cake. Good lord, you're making me feel like we're starving you or something."

"I don't want to interrupt your conversation," I explain.

"You're old enough to hear anything we talk about," she replies. "If we want to talk about you, we'll tell you."

Mom smiles. "She would too. Scarlet's been getting ready for the party tonight."

"Oh, yeah. Maxi's doing the same thing." She glances at me. "You know this girl she's all infatuated with?"

Mom straightens. "Maxi's got a crush? On who?"

"Darcy Logan," I tell her, cutting into my cake with a fork. Oh, it smells so cinnamony and sugary.

Her eyes widen. "Really? Well, maybe something good came out of this after all."

"They already knew each other, Mom." I roll my eyes. "Not like I single-handedly brought them together."

"No, but you gave Maxi an opening. She can be really shy when it comes to her heart. Can't say I blame her. It might be the twenty-first century, but not everyone in this neck of the woods is as open-minded as they ought to be."

I shake my head. "I don't get why anyone would care who I—or anyone else—have sex with. As long as it's consensual, what does it matter?"

My aunt's eyebrows lift. "Are you having consensual sex with anyone interesting?"

"Cat!" Mom exclaims, but there's a gleam in her eye . . . she's interested in the answer. Seriously, what kind of pod person have the aliens replaced my mother with?

"No," I reply honestly. "There was a guy at home that I was interested in, but that juice turned out to be not worth the squeeze."

"Anyone here caught your eye?" That comes from Mom, with a very leading edge in her tone.

I meet her gaze with a roll of my eyes. "You mean Luke?"

"Yeah, sure. He's really cute."

Again, calling Luke Logan "cute" is a gross understatement.

I humor her. "He is. And guys like that are often more trouble than they're worth."

"Oh, but the trouble is the fun part," Aunt Cat interjects. "Am I right, Gee?"

No one else has ever called my mother "Gee." It's obvious she likes it. I guess it means something that someone she used to know has embraced the "new" her. "Unless he turns out to be a serial killer. They're definitely more trouble than they're worth." I gasp and she looks between me and my aunt. "Too soon?"

No one ever expects their mother to make that kind of joke. Although no one ever expects to find out their father is a monster either.

I start laughing. Aunt Cat does too, then Mom. We laugh longer than we probably should, but I guess we needed it.

"Back to Scarlet's love life." Cat wipes her eyes. "Do you like this boy? I'm assuming he's Andrew's son—the tall drink of water?"

Mom winks at her when I nod. "Yeah, he's been . . . nice." What am I supposed to say? That I'd really like it if he made a move? That there's a part of me that wants to climb him like a tree and do all kinds of things I've only read about? I'm not sure I want to admit that, even to myself.

"'Nice.'" Cat shakes her head. "I give up. Gee, I'm going to have to live through you. You getting any?"

I almost choke on my coffee as my gaze snaps to my mother.

Her cheeks flush a brilliant red. "Uh, no. There were a couple of guys in Connecticut, but nothing serious. I couldn't let that happen."

"Well, now you're home. We should go out tonight. Let's find you some young stud."

"Yeah, Mom," I encourage with a grin. "Maybe *you* could go after Luke."

She looks horrified. "Don't even joke. I'd feel like a dirty old woman. Cat, you're sweet, but I'm not interested."

"Why not?" I ask. "The secret's out. Not like you have to worry about someone finding out who you are. Not like you have to protect me anymore. Why shouldn't you go out?"

"Because I look like I got in the ring with Rocky?" She gestures to her face. "No one is going to want to hook up with this!"

Aunt Cat's shoulders slump. "My God, you're right. We'll have to wait until you've healed."

"We might be back north by then. Andy says it doesn't look like Jeff has long."

I freeze. "He said that?"

She nods, her expression turning wary. "His cancer's pretty advanced. I think he only made it this long because he knew you were coming."

Ha. Anyone eavesdropping on this conversation would think she was talking about a doting dad, not a manipulative asshole.

"I've only gotten four names from him."

My aunt reaches across the table and places her hand on mine. "Honey, he was never going to give you all those girls, so don't you take that on yourself."

She's right, so why do I have this feeling of dread all of a sudden? It's not like I'm going to be sorry to see him go.

I don't want to go back to Connecticut yet.

"The Mitchells have agreed to meet with Scarlet for the documentary she wants to film about her father's victims."

Thank you, Mom, for changing the subject as much as you can.

"Really? How do you feel about that, Gee?"

"I think it's good. I'm trying to decide whether or not to go with her. I never got to tell them how sorry I was."

"You should totally come with, if you want to," I tell her. "You need closure even more than I do."

"She's not wrong," Cat agrees. "Hey, did I tell you that crazy wife of Jeff's tried to talk to me about his last wishes? Apparently he wants to leave something to me. I told her to go eff herself. I am not interested."

I don't even want to think about what my father might possibly have to leave anyone. More jewelry from dead girls?

I finish my cake and get up from the table. I take my coffee to my room and listen to some music while I start to do my makeup. God, it's boring here. No, not boring. I just find the time long. Once schoolwork and prison visits are done, there's not much else for me to do. I really need to get going on this documentary. All I have is the footage from the school. I need to get more on the other victims.

I send Agent Logan a text asking if he could share some archival stuff with me when I see him next. It's not like he can email me anything. The FBI probably frowns upon that. He texts me back a few minutes later saying he'll see what they've got in terms of video and audio.

Having someone on the inside at the FBI is going to be so helpful with this project. Like, I can't even begin to explain it.

After finishing my makeup, I get dressed. Jeans, boots, and a light sweater. Hair loose, silver hoops in my ears. Nothing too crazy. My leather jacket will help ward off the chill. Maxi said there's always a fire at these things, so I probably won't get too cold.

And maybe Luke will keep me warm. Ugh. I am so thirsty.

Last thing I do is make sure my phone is fully charged.

Aunt Cat is gone when I walk into the kitchen. Mom's just getting dinner. "You look nice," she says.

"Thanks. So, my phone is charged, and I've got it on vibrate so I'll know if you call. I'll text you if I'm going to be late, and GPS is on."

She takes the pot holders off her hands and sets them gently on the counter. "About that."

Here we go. I brace myself.

"I don't need to check up on you. You'll be with kids you can trust. Kids I trust. Text me if you're going to be late, but otherwise, just go have fun."

I stare at her. "Seriously?"

She nods. "You're going to be eighteen soon. I need to give you your freedom."

I glance down at my feet. I'm not sure how I feel about this. I mean, it's great, but . . . it feels wrong somehow.

I shrug one shoulder. "I could maybe check in? To let you know I'm okay or whatever."

She looks relieved. "Sure. I'll be at Cat's drinking wine and probably setting up a dating profile or something."

"Do you want to date?"

"Maybe." She smiles. "What about you?"

"You said we'd probably leave soon."

"Probably. But we could always come back."

"For a visit, or for good?" I'm not quite sure what she's getting at, but the idea is . . . intriguing.

"Either. I don't know how you feel about it, but once you

go to college, I'm thinking about moving back. This is where my family is. My friends."

Whoa. After I spent my entire life being stalked by her, she's suddenly letting go of the reins completely? Like, she's ready to abandon me. I don't know how to process this.

"I'd love it if you decided you want to make this home as well, but I realize you might not want to leave your friends behind." There's an element of hope in her expression that soothes the anxiety souring my stomach. She's not trying to abandon me, she's just . . . trying.

Ash and Taylor were going to be going away to different colleges next year anyway, and it's not like we can't video-chat whenever we want. I'm going to be applying to film schools across the country, but there's a good school here, and there are schools in Florida and Georgia. Not like I couldn't jump on a plane from Connecticut or California.

This is what I've been wanting for years—for her to ease up and let me make my own decisions. This is a good thing.

"I'll give it some thought." It's all I can promise at the moment.

We eat dinner and I help her clean up.

"You're not driving tonight, are you?" I ask.

"No. I'll call for a car. Don't worry."

"It's nice, you know."

"What?" she asks as she closes the dishwasher door.

"You finally letting yourself have a life. It's good. Weird, but good."

"I never realized just how much I denied myself—denied us. I thought I was keeping us safe, but safe isn't the same as hidden. I've missed these people. I've missed home and having friends." She touches her swollen eye. "I don't even care about this. If this had happened ten years ago, I would have freaked out, but now . . . I'm done being Jeffrey Robert Lake's ex-wife, you know? I'm done with him. If people want to think I helped him, I can't change that."

"We could do a video about it," I tell her. "You could be in my docuseries. Give your side."

Her bright eyes narrow thoughtfully. "Yeah, maybe."

We're interrupted from further talk by the doorbell. Mom checks the security camera. "It's Maxi." She gives me a hug. "Have fun tonight."

"You're not going to ask if I have my Mace? Tell me to be careful?" I'm only half joking.

"I don't have to. I know you will be. Tell Maxi I said hello. I'm going to go change before I head over to Cat's. See you later."

I grab my jacket and keys and head out with Maxi. Mom was right. I should have fun. I should live a little.

I leave the GPS on my phone on, though. Just in case.

Chapter Twenty-Two

Excerpt from *Dear Lucy: Letters from the Gentleman Killer* by Lucy Gronan, 2010

May 5, 2008

Dear Lucy:

Thank you for your recent letter. As always, you remain a beacon of hope to which I cling in this dark, cruel place. My days are solitary and confined, like that of a tiger in a city zoo. I find the days bleed together into one constant, rigid spiral of excruciating loneliness. Hearing from you breaks that spiral, like a spring sunrise after a week of rain. I do hope you will forgive my tendency to ramble, as I so rarely get the opportunity to express myself to another human being in a personal and intimate manner. In this technological age, I am so very pleased to discover that letter-writing is not a dead art, though it certainly could benefit from a little resuscitation!

In your last letter you asked, "How do I [sic] get through the day knowing I have been so failed by the very system of justice I [sic] studied to uphold?" To be honest, I have no simple answer. Every day is a struggle of great personal pain. I believe in the justice system of the United States of America. I have dedicated myself to upholding the tenets of it and defending those who have been falsely accused of wrongdoing. The irony of that is not lost on me. I suppose there are some who might think my current predicament was a universal response to defending those who were indeed guilty souls. Karma, if you will. However, I uphold that I did not endeavor to allow the guilty to walk free, only to ensure they got the fair and just trial they deserved. I rest easy at night knowing that I did my job, but that the prosecution did not do theirs.

However, in my case, I have been egregiously let down by my own defense. The prosecution chose to believe lies and strove to ruin me instead of searching for the true culprit. Whoever killed those poor women wanted to use me as his scapegoat, his sacrificial lamb, and he certainly succeeded. However, I will not give up the fight to prove my innocence, even if others have. I am *not* the monster the press would have you believe me to be. . . .

"The pit" lives up to its name. That's all it is. An old gravel pit in a less populated area just outside the city. It's far enough away from houses not to cause a disturbance, but not quite in the middle of nowhere.

We park next to a bunch of other cars. There are more pickup trucks than I'm used to seeing, but other than that, it's a lot like parties back home. I can see the bonfire from the passenger seat. Maxi picks up her phone, shuts down Taylor

Swift's new album, and disconnects from her car's Bluetooth. "Darcy said she'd meet us by the fire. I'll text and let her know we're here."

I smile under the dome light. It's kind of cute how much she's into Darcy and vice versa. I have to bite my tongue to keep from asking about Luke. Is he here yet? Is he waiting for me? This part of me that thinks he wants me is still new enough that I'm not sure if I should trust it, even though he's been pretty obvious. What I do know is it's easier to take a chance when you think a situation is temporary. I don't know how long I'm going to be here, and if I have a chance with him, I want to take it.

Maxi's phone pings and she smiles. "She says Luke and her just got here too."

My heart gives a happy thump. We open our doors and step out into the cool night. I'm still amazed how much warmer it is here than Connecticut. An outdoor party in late February? Crazy.

"There they are!" I hear Darcy exclaim. I see the flashlight of her phone punctuate the dark as she and her brother approach from where they parked a row away.

I get a hug from Darcy, but then she immediately falls into place at Maxi's side. The two of them start talking, leaving me and Luke to greet each other.

"Hey, you," I say, opening my arms.

He gives me a hug that smells like vanilla and spice, warm enough to make my head spin. His shoulders are spectacular beneath my hands. "Hey, Scar."

"You smell good," I tell him as I step back. "Did you shower?"

He laughs. "And I put on deodorant."

"You trying to impress someone?"

"I always strive to be impressive," he quips, taking a step closer.

"Well, consider me impressed," I reply, swallowing. Is he lowering his head . . . ?

"You guys coming?" Darcy yells back at us. It's like a bucket of cold water.

We fall into step, close together, following his sister and Maxi toward the music and fire. I can't second-guess it anymore. Luke is into me and I am so very into him.

As soon as we're within the glow of the fire, we encounter the friends I met with him and Darcy during my first visit. They greet me with smiles and hugs. Do I want to smoke a blunt? Maybe later. It would take the edge off, but I'm kind of enjoying the edge and being on it. Being near Luke is like having a low hum of electricity running through my veins, and I like it.

Mazy offers me a soda from the cooler beside her and I take it. Luke takes one too. "You don't drink?" I ask.

"Not when I'm driving," he replies. "You?"

"Drunk Scarlet is not something you need to see tonight."

He smiles. The flicker of the fire reflects in his eyes. "I bet drunk Scarlet's fun. I like sober Scarlet too, though."

I bat my eyelashes at him. "Why, thank you, kind sir."

He groans at my horrible attempt at imitating his accent. I watch his grin fade as his gaze lands on something—someone—on the other side of the fire. "Shit," he mutters.

"What?"

"The ex," he says, giving me a tight smile. "Is she coming over?"

How the hell should I know? I don't know what she looks like. I don't say that, though, because just then I spot a girl coming at us like she's on a mission. She's little and blond and as pretty as I would expect Luke's ex to be.

"Here comes trouble," Ramon remarks, turning his back to her.

"Do you want this?" I ask Luke, quickly.

"What? Krystie? No." He shakes his head, and his gaze locks with mine. "There's only one girl here I'm interested in."

Okay then. I flash him a huge grin right as the girl reaches us. "Luke!"

I watch his shoulders sag slightly and wonder what kind of number this girl did on him. Still, he turns and greets her with a pleasant expression. No smile, though. "Hey, Krys."

She bounces on her feet a little, like she's expecting him to say more. "What are you doing here? I thought you hated these things."

Taking a deep breath, I slip my arm around his lean waist. "I talked him into coming," I tell her in my friendliest voice. "Hi, I'm Scarlet."

Immediately, Luke puts his arm around my shoulders.

"Oh my God," she breathes, staring at me. "You're that killer's daughter."

Well, shit. "I'm also a fully formed person all on my own." Ramon chokes on his drink. "Nice to meet you."

She stares at me, her gaze eventually drifting up to Luke's. "Did your dad ask you to bring her?" She doesn't ask this with any sort of nastiness, which makes it worse, really. She obviously doesn't think Luke could have any interest in me. I may not be a gorgeous little Southern flower, but I have enough confidence to know I'm not ugly either.

His grip on my shoulders tightens. "No. I'm here because I want to be. Where's Brad? Shouldn't you be with him?"

"We broke up. Turns out he wasn't who I thought he was." Her gaze drifts back to mine, wide and full of questions.

"Tell me about it," I say. "A couple of weeks ago I found out I'm not who I thought I was either." Someone behind me snorts. Beneath my hand, the muscles of Luke's stomach contract, as though he's trying not to laugh.

Krystie's expression turns uncertain. "Yeah . . . I bet. Um, well, it was nice to meet you, Scarlet. Luke, call me sometime if you want."

He smiles tightly. She gives me yet another glance before walking away.

Laughing, Ramon sticks his face way too close to mine. "That was awesome!"

I wince at the alcohol on his breath but manage to smile. Luke draws me back a step, so his friend is no longer in my personal space. I start to drop my arm from around his waist, but he doesn't seem to be in too much of a hurry to let me go. Okay, that's cool.

In that case . . . I keep my arm where it is, tucked under his jacket. I can feel the warmth of his skin through our clothes. His hand is big enough to engulf my entire shoulder. I have to really tilt my head to look up at him. He happens to look down at the same time. "Is this okay?" he asks, giving me a squeeze.

"Yeah." And then, because I'm embarrassed by the breathiness of my voice, "I'm so glad you decided to wear deodorant."

He laughs and kisses the top of my head. A wave of warmth rolls all the way down to my toes.

We stay like this for at least an hour—long enough for his friends and Darcy and Maxi to notice. Long enough for word to get around that Luke Logan brought a serial killer's daughter to the party. A few people approach under the guise of saying hi, but it's obvious they want to check me out. No one's rude, though. That's nice.

What's important is that I don't feel threatened. No one seems to want to do me harm, they're just . . . nosy. As long as it stays that way, I'm good. It helps that most of them seem to know Luke. I guess if he trusts me, they do too.

Luke lets me go long enough to help a couple of friends carry in some beer. When he returns to my side, he takes my hand. Something deep inside me shivers in a way that's almost palatable. Delicious. The excitement I felt around Neal is *nothing* compared with this. There's a comfort—a rightness—to this that not only feels good but gives me a certainty I've never had before. Luke is mine if I want him, and he knows I'm his if he wants me. It's not an attraction thing. We actually like each other. Even if he wasn't hot, I'd want to know him. It's like something just clicked the first time we met.

He's good. Sofie would dismiss him as "too nice." Too clean-cut. Too much. Too big, probably. He makes me feel like I'm standing on even ground. So does his sister. That's not something I've experienced much in my life. They've known about my father from the beginning and don't care about him. They care about me.

Some people brought snacks—chips and marshmallows for roasting. Someone even brought stuff to make s'mores. Luke and I share a stick for marshmallows, as do Maxi and Darcy, who attempt to make s'mores dip in a ripped-apart beer can. It's not half bad.

Eventually I have to go in search of the porta-potty I'm told is at the edge of the pit crater. Darcy has to go too, so she comes with me. Of course, there's a line.

"Hi, Darcy," says the guy in front of us.

"Hey, Scott," she replies.

He glances at me. "Hi."

I nod, feeling slightly awkward. "Hi."

"I'm Scott."

"Scarlet."

He bobs his head. He's obviously had too much to drink. "You guys havin' fun?"

"Yeah." Darcy shoves her hands in her pockets. "You?"

More head bobbing. He looks at me. "Is it true Jeff Lake is your father?"

Okay, I wasn't quite expecting that. "Yep."

"Cool." He turns away.

Darcy and I share a look. WTF?

"I saw what you did when Krystie showed up," she says to me. "Nice work."

I shrug. "I saw an opening and I took it. It's not going to make things weird for us, is it?"

"Dude, I'm crushing on your cousin."

"Yeah, but it's not quite the same thing, is it?"

She shakes her head. "We're fine. You don't even know what a step-up you are."

I laugh, but it shakes my bladder. "That doesn't say a whole lot for him."

"I love my brother, but sometimes I don't know where his head's at. In his crotch, I guess."

"Don't make me laugh," I warn.

Finally, we get to the front of the line. Scott comes out of the porta-potty rubbing sanitizer on his hands. "I wiped the seat for you," he says to me.

"Uh . . . thanks." I shoot Darcy another glance before stepping inside.

"Someone puked," I hear Scott explain to Darcy. "It wasn't me."

The smell hits me when I close the door. Oh, God. Shit,

piss, and puke. What an absolutely glorious sensory experience. Ugh. I hold my breath and do my business as quickly as possible—touching absolutely nothing. It's a workout for my thighs, but there's no way I'm sitting down.

At least there's sanitizer in the dispenser. I grab a palmful, open the door, and rub my hands together as I step out into the fresh air.

Darcy grimaces. "That bad?"

I nod. "That bad." I step aside to wait for her.

Suddenly, Scott comes out of the shadows. "What's he like?" he asks.

I blink at him. "Who?"

"Your father."

"Did you . . . were you waiting for me?"

He nods. "Yeah. Sorry. I just need to know what he's like."

This is weird. Like, really weird. I hope it's only because he's drunk. "He's a jerk, actually."

"But . . ." He stumbles closer. I can smell the booze on him as he blinks heavily at me. "You were in the same room as him. Did he, like . . . tell you about what he did?"

"Some, yeah. Listen, Scott, I really don't like talking about him, if that's okay—"

"You're half him. Half of you is him."

I take a step back. "No. I'm nothing like him."

He lurches forward, grabbing me by the arm. "Did he tell you what it was like?" Beer breath blasts me in the face. "I've . . . I've always wondered what it would be like to, you know." His gaze is intense but unfocused as it meets mine.

My chest squeezes. *To kill someone.* That's what he's not saying. That's what he wants to know.

The door to the porta-potty flies open and Darcy bolts out

like an Olympic sprinter. "Oh my God! That's so gross. Scott, there's such a thing as personal space, buddy. There you go."

She slips in between us easily and takes my arm, steering me away from drunken Scott.

"Did he creep you out?" she asks.

"He's not right," I tell her, cold to the bone despite the mild night. "There's something wrong with him, I think."

"Yeah, I know. Keep walking." She doesn't glance behind us, making a beeline for her brother and Maxi. I have to hurry to keep up with her long strides.

I shouldn't be so shocked by his interest but I am. Shocked and alarmed. Is Scott just weird, or is he something darker? Psychopaths can't be that common, can they?

Luke's laughing at something someone said to him as we approach. He looks at me and the humor drains from his face. "What happened?" he demands.

"Scott Schneider," Darcy tells him. "Creeped her out."

"Oh, *that* guy." Maxi shudders. "He's a weirdo. You okay, Scar?"

I nod. I'm not, but I will be.

Maybe half an hour later, standing with my back against his front to warm me up, Luke leans down, his mouth close to my ear. "Wanna get out of here?"

I turn my head. His face is so close to mine. . . . I have never wanted to kiss anyone like I want to kiss him. It's almost painful. "Yeah. I do. What about Darcy?"

"Hey, Maxi," he calls out, straightening.

My cousin turns her head. "Yeah?"

"We're gonna head. You mind giving Darce a lift home?"

"Nope." The idea of time alone looks like it appeals to both of them. I'd be happier for them if they weren't smirking at me like that, though.

We hold hands on the way to his car. He even opens the door for me, which no one has ever done before.

Neither of us says much on the drive. Anticipation or nerves, I'm not sure. I don't mind the silence, though. It's comfortable, even if I am incredibly aware of the guy a foot away from me.

We end up at the park he took me to the first time we met. There's one other vehicle there, but it's at the other end of the lot.

"Wanna go for a walk?"

I look out into the dark. I never used to be afraid of it. I used to brazenly go out into it just to prove my mother wrong about the danger there. I don't feel so brave right now.

"Can we just stay here?" I ask.

He frowns. "Are you okay?"

I nod. "After what happened with Scott at the party, the outside feels . . . unsafe. Does that sound stupid?"

"Not at all. Music?"

"Sure."

He finds something for us to listen to and we both unfasten our seat belts, shifting to face one another. In the moonlight he looks like the hero of a romance novel.

"Are you ever going to kiss me?" I ask.

Luke goes perfectly still. A slow smile curves his lips. "I was thinking about it, yeah."

I grin and lean across the center console toward him. "Stop thinking."

He takes my face in his hands and looks at me, as if memorizing my features. "You're beautiful," he murmurs.

"So are you." I don't even feel foolish saying it.

My eyes close as he lowers his head, and when his lips touch mine . . . *oh*. Oh, wow. The taste of soda clings to his lips as I touch them with my tongue. His fingers are in my hair, holding my head as if he thinks I might suddenly try to run away. Idiot boy.

I wrap my arms around him, dragging my body closer until I'm on my knees, straddling him, the steering wheel digging into my low back. Suddenly, we fall as he puts the seat back and down. I yelp. Luke laughs and kisses me again.

I'm draped over him like a blanket, his hips between my thighs. He feels so good. Smells so good. Tastes so good. I move—just a little—and smile against his mouth when he groans.

He doesn't try to stop me when I slide my hands under his shirt. His skin is warm, the muscles beneath firm. He's perfect. So perfect.

His hands run up my thighs, stroke my hips, holding me tight against him until my head spins. And then his thumb strokes my breast, and my breath catches in a rough gasp as a shiver races through me.

"Scarlet," he murmurs against my mouth. "We should stop."

Oh, he really is too good to be real. My hair falls around us like a curtain as I smile down at him. "Do you really want to stop?" I ask.

Luke grins. "Hell no. But I don't want you to do anything you don't want."

"I want," I tell him, and lightly brush my lips over his. "I really, really, *really* want."

He pushes my hair back. Moonlight filters through the window and I know he can see me as clearly as I can see him. I wonder if I look as magical to him as he does to me.

"Girl, my life was not expecting you to walk into it."

"I know." I slide my hand over the outside of his T-shirt,

up to cup his jaw. Stubble prickles my palm. "Do you want this?"

"I think it's pretty obvious what I want," he answers in a low drawl that sends a shiver down my spine. His hand cups the back of my head, bringing me closer for another kiss.

It's not the most romantic of settings, but I don't care. I feel incredibly empowered and sexy in the moment. Clothes seem to melt away and we laugh when jeans refuse to come off easily. I don't have any embarrassment or shame with him. I don't even have to ask if he has a condom, because he produces one.

Our bodies move together like one. I don't have a lot of experience—I've never even had an orgasm during sex before. But I do with Luke.

Afterward, we get dressed and cuddle. Kiss some more. I didn't have anything to drink or smoke tonight, but my head is light. It's got to be because of him.

Eventually, it's late enough that I yawn.

Luke chuckles. "Guess I should get you home."

"I guess."

"We'll see each other again in a few hours." I feel like he's saying it for his benefit as much as mine.

I buckle my seat belt with a sigh. He holds my hand the entire drive, steering with one hand. The familiar sight of the unmarked police car in front of the house is welcoming even though it's a reminder of all the weirdness of my life.

Luke walks me to the door, even though I tell him he doesn't have to. The cops wave, then politely look away.

"I'll pick you up around ten to head to the cabin?" he asks. I nod.

He smiles self-consciously. "I don't want to leave."

"I don't want to go inside," I confess with a grin of my own. "You could always kiss me again, if you want."

He arches a brow. "I really, really, *really* want."

I blush at my words being repeated back to me, but then he kisses me again and I don't think of anything but him and how this night turned out to be really, really, *really* good.

Chapter Twenty-Three

A road trip to a kill site and former mass grave is hardly what I'd call a romantic outing, but the four of us make the trip the following morning, regardless. I sit up front with Luke, while Maxi and Darcy hold hands and sing along with the radio in the back. They are in their own little world and I envy them.

As if reading my mind, Luke shifts the hand that rests on the console between us—just enough that his pinky brushes mine. My breath catches at the contact—like a spark. I slide my finger under his, hooking the two together. My heart keeps a tight, heavy rhythm, like when I'm about to panic, except this feels good.

I glance at him. He smiles at me, dark eyes sparkling in the late-winter sunshine. I give an almost shy smile back. Is he thinking about last night? Because I am. I haven't thought of anything else since he reluctantly left hours earlier. I thought maybe daylight would make things awkward, but it hasn't. Being with him feels completely right.

Maxi said the cabin was near Fayetteville in some rural

area where the Lake family originally came from, set on a plot of land that had been divided up among our ancestors a century ago. To be honest, I only followed the history lesson for about five minutes before my mind wandered. It's a nice drive, though. I gawk at the scenery—redbrick buildings, rolling green hills. It's got that same colonial feel as a lot of Connecticut, but it's warmer. And people don't rush around here like they do up north.

Listen to me—"up north." I'm starting to sound like Mom and Cat, talking about the place I grew up like it's some strange land.

We stop at a small gas station to fill the tank and use the restroom. It's one of those mom-and-pop things that has a little diner attached.

"They have the best doughnuts here," Maxi says. "Coffee's good too. Let's get some."

Luke claps his hands together. "Dude, you had me at doughnuts."

I don't need the energy that comes with sugar and caffeine, but fuck it. We get a dozen of golden, deep-fried deliciousness and four drinks. We eat and drink for the rest of the drive, Darcy making her brother turn up certain songs so we can all sing along.

I feel like I've known these people forever—especially Maxi. I guess that makes sense. She's family. The only other person I've ever felt this comfortable with is Taylor, and maybe Ash. It's odd for me to feel at ease with people who are still strangers for the most part. But they know who I am and opened their lives to me anyway. That means something. I didn't have to wait for something to test their friendship—it was offered to me at a very, very low point.

And Luke . . . well, he was probably the most unexpected

development. He's not as extroverted as Neal, but there's a solidness to him that goes beyond his six-four Captain America build. He could have his pick of girls, but he likes me. And I'm going to enjoy it.

Eventually the GPS on Luke's phone tells him to turn right onto a dirt road that winds into the forest. We drive for what feels like forever but is probably only about ten minutes before Maxi cries out, "There it is! Pull in here!" Like the chain-link fence and gated driveway weren't indication enough.

Maxi jumps out and unlocks the gate so Luke can drive through, then locks it behind us.

It's not what I expected, though I can't say what I thought I'd find here. It's a nice but weathered cabin with a peaked roof and wraparound deck. It was probably really nice before my father ruined it for everyone.

I grab my camera and get out. As I turn to watch Maxi approach, I notice that the fence is littered with flowers—fresh and wilted—and other trinkets and stuffed animals. Some of it has blown into the yard. I pick up a card lying by my boot.

In loving memory of Tara Miller. Gone, but not forgotten.

My throat constricts. She's one of the fourteen. She was found here. I film the card, dirty and crumpled as it lies in my palm. Then, I let it float to the ground. I can't bring myself to take it or throw it out. Let it stay here, until the words on it can't be read.

I pan along the fence. I'll have to get the view from the outside before we leave.

"I'm surprised there's no one here," Maxi comments as she joins me. "Usually there's someone on the road."

"Looks like there's been a party here recently," Luke comments from where he stands, closer to the building. "Some beer bottles out back."

"Yeah, they jump the fence," Maxi explains. "Or cut through it. Mom's already replaced it three times. I think she's done trying to protect it now, though. At least no one's broken the windows again. Couple of years ago someone got in and vandalized it real bad. That's when Mom got the security system."

I look up at where she points and see a camera aimed our way. I wave.

"They're all over the property," she says. "Mom doesn't care if people are nosy, but she draws the line at destruction, you know?"

"I'm surprised she hasn't torn the place down."

"It's not the cabin's fault," my cousin counters. "I think she's hoping one of us will want it or something. I don't know. I don't ask, to be honest. Wanna go in?"

I gesture for her to lead the way. We walk up the steps to the front door and she slips keys into the numerous locks. Once we're inside, she punches a code on a keypad by the door. The air is close and musty in here—disuse and dust. Moisture and mold.

It's nice. Cozy and welcoming. It really is too bad my father ruined it for the family. It would probably be a great place to chill out for a weekend.

Maxi gives us a tour of the place. No trace of my father has been left here. No photos, no belongings. I suppose Cat didn't want to give memorabilia hunters anything to steal. The only hint of him is a photograph of me and Mom sitting on top of the mantel in the main living area.

"We looked so much alike as babies," Maxi comments as she looks at it.

"You still do," Darcy informs her. "If Scarlet were blond, you'd look like sisters."

That makes me smile—Maxi too.

"Let's go outside," I suggest. "I don't want to stay here any longer than we have to."

The backyard is what I've dreaded. Out there, the lawn has dips in it where bodies were—where my father planted his fucking rosebushes to hide them. There's only six, though. He couldn't even be bothered to give them their own graves. He made them share.

I film it all, get close-ups too. I'll cut in images from the original excavation when I edit. I'm not going to show the bodies if I can help it. I don't want to glorify the deaths of these women, or let people linger on what my father did to them. I want the focus to be on their lives.

A large, warm hand comes down on my shoulder. "You okay?" Luke asks, his voice low and rough.

Shivering a little, I lean back against him. "It's surreal."

He points up at the cabin. "Look."

I follow his finger with my gaze. It takes me a minute to see it, but then it comes into full focus. It's faded, but the word MONSTER is spray-painted on the back wall, underneath the picture window. It looks like someone tried to scrape it off, but the paint seeped into the wood and stained it. I film it. Maybe after I pay my respects to his victims, I'll do a segment about what it's been like to find out Jeff Lake is my father. It might be good therapy. There will be those who accuse me of trying to profit from his crimes, but I don't care. I'm not doing this for them.

We stay another hour, poking around and filming. We find the place in the fence where the partiers probably snuck in.

"Bolt cutters," Luke comments. "They came prepared."

"Morbid asshats," Maxi mutters. "They bring their girlfriends up here and try to scare them. As if the girls haunt this place."

"If they do haunt it, it's not their girlfriends those guys have to worry about." I let my gaze drift around us. I don't know if I really expect to see one, but there aren't any ghosts. Under my breath I add, "I hope you're someplace better than this."

Maxi unlocks the front gate for me so I can film the outside of the fence. I try to get details on the offerings left. Most don't seem to have been left for anyone in particular, though a couple, like the card I found, are inscribed with a name. Someone even left a love letter for my father.

I crush it in my fist with a snarl.

"Want to burn it?" Luke asks.

I nod. He takes the letter from my hand and crouches in the gravel drive. He takes a lighter from his pocket and flicks his thumb over the wheel, lighting the paper. There's no wind so there's no worry of starting a forest fire. Plus, I'll double-check it's out before we leave.

There's something satisfying about watching those stupid words, written in ridiculous red ink, singe and curl, burn and turn to ash. What kind of person would leave something like that at this place? It's inconsiderate and tasteless. Cruel, even. If I could, I'd piss on it. I'm tempted to ask Luke to do it for me.

When there's nothing left but blackened ash, Darcy dumps water from the bottle she has with her on it. None of us says anything.

"I'll get the car," Luke says.

I hold the gate open for him as Maxi pulls the keys out of her jacket. "There's someone coming," she says.

I listen and hear tires on the gravel road, the low rumble of an engine. As Luke pulls the car out, I close the gate and Maxi locks it. I open the passenger door right as a car pulls across the drive, blocking us in.

The woman driving rolls down her window. There's a guy with a camera in the passenger seat. He's filming us. Me.

"Britney!" the woman exclaims, like she knows me. "We heard you might be here! Come to see the scene of your father's atrocities?"

"My name's not Britney," I say, dumbly.

Luke sticks his head out of the driver's window. "You need to move your car."

"Oh, we will," the woman says as she opens her door. "One minute."

I back away as she steps toward me. Suddenly, a door slams and Luke is right behind her, a fierce expression on his face.

"Lady, get back in your car."

She turns on him with a sneer. "I said one minute, boy. What part of that don't you understand?"

Right, because he's big and pretty, she's going to treat him like he's stupid?

"Please," I say. "Please go."

Now that predatory look is fixed on me. "Sure—as soon as you answer a few questions."

Luke puts himself between us, staring down at the woman. She doesn't seem the least bit intimidated. From the road, her cameraman films everything. Maxi and Darcy descend upon him.

"Here's what I understand," Luke tells the woman in a low, calm voice. "I understand that you are trespassing on private property. I understand that if you followed us here, that's akin to stalking. What you're doing right now is harassing a minor, and by blocking the drive and preventing us from leaving, you are essentially threatening us."

The woman smirks at him. "What are you, a lawyer?"

"Soon enough," he says. "But my father is also a senior

agent with the FBI, so I've picked up a few things. If you don't want me to call him with your license plate number and photos of you both, I suggest you leave. Now."

That's when I notice that Darcy has not only taken pictures of their car, but of each of them. "Say the word and I send them to Dad," she calls to her brother.

The reporter—or whatever she is—backs down. She hasn't even given us any credentials. She could be in love with Lake for all I know. "Fine," she says. "We'll leave. For now. You won't always have your Prince Charming here with you, Britney."

I meet her gaze from around Luke's shoulder. "My name is *Scarlet.*"

She merely smiles before pivoting on her heel and prancing back to her car.

"Get in," Luke urges, opening the door for me. He has to help me inside, my legs are shaking so bad. God, I wish I weren't so afraid of these people! I said I would talk to the next ones that approached me, but this woman was too aggressive.

We wait for them to leave before closing the gate and leaving ourselves.

"I don't know about you guys, but I could so smoke a bowl right now," Maxi comments once we're on the road.

Luke laughs as he reaches over and takes my hand. Mine is freezing compared with his, and I'm grateful for the warmth. "Let's get back into our own territory first." He glances at me. "You okay?"

I nod. "Thank you for what you did back there."

"Yeah," Darcy agrees, sticking her head between our seats. "You were awesome, bro. I got it all on camera too so I can show Dad. He'll be so proud."

"I'm sorry that happened, Scarlet," Maxi says. "I thought we'd stumble upon the usual nosies, not that."

"It's fine," I deflect. "It's going to happen, so I have to get used to it."

"No," Luke retorts with a frown. "You don't. No one has the right to follow you or harass you, Scarlet. No one. It's not your fault your father's a douche, and you don't owe anyone a fucking apology for being you."

And this is the moment I fall in love with Luke Logan.

"I didn't ask to be born this way, you know," my father says the next time I see him. I don't think he has much time left. He's wasted away even more since the last time. And the smell . . .

"If you were given the chance to change, would you take it?" I ask, taking shallow breaths.

"I do not know. I like the attention, but I do not care for the accommodations." He smiles slightly. I'm not going to lie, part of me is tempted to smile back, but then I remember he's a monster. There is no goodness in him.

"Being locked up must be hard for someone like you."

He shrugs. "I thought it would be better than the alternative. I was wrong."

I don't know what to say, so silence hangs between us as he draws a raspy breath.

"Look at me." I do—it's not easy. "I used to be a lion. I used to be muscled and sleek—pretty but deadly. I'm not even going to be a shell of my former self when the end comes. I'm already a ghost. I used to think if the FBI took me, they'd have to kill me, and at least I'd leave a beautiful corpse. But I messed up and hinted that there were other girls because I wasn't ready to die. They've kept me alive ever since. I should have kept my mouth shut."

"But you didn't," I remind him.

"That was my first mistake. Overestimating your mother's devotion was the second. If I really wanted to keep her close, I ought to have implicated her. I told Logan she didn't know anything about what I was, though. I suppose that was the closest I ever came to actually loving her." He sighs, closes his eyes. His orbital bones stand out in sharp relief, the thin skin of his face draped over his skull like a sheet of damp tissue. "Is there anything about me you like?"

His eyes are still shut. He can't see me shake my head, but he smiles slightly. "Didn't think so. Your aunt Cat—she ever say anything about that boy of hers being like me?"

An icy finger drags down my spine. "No."

"I don't know if this sort of thing runs in the blood, but if you ever have kids, you might want to watch for it."

I can't tell if he's trying to be helpful or playing with me. Either way, I say, "That's not anything I can control."

"Suppose not." His eyes open. There isn't a gleam of malice in his gaze, but there isn't much of anything, except the glaze of morphine. "Your mama was right to take you away from me. I hate her for it, but she was right. God knows what I would have turned you into."

Would I be more of a mess or less of one if I'd grown up in his crazy shadow? Maxi seems okay. She has less anxiety than I do. She wasn't raised to be afraid of everything and distrust everyone. But I'm not going to let myself be bitter toward Mom. She did what she thought was right, and I'm old enough to take responsibility for the person I want to be. That's not on her.

"Are you glad you met me?" he asks.

"Honestly? I don't know. I think so. I don't like you, but

good things have come out of it." I can't help but think of
Luke. "What about you?"

"I would have liked to have more time. Maybe for you to
meet me in my prime, when I was something to be feared or
at least respected."

"You still are something to be feared," I tell him, not caring if it panders to his ego. "You are a despicable person, and
I have no doubt you'd kill again if you were able."

He chuckles. The sound makes my skin creep. "It's been
the only thing I've thought of since they put me in here—what
I'd do if I ever got out. The memories of what I've done are the
only things that have given me solace. Them, and the thought
of getting revenge on your mother."

Am I upset that he doesn't include me in that list? Not at
all. "You should really let her go, you know. You did your
damage. You're the one who remarried."

"It's a sad thing to admit to my daughter, but I had to re-
marry. I needed the attention. It's better than sex."

"Does she love you?"

He shakes his head. "I'm not sure she ever did. She loved
what I was—the idea of that apex predator you and I have discussed. She loved that lion. I imagine she feels hardly anything
for me now. It used to anger me—how she could sit across
from me, see the things I wanted to do to her in my eyes, and
not run away, screaming. She didn't understand me. She just
wanted to make herself feel stronger by being mine. If I'd had
the strength, I would have killed her just for being a fucking
leech." His gaze latches on to mine. "Does that upset you?"

"No. It's not like you were able to do it."

He holds up the hand that isn't restrained—it's almost
skeletal. "Look at it. I used to be able to deny breath with

these hands. Now, I can barely hold a glass of water." He makes a scoffing sound. "Punishment for my sins, I suppose."

"We all die," I remind him. "You getting cancer is hardly the same as what you did to those girls."

"What do you think would be a more appropriate way for me to go?"

"I'd hand you over to Britney's family, personally."

My father laughs. "Yes. That would suit." After a moment, he holds out his free hand. It takes me a second to realize he wants me to take it. It's not a good idea, but Agent Logan is outside and help is only a scream away.

I take his hand—against my better judgment. His fingers feel papery and dry, but there's more strength in them than I first thought.

"You have hands like my mother," he says, stroking his thumb across my knuckles. "She was a useless gash too."

I jerk my hand back, but he's fast. Even drugged, he's fast as a snake. He grabs my wrist tightly, the bones of his fingers digging into my skin. He pulls me forward, almost out of my chair. The door to the room flies open and Agent Logan shouts for him to let me go.

My father's lips peel back from his teeth. His breath smells like rot. It's hot and moist on my face. "I fucked and murdered fifty-seven girls not much older than you, darlin'. I was going to let you have them, but I'm taking them with me. You failed, bitch."

Agent Logan grabs me by the shoulders, pulling me back. Guards restrain my father as I'm whisked away. My wrist throbs where he held it. Red welts fill the void where his fingers had been. My heart pounds so loud I can hear it.

"Breathe," Agent Logan commands as he rubs my back. "You're okay. I've got you."

Hands on my thighs, I bend slightly and suck in a desperate breath. In through my nose, out through my mouth. He's right. I'm okay.

The panic fades faster than I expect. I'm still shaking from the adrenaline, but I'm not nearly as freaked out as I ought to be.

Lake is silent. A nurse is there and it's obvious they've sedated him. He's almost unconscious.

The bastard is smiling.

Chapter Twenty-Four

I want to see Luke.

I text him while I wait for his father to finish up in the prison. I guess he has to make an incident report, or something. Regardless, he decided I didn't need to be there for it. Luke responds within minutes, telling me that he just got out of his last class of the day and will meet me at his place.

Agent Logan has no problem taking me home with him. He doesn't tease me about it, like some adults do, reducing teenage feelings to something "cute" and Disney. He just turns on the AC and leaves the tinted windows up so any vultures hanging around can't see my face as we leave the prison grounds. There's a small crowd out there—not just reporters either. People hanging around, carrying signs with my father's name on them. I wonder if one of them is Scott. Creeper. I think maybe he's what will linger the longest after all of this—not the horrible things people did or said, thinking Mom and I were monsters, but Scott wanting to be close to me because he admires Lake.

I call Mom on the way and tell her what happened—leaving out some details. She doesn't need to know the names he called me. All she needs to know is that he grabbed me, and I want to hang out with friends. "Be careful," she says. "Don't go anywhere. If Luke can't bring you home later, I'll come get you, okay?"

I promise her I will and disconnect.

"You're not going back," Agent Logan informs me, his gaze intent on the road. "I appreciate what you've done to help us, but I'm not letting you in that room again. I shouldn't have let you in at all. This is on me."

"No, it's not. It was my decision and I'm glad I did it."

"You're a brave girl. Your mother did a good job."

"She didn't make me brave. She wanted to make me smart and suspicious, but she made me afraid too. Coming here—facing him—that's what made me brave. Thank you for that."

He looks like he doesn't know what to say. "He'll be dead soon and this will be over."

"Will it, though? Be over, I mean? People will always be fascinated by him."

"Yeah, but your face won't be everywhere. They'll forget what you and your mother look like. You'll be able to have a life."

"Maybe."

"Rosa Bundy has done it."

I've heard Ashley mention her. "People still wonder about her, though."

"Yeah. There will always be people like that, but you can handle them. With him gone, it will be different. Trust me. I've seen enough of his kind die to know."

I shrug. "It doesn't matter. I can own being his kid a lot easier when I start putting my videos up."

"How are those going?"

"Good. I don't have enough footage to start uploading yet, but the information you, Mom, and Cat have given me is a huge help. Once I talk to the Mitchells, I hope to get Britney's video done. I want to have a few ready to go before I start uploading."

"You should be proud of what you're doing. Michelle Gordon's sister said she'd be willing to speak to you if you want. Just voice, but she's willing."

"That would be great. Thanks." He gives me her contact information when we get to the house.

"Luke should be home in a few minutes. You can hang out in his room if you want. I need to get back to the office. Help yourself in the kitchen if you're hungry or thirsty."

"Thanks."

He hesitates. "You sure you're okay being alone here? It should only be twenty, maybe thirty minutes."

"I'm good. I promise." I am, that's the weird thing. Yeah, still a little tingle or two, but nothing I can't handle. I don't even consider taking a pill.

After making sure—again—he finally leaves. I'm flattered that he trusts me enough to leave me alone in his house. It's only one o'clock in the afternoon; Moira is at work and Darcy is still at school. I have my backpack with me, so I grab a "coke" and head up to Luke's room.

As far as a guy's room goes, it's pretty clean. He even makes his bed. Not great, but it's made.

I sit down at his desk. Before even attempting to work on school stuff, I text both Ash and Taylor asking to video-chat later. It feels like forever since I spoke to them. I've missed them, but not as much as I should have.

I'm working on an English assignment when Luke comes

in. His cheeks are flushed, and he's breathing like he ran all the way from his car. He drops his backpack on the floor and comes toward me.

I stand. He lifts me off my feet into a fierce hug. I wrap my arms and legs around him, trusting his strength. Trusting him. Tears flood my eyes. I can cry now. He won't out me, won't tell anyone I'm not as strong as I want to be. That my father's cruelty got to me more than it should have.

"It's okay," he murmurs. "It's gonna be okay."

I nod, my face buried in his neck. I sniff. The tears don't last long.

"You can set me down," I say after a bit.

He smiles. "I kinda like it. It's sexy." He waggles his eyebrows.

I laugh. "Having a crying girl cling to you like a koala is sexy?"

"Not when you put it that way, no." He squeezes my thighs before setting me on my feet. Kisses the top of my head. "You okay?"

I sigh. "Yeah. Lake got to me today, that's all. Like, he grabbed me." I show Luke the marks on my arm.

His expression darkens. "Fucker." His fingers are gentle as they touch my skin. "Does it hurt?"

"A little. I'll probably bruise. Your dad said he's not letting me go back."

Lifting my arm, he presses a light kiss to one of the marks before meeting my gaze. "What do you want?"

"Lake said he wasn't giving me any more names, and I'm . . . Luke, I'm done." My shoulders slump. "I should feel worse than I do."

He frowns. "Feel worse? For what?"

"Letting down those other girls."

"You can't let down the dead, Scarlet."

"Their families, then."

"You did what you could. You're making your films, and that's going to have to be enough. You can't live your life in debt to strangers."

He's right, but I still feel like crap. "Thanks for being here."

Luke smooths back my hair. "You don't need to thank me. I like being the first person you call."

"Really?"

He nods, a little smile creeping in. "Uh, yeah. I like you. I think I made that pretty obvious."

I grin. "I like you too."

"I figured that out Saturday night."

"Maybe I was just using you for sex."

His smile spreads. "You don't strike me as the type, but by all means, use away."

An image flashes in my head—him standing with me wrapped around him while we . . . *oh*.

"Keep looking at me like that and you can use me right now," he says softly.

I smile. "I can think of worse ways to spend the afternoon."

He shuts the door, hesitates, then locks it, before walking toward me like a cat stalking a bird. I don't feel like prey, though. I feel safe and wanted and so incredibly unbroken. He pulls his shirt over his head, revealing the chest I've longed to see in the light of day.

"Lucky me," he says, taking me in his arms. "I happen to have the afternoon free."

The Mitchells live in a newer suburb in an affluent part of the city.

"They moved before Lake's trial," Agent Logan explains to me as he unbuckles his seat belt. "Once they knew Britney wasn't coming home, they couldn't stand to live with the reminders. They needed a fresh start."

A fresh start would be nice. If anyone deserved one, it was them.

"Are you ready for this?" he asks. "There's no shame in changing your mind."

"No, I'm good. Can you help me with my equipment?" I rented a couple of ring lights for filming and tripods and screens in addition to my other equipment. I want this to be as professional as possible. Thank God that Mom lent me her credit card.

The house is light gray brick with white trim. It has a cute little veranda with two rocking chairs and pots of pretty hanging flowers.

I wipe my palms on my hips as we walk up the front steps. I'm more nervous about this than I had been about meeting Lake. He'd just been frightening. This is . . . important.

Agent Logan rings the bell. A few moments later, the door is opened by a tall, thin man probably in his seventies. His hair is mostly gray, with shades of ashy brown mixed in, and his eyes are a warm hazel.

"Andy," he says. "Welcome. And you must be Scarlet." He offers me his hand.

I accept the handshake, hoping he doesn't notice the humidity of my palm. "Thanks for agreeing to meet with me," I say.

He gives me a gentle smile. "Of course. Please, come in. Camille is making tea. I'll show you where you can put that gear."

We follow him into the house—it smells like sugar and

baking—and to the right into what appears to be a parlor. I've never been in an actual parlor before.

"Do whatever you need to do," Mr. Mitchell tells me. "I'll be right back."

Agent Logan helps me put together the lights and sets up the screens so I can arrange them how I want.

"This looks like quite the production," he comments with a smile.

"I want it to look good," I reply, trying not to sound defensive. "They deserve that."

I'm untangling wires for the mike packs when Mr. Mitchell returns with his wife. She's a shorter woman with dyed blond hair and pretty blue eyes. She has a plate of sandwiches in one hand and a plate of cookies in the other. Mr. Mitchell has a tray with four tall glasses on it.

Iced tea. Not hot. Right.

"Oh, Josh. She looks a bit like Brit, don't you think?"

Mr. Mitchell sets the drinks on the coffee table and takes the plates from her. "Camille, this is Scarlet."

She hugs me. I'm not prepared for that. She smells like vanilla and my throat tightens. She should be a grandmother, but Britney was their only child. Maybe Britney wouldn't have had kids, but they probably wonder about it.

I blink back tears as she releases me. "Your mother. How is she?"

I search her face for distaste or any hint of bitterness, but there isn't any. Good. "She's well, thanks. I guess as good as to be expected?"

Camille's smile is kind. "I suppose this must have been a big shock to you. Andy tells us you didn't know about . . . Jeffrey."

I wonder what she wanted to call him. "I didn't. It was a shock, actually. But it's made me understand why my mother has been so strict with me. Careful."

She nods. "I wish I'd been more cautious with Britney. She was such a sweet, trusting thing. Maybe if she hadn't been—"

"He fooled us all, Cam," her husband interrupts—gently. "There's nothing anyone could have done." His gaze meets mine. "But we do appreciate what you aspire to do, Scarlet. I'm sure a lot of the other families will as well. It means so much to us that you want to add to Britney's legacy."

"Thanks." It's not much, but I don't know what else to say. I hold up one of the microphones. "Have you worn one of these before?"

After getting them miked, I put two chairs together in front of the coffee table, facing the sofa where I plan to sit. It's the best setup given the direction of the natural light coming into the room. I get the lights and screens situated, and then position the two cameras I have. I put one almost straight on and another from an angle to break up the point of view every once in a while. I'll decide where to add those switches when I edit footage together.

"Have a cookie," Camille urges when I sit down. I take a sugar cookie off the plate and bite into it to humor her.

"I don't have many questions," I confide after I swallow. I'm tempted to take another bite, they're really good cookies. "The whole point of this is for me—and anyone watching—to get to know Britney. I'll leave it up to you what you want to share. Please don't feel like you need to talk about anything that might be difficult. I don't want to upset you."

They smile at me. "It's been a long time," Josh tells me, "but it still hurts, so thank you."

I nod. This is not going to be easy, but that's the point. "Why don't we start with what Britney was like as a child?" That's always a good place to begin.

I sit on the edge of the sofa, listening to them talk about their daughter. It's obvious how much they adored her. What I'm not prepared for is how much they adored my father.

"We thought they were going to get married," Camille confides, a sad expression on her face. "He was such a doting boyfriend. When Britney told us he'd gotten violent with her, we could hardly believe it." She looks to her husband for confirmation.

"But we knew she wouldn't lie," Josh adds. "When she went missing, we told police how their relationship had ended, but they didn't think he was a suspect." His mouth turns down as he says this.

"Jeffrey had moved on by then," Camille continues. "He was dating your mother, er, Allison. He cooperated with the investigation. He seemed as distraught as we were, and Allison and Britney had been friendly despite Brit being a couple of years older." She shakes her head.

I give them a minute. "Were you surprised when the two of them got married?"

"A little," Josh tells me. "We didn't think Allison was really Jeffrey's type. She was ambitious and outgoing. Brit had been quieter. We weren't surprised it took them a few years to have a child. Allison wanted to get her career on track first."

Camille looks at me. "We thought you were named as a tribute to Britney by a young man who cared about her very much. When we found out the truth, we hated him even more. We hated you—an innocent child. I'm so sorry for that."

Her sincerity—her blunt honesty—throws me for a moment. "I'm sorry for all you've been through."

She gives me a sad smile.

"And then he got up at the trial and denied having done anything to her." There's heat in Josh's tone. "He stared right in my eyes and lied. He said he could never hurt Brit, that he was horrified someone could have done that to her. He said he was being set up."

"But he never asked how we were," Camille chimes in. "That's how I knew he was lying. It was all about how *he* felt. He didn't care about our suffering. I remarked upon it, remember, Josh?"

Her husband nods. "Finding out he killed her was almost as horrible as finding out she was dead."

They look at each other. He takes her hand in his. The pressure in my chest grows.

"He betrayed your trust as well as hers," I say.

Camille nods and looks off into space for a moment before turning back to me. "This is where it gets hard. I have some photos. Would you like to see them?"

I force a smile, because she's breaking my heart. "I would, yeah."

We stay for another forty minutes. I make sure I ask for copies of some of the photos and give them my email so they can scan and send them to me. Then, when I can't stand their sadness anymore, when I can't stand how they don't seem to blame me or Mom, I decide I have everything I need.

Camille makes me take cookies home with me.

"Thank you for honoring our daughter this way, and the other victims." She places her hand on my arm. She's so petite. "This goes a long way toward our healing."

Her husband puts his arm around her, and I think about how Luke had done the same thing with me at the party. They just fit together.

"I'll send you a copy of the video when it's done if you want."

"Just let us know when you upload it," Josh says. "And thank you again. Andy, don't be a stranger." The two of them shake hands and I get another hug before we leave.

"That was hard," I tell Agent Logan once we're on the road. "I feel so bad for them."

"You just gave them something positive. Remember that." His phone chimes and he glances at it quickly. "Huh."

"Anything wrong?" I ask.

He shakes his head. "No. Nothing. A text from the warden at Central. Wants me to call him." His smile is just false enough that I wonder if there's something he's not telling me.

When I get home, I find out what. Mom is in the kitchen opening a bottle of wine. She pours two glasses and hands me one. "We're celebrating," she says, but there's tension around her eyes.

"What?"

"Your father's not expected to make it through the night."

Letter to the Editor, *Entertain Us* magazine, February 21, 2022

Who the Hell Does Jeffrey Robert Lake Think He Is? And Why Do You Care?

I write this letter in a state of cold rage. I've just finished reading the article ("A Killer's Regret," Mark Rylen, Feb. 15, 2022) you published about Jeff Lake dying of cancer and cannot believe your reporter tried to garner sympathy for

the soulless monster who robbed the world of so many
daughters, including mine.

Tracey was a bright and beautiful girl who had her entire
life ahead of her—until she was kind to the wrong man.
Jeff Lake tortured and killed her. Defiled her. Robbed her of
any dignity in death. He kept her from us for years before
she was found in his "garden" and finally brought home. He
has been the source of the worst pain my family has ever
endured, and why? Because he couldn't control himself.
Because he is inhuman, and yet your magazine wants
America—the world—to feel sorry for him because he's
dying a horrible death? My daughter died a horrible death.
Jeffrey Lake isn't getting nearly the end he deserves.

You bring up how his former wife and estranged daughter
have reunited with him on his deathbed. I remember Lake's
trial. I remember his wife's reaction to finding out what he
truly was. I saw her that day in court. The best thing she
could have done for that child was take her away. She didn't
come back to North Carolina out of fond feeling for that
man. She came back as much a victim as my daughter, and
she brought that little girl with her because Lake's playing
games with the FBI, dangling other missing girls in front
of them like bait instead of daughters who are loved and
missed with every inch of a mother's heart.

How dare you insinuate that anyone should feel anything
but contempt for Jeff Lake. How dare you ask me to forgive
him and open my heart to that fool woman who became
wife number two. How dare you even suggest that he has
remorse for what he's done. This isn't the '70s—we all know

what a psychopath is, and Lake is one of the worst. He has no remorse for what he did to my daughter. He has no remorse for what he's done to his own.

Shame on you. Shame on the author for writing such a horrible, harmful article. Shame on you for printing it. Shame on everyone who read it and felt a stirring in their heart toward Lake. You owe the mother of each of his victims an apology for the harm you've done. And you owe an apology to Lake's daughter for printing her photo. I will never read your magazine again.

Madeline Hart
Chapel Hill, NC

Chapter Twenty-Five

Saturday, February 25, 2022

Lake Dies Alone: No Tears for Killer

RALEIGH, NC—Jeffrey Robert Lake, convicted serial killer, died late Friday night after a battle with pancreatic cancer.

Officials within Central Prison, where Lake has been incarcerated since his arrest in 2006 for the murders of 14 women, said that Lake slipped into a coma on Thursday and never woke up.

Wife Everly Evans was by his side during Lake's last moments. She was dry-eyed when she left the prison hospital.

Prior to his death, Lake revealed the names of four more victims to authorities, but refused to give more, citing that he planned to take the remaining identities to his grave.

Lake's final words were a request to see his daughter, Scarlet, whom he had with his first wife, Allison Michaels, aka Gina Murphy. Murphy divorced Lake during his trial in 2007.

A crowd of approximately 200 people gathered outside Central Prison when word of Lake's imminent death leaked. Some held candles, others had signs that read BURN, LAKE, BURN and ROT in HELL, JEFF.

"He got off easy," said one bystander. "If there's a hereafter, I hope he finds a harsher judgment than he did on this earth."

FBI agent Andrew Logan, who was instrumental in Lake's arrest, was there at the time of death. He said Lake's passing was a "relief." "I don't ever take pleasure in the loss of human life, and Jeff Lake left us with more questions than answers, but I cannot deny that a part of me will rest easier knowing he's gone."

Lake had been serving a life sentence on death row and had bartered for visitation rights with his daughter in exchange for giving up the names of his remaining victims. While there are many families who will finally find peace at his passing, there are many others who may never know what truly happened to their loved ones.

Lake was arrested in 2006 after police caught him with the corpse of a recently missing young woman. An investigation of the area revealed 13 more bodies in various stages of decay. These new victims were from New York, Virginia and South Carolina, leaving law enforcement to speculate that Lake may have victims up and down the East Coast.

Per Lake's wishes, he will be cremated.

He's dead.

And I didn't get to see it happen. My last memory is of him as a snarling beast that left bruises on my wrist. I suppose none of my other memories are any better. I probably wouldn't have gotten any pleasure in watching him die, but at least I would know it was true. It feels so impossible. Evil like that doesn't just stop breathing, does it? Rasputin was harder to kill than my father.

"I'll book flights for Hartford later this week," Mom says on Sunday. "You okay with going back for a bit?"

"Yeah. School's done in May. It's only a couple of months. Plus, I miss Taylor and Ash." They're all I miss, though. I'm really not looking forward to going back to a New England winter.

And I don't like the idea of leaving Luke. Turns out I'm not a casual-dating person after all. I like him. I'd like to hang on to him a little longer, but I can't expect him to do the long-distance thing. Can I?

I guess I owe it to him to at least ask.

"I'm thinking we should still take that trip to England," she says. "It might be nice to get out of the US for a bit. Go somewhere they don't care who we are."

"Can we?" Forget trying to play it cool. "For reals?"

Smiling, she pulls out her phone. "Let's check prices." She

plunks herself down on the sofa beside me and goes to a travel site to check out airfare and hotels.

"This one looks nice." It's a hotel not far from Westminster Abbey. It's right on the Thames and next to the London Eye. It's the most perfect location ever.

"Can we afford that?" I ask.

She laughs. "Sweetheart, that's why God made credit cards, but yes. We can afford to make our mother-daughter trip memorable. Besides, after all this, we deserve it."

I throw my arms around her. Her still wanting to go means so much to me. "We have to go to Covent Garden and the abbey and Buckingham Palace, and we have to do the Jack the Ripper tour . . ."

She arches a brow. "Seriously?"

I make a face. "Yeah, you're probably right. Kinda done with serial killers for the time being. But maybe we can check out some National Trust houses?"

"We can do whatever you want. It's your trip. Although, a little shopping would be nice. And maybe a night at the theater."

She books everything right then. Well, after she does a Google search on the hotel and is fairly certain it's as good as it looks. I can't believe it. I just sit there, stunned.

I'm going to England. It definitely takes the sting out of leaving Luke behind for a bit.

"Oh, my God." I can barely stand it. I have to text Taylor. She's still in class, but that's okay. She'll see it when she's done for the day. I start to text Maxi and Darcy too, but I don't want Darcy to say anything to Luke before I do.

I'm on the sofa, making a list of the things I want to do while we're in England, when I hear Mom's phone ring. I can't make out what she says, but I hear her talking in the other room. A few minutes later, she comes to stand in front of me, still holding her phone, a bewildered expression on her face.

My hope falls. "Tell me that wasn't something that will stop us from taking our trip."

"It wasn't." She lifts her gaze to mine. "It was Cat. Apparently Everly wants me to call her."

"Everly Evans? As in the stepmonster?"

Mom laughs. "You probably shouldn't call her that, but yeah. I wonder what she wants."

I shrug. "Maybe she wants to apologize for siccing the media on us. Oh, maybe she wants to tell you how right you were about him. Whatever, who cares, right? Are you going to call her?"

"I think I will. I'll just obsess over it until I do." I watch as she taps the screen on her phone and lifts it to her ear.

"You're calling her *now*?"

Mom brings her finger to her lips to shush me. "Hello. Is this Everly . . . ? Hi, Everly. It's Gina Murphy. . . . Oh, it's no trouble. Cat said you wanted to talk. . . ." Her gaze flicks to mine as she listens to the woman on the other end of the connection. "Really? I can't imagine what it would be. . . . Yes, we can meet."

I start shaking my head, but Mom ignores me. "Why don't you come here? It's probably safer for us all that way. We still have a detail on the place. I'll text you the address. . . . Sure, see you in a bit." She disconnects.

"Are you crazy?" I demand. "You invited her here?"

"We're not going to her house, and I'm not meeting her in public—that's begging for front-page coverage. What would you have me do?"

"Not call her at all."

"She has something for you."

My eyes narrow. "What could she possibly have that I would want?"

"I don't know. She just said she had something for you that was important and she had to give it to you in person."

"That sounds ominous."

"I know." Mom chews her bottom lip. "I'm going to call Andy. Make a pot of coffee, will you? And throw some of those frozen scones in the microwave."

The only reason I get off the sofa is because coffee and scones sound good. I have no desire to impress my father's widow. No desire to even lay eyes on the woman. I don't care that she apparently saw him for what he was before he died. I have zero sympathy for her that he wasn't the man she thought. He'd already been convicted when she met him. The whole world knew what he was.

I make the coffee first so it will be good and hot by the time we drink it, then I get one of the boxes of scones Moira made out of the freezer. Mmm. White chocolate almond. So. Freaking. Good.

Is it wrong that I feel like a weight has been lifted off my shoulders? I mean, it hasn't even been a whole day since we heard that he was gone. Agent Logan called last night with the news. Mom and I cried with relief. It's like a blight has been lifted. Like the sun has come out after a month of rain.

My phone pings. It's Luke, asking if I want to go for celebratory nachos tonight. Yes, I do. And then he and I can talk about how we want to go forward. I've had a lot of fun with him, and the sex . . . well, the sex is awesome. I really like him, but a month ago I thought Neal was the best thing to ever walk the earth. Chances are I'm going to meet a few of those kinds of guys over the course of my life. Some I'll be wrong about, like Neal, and others will be exactly what they seem, like Luke.

That's not to say it wouldn't be awesome if Luke ended up being my forever-guy. But I'm not putting all my hopes into it at this point. I just want to spend time together and get to know him better.

And jump his bones every now and again. I smile at the thought. He really is extremely fun to get naked with. And a good kisser. And fun to hang out with. And easy to talk to.

Okay, yeah, I'm not infatuated *at all*. Giving my head a shake, I put several scones on a plate and set it beside the microwave. I'll wait until Everly gets here to heat them up.

Twenty minutes later, when I'm putting on a little makeup for seeing Luke after, the doorbell rings.

"That's her," Mom says, going to check the camera. "Whatever it is she gives you, we need to hand it over to Andy, okay? It could be important for the continuing investigation."

"He's dead. Not like they can press charges," I counter. But I get it. It might help with victim recovery, and I'm all for that.

Mom rolls her eyes at me. "Finish your makeup and come out. I'm not facing her alone. It's you she wants to see."

I like this new side of Mom. Sarcastic and teasing. Lighter. She went shopping the other day for new clothes even. Every part of her is more vibrant. She looks amazing, and I love watching her emerge from her self-imposed cocoon like a badass butterfly.

As I put on mascara, I hear voices out in the entryway. Everly sounds . . . normal. I put my makeup away and leave the bathroom. The sooner we get this over with, the better.

Everly Evans-Lake is tiny. Short and thin. She might weigh a hundred pounds, if that. Her shoulder-length hair is a high-lighted toffee color, and her eyes are a very similar shade.

She looks nice. She also looks wrecked. There are dark circles under her eyes, and she's pale and drawn, like she hasn't slept well for a while.

No, I bet she hasn't. I can't even bring myself to think meanly of her. I pity her.

"Oh," she says when she looks at me. "There you are." Her voice trembles.

"Come in," Mom says. "Scarlet made coffee."

"Oh, I don't want to trouble you." It's obvious from the shakiness of her voice that she's a mess.

Mom takes her hand. "Everly, I might be the only person who knows what you're feeling right now. You're not trouble. Come have a coffee and something to eat."

That's my cue to heat up the scones. I am all too glad to make a run for it. A few minutes later, the three of us sit at the kitchen table. We have full mugs of coffee and a plate of warm scones in the center of the table. I grab one and take a bite.

"Thank you for your kindness," Everly says. "Lord knows I've done nothing to deserve it."

"Hush," Mom chides, offering her a scone. "You trusted the wrong man. There aren't too many of us who get through life without saying that."

"I didn't just trust him, Gina. I loved him, but the things he said to me the last time I saw him . . . he wasn't who I thought he was."

"You were manipulated," I correct her, surprising Mom and myself. "He was good at that."

She gives me a weak smile. I don't think she believes that any more than I do. "I have something for you. Something your father wanted you to have."

Since she only has a small purse with her, I can safely assume it's not a human skull or something equally macabre. She lays her hand flat on the table and slides it toward me. When she lifts it, there's a key on the scarred wood.

I frown. "What is it?"

Everly clears her throat. "It's a key to a storage container downtown. It's in your name."

A chill goes down my spine. "My name?"

She looks pained. "Under the name of Britney Lake. That's how he managed to keep it a secret, I suppose. He said he leased it shortly after you were born."

"Why?" I ask, glancing from her to Mom. "Do you know anything about this?"

Mom's lips draw into a thin line. "This is the first I've heard of it. Everly, did he give you any idea what's inside?"

She shakes her head. "Only that it holds some of his most prized possessions. He said to tell Br . . . Scarlet that it's her legacy."

This cannot be good. I'm thinking it's a crate of trophies, probably? Newspaper clippings and articles about his kills? Things that made him feel like a big man?

But maybe there's evidence that will lead Agent Logan to finding more of his victims. Look at me, still trying to find some shred of decency in the motherfucker.

"I didn't know anything about it. Jeff's lawyer handled the payments for the rental." She glances at Mom. "I was thinking maybe it contains things that got left behind when you left?"

"Maybe," Mom allows. "I only took what was mine and what I could pack in a car. There was plenty left behind. I always thought Cat took care of it, but I never asked." She shrugs, which means she never really cared to know.

"Here's the address." Everly hands me a bright pink sticky note with writing on it.

"Thanks." I put it with the key and take another bite of my scone. It tastes a little like sawdust now, but I keep chewing.

With her task completed, Everly doesn't seem to know what to do with herself. She sits there, across from me, small and silent, her hands wrapped around her untouched coffee. When a tear drops from her cheek, I nudge Mom with my foot under the table.

She immediately reaches out and touches the other woman's arm. "Everly, sweetie? Are you all right?"

Everly lifts her head. Mascara tears streak down her face. She doesn't try to wipe them away, as if she knows there will be more. "How do I go on knowing how little I mattered to him?"

"Oh, sugar. You just have to get through today, and trust tomorrow will take care of itself."

Everly shakes her head and sniffs. "I'm so ashamed."

"Yeah." Mom's voice is soft and entirely too understanding. "If it's any consolation, it will get easier with time."

"I've been such a fool."

"Yes," Mom allows. I raise my eyebrows but say nothing. "You were a fool, but there's a big difference between foolish and cruel, Everly. A universe of distance between trusting and manipulative. He chose you because he wanted to hurt someone. It's what he does."

"Did," I correct. "It's what he did. He liked having someone he could project onto, but he's dead and we're not. So, dig a hole and put him in it and get the fuck on with your life."

Both women stare at me. I shrug. "It's true, and I'm not sorry for saying it, though I apologize for my language."

Mom starts to snicker first. I'm not really surprised at that. I am surprised when Everly gives me a shaky smile.

"You're right," she says. "I can only go forward. There's no going back."

Yeah, that's what I meant, though she said it a lot more eloquently.

She blinks and wipes at her face. Mom offers her a napkin to use as a tissue. "I don't even have anyone I can talk to," she admits. "I lost all my friends because of this. Not that I blame them. I should find a new therapist, I guess."

Mom gives her a sympathetic smile. "You've got us. Scarlet has plans soon, but why don't you stay for dinner? I have a bottle of wine. We can talk about Jeff as much or as little as you want."

I'm so freaking proud of my mother. There is absolutely no reason for her to do this, other than that she's a good person.

Everly nods. "I'd like that. Thank you."

I raise my mug. "To the first meeting of the Jeff Lake Survivors Club."

Mom looks at me in surprise. "Seriously, Scarlet?"

"What? It's true, isn't it?" She shakes her head. But Everly, she lifts her mug and clinks it against mine. "Here's to survivors," she says, her voice the strongest I've heard it since she arrived.

Shrugging, Mom lifts her mug with a smile, and we drink. He's dead. We're not, and that's good enough for me.

Chapter Twenty-Six

The storage locker is old. It hasn't been opened since before my father went to prison. The guy at the office was surprised that someone actually claimed it. The fee had been paid every month, but no one had ever come by. No one got suspicious. Why would they? Not one person looked at the name Britney Lake and did the math.

I give Agent Logan the key—mostly because I've never opened one of these before and have no idea how it works.

The steel door rolls up.

I wrinkle my nose. "What's that smell?"

Agent Logan grabs me and pulls me away. The door falls shut with a loud clattering crash. "Get forensics out here," he cries. "*Now!*"

I turn my head to look back as he drags me away. I only catch a glimpse of a police detective, blood drained from her face, pulling out her phone.

"Jesus Christ," Agent Logan swears. He's pale as he drags a hand through his hair. "Scarlet, I'm so sorry. I didn't think—

God damn that asshole!" He crushes me to his chest in a
fierce hug. Stunned, I stand there with my arms at my sides.

"What's in there?" I ask.

He just shakes his head. "When forensics gets here, I want
you to leave, okay? You don't need to be here for this."

A horrible feeling settles over me—a certainty that chills
me right to the marrow in my bones. "How many?"

His jaw tightens.

"Agent Logan, how many b-bodies are in that locker?"

"I'm not sure," is his quiet reply. "I saw two, but I'm thinking there's more."

The heaviness in the pit of my stomach is like a bowling
ball, spinning and hurtling toward the gutter. I slide down
the wall to the dirty floor. "He wanted me to find them." My
father literally left me corpses.

Part of me wants to get out my camera and document this,
but I can't make my hands work. I just sit there, my back
against the wall, unable to move. All I can do is breathe and
stare at the closed bay. Police and agents stand in front of it,
looking tense and shocked. The lead detective is still on her
phone.

How can you store people like old furniture? How can you
leave it for your daughter to find? My father's sickness—his
cruelty and lack of feeling—truly knew no bounds.

I look up at Agent Logan, the man who stopped me from
seeing my "inheritance." He kept me from being forever—
forever—damaged by my father's legacy.

In the few short weeks I've known him, he's been more of
a father to me than anyone else.

"Thank you," I say.

He nods. "You want me to call Luke to come get you? You
shouldn't be here when they . . . when forensics is at work."

"I want to stay." Slowly, I push myself to my feet. My legs are a little shaky, but they hold. More importantly, I don't feel that sickening panic anymore. If my father did one thing good for me, it was that dealing with him changed my fight-or-flight reflex. I'm more fight now.

"I owe it to his victims to stay. To myself."

He pats me on the shoulder with a tight smile. "You're a lot like your mother."

I want to tell him to call her. I want my mom. I don't say anything, though, because she'll come, and she doesn't need this. I know she'll blame herself somehow.

But he must, because she's there a little while later. The police let her into the area—it's taped off, obviously. We don't run, but we walk quickly toward one another.

I grab her in a tight hug.

"Oh, my sweet girl," she says, smoothing her hands over my hair. "I'm so sorry. I shouldn't have let you do this alone. I should have known he'd have something planned."

"It's not your fault," I tell her. "None of this has been your fault. It's *his*." My voice shakes with anger.

She looks at me a moment—like, really deep into my eyes. "Okay," she says. "You are one hundred percent right." Then, she releases me, only to take one of my cold hands in hers.

We stand together, out of the way, but within sight of the container. Forensics arrives as a four-person team. They completely gear up with masks and protective gear before going inside.

I don't know how long it is before they start bringing out body bags. It feels like a long time. It feels like time stands still.

Eleven. That's how many they bring out. How did he manage this without anyone seeing? Without anyone wondering about the smell? I don't want to know. He obviously put a lot of thought into it.

He told me fifty-seven. Even with his original fourteen, this brings the total to twenty-nine recovered. Twenty-eight women are still unaccounted for.

"My God," Mom whispers as they bring the last one out.

Agent Logan approaches with a paper cup in each hand. "How you ladies holding up?"

"We're managing," Mom replies, taking the coffee he offers. She hands one to me. It feels good in my hands. "Is that the last of them?"

He nods, glancing over his shoulder. "Now we start processing the container itself. Aside from what he used for biological storage, there are several boxes. Mementos, we believe. Hopefully those will lead to further identifications."

Biological storage. I'm hung up on that. It's going to take a while for me to stop wondering about what sort of storage my father used for all this "biology."

"You should go home," he tells me. "You did what you needed to. Those girls are one step closer to going home themselves. I'll come by tomorrow and bring you up to speed, okay?"

I take a shaky breath. "Okay."

Mom and I walk to her car in silence. I sip at my coffee and nod at the police as we pass.

"Careful out there," one officer advises. "Someone alerted the press."

"We have a detail," Mom replies. "But thanks for the heads-up."

As soon as we step out of the labyrinth of containers and into the waning daylight, we see the crowd. Finding one body is news. Finding eleven in a unit belonging to a dead serial killer is an even bigger story.

"He really knew how to make it all about him, didn't he?" I ask as they start shouting our names.

"One last fuck-you to the world," Mom replies.

"To us," I correct her. "He could have turned that over years ago. He saved it for us." For me. I don't even think it's because he hated me. I'm not sure he was any more capable of hate than he was love, because you have to be able to feel to hate someone. I was nothing but an extension of him, like an arm. I was a piece to play his game.

"He died thinking he'd won."

Mom shakes her head. "He's dead. It doesn't matter what he thought. He doesn't matter anymore." She gives me a little smile that I do my best to return.

"C'mon," she says, holding out her hand. "I feel like pizza. We need to make this a celebration. Eleven more girls found, and Jeff Lake has been burned to ash by now. I no longer have to carry him with me wherever I go. No more glancing over my shoulder. We're free, babe. Time to act like it."

I don't feel much like celebrating, and I don't really think she does either, but we silently agree to fake it until we make it.

Inside the car, the cries of the reporters are muffled. Mom calls Aunt Cat before starting the engine, and I text Luke and Darcy.

"Cat's going to pick up the pizza," Mom says, putting the car in reverse. "Save the delivery guy the hassle of having to deal with the press."

I acknowledge this with a sigh. Fortunately, the police parked outside our house do a good job of keeping them from knocking on the door, but they can't stop them from sitting down the street and taking photos with telephoto lenses.

It's not even like Mom and I are that interesting. Media

has a lot in common with psychopaths—it's all about attention and who can do the most for you. They don't care about us, we're just extensions of Jeffrey Robert Lake, and he sells papers and gets ratings and clicks.

It's all pretty sick. I swear I'll never watch someone else's public suffering again. Not if I can help it.

My phone pings as soon as we walk through the door. It's a text from Ashley.

Ash

Just saw on Twitter they found more
bodies???? In a storage locker???
WTF? U OK?

I text her back: I'm OK. Will explain later. Tired. <3

Taylor texts as well, but it's just a bunch of emojis. I send her back a heart and set my phone aside. I need a shower.

In the bathroom, I look at myself in the mirror. The burgundy is almost completely gone from my hair. I look like the old me—pale and kind of freaked out. Maybe I'll try another color. Blond, maybe, and see how much Maxi and I really do look alike. Or maybe vampire red. Something bold and totally unlike me. And maybe I'll get it cut.

Or maybe I'll get a tattoo or a new piercing. That makes me smile.

I hold on to that smile. The old me wouldn't have been able to smile right now. The old me would be sedated somewhere—smoked up or zoned out. The old me had no idea life is about so much more than what people think of me.

It's what *I* think of me. You can go to parties and travel and have lots of friends, but if you don't like who you are, none of it matters. I think I've always secretly been afraid of who I really am. I mean, I knew Mom was paranoid for a reason, right? It made me afraid too. Made me bitter and small.

I'm not afraid anymore.

I step into the warm spray still holding that smile. Today had freaked me out, but I'm going to look at it as a good thing, like Mom said. More girls brought home. My father dead and gone. I have no intention of letting him poison the rest of my life. Today is the day I stop being one of his victims.

I reach for the soap and wash the rest of the old me down the drain.

"When do you leave?"

It's just me and Luke in the house. We're on top of my bed—fully clothed. Mom went out with some old friends for dinner and drinks. One of them is a guy she used to date; she was nervous about seeing him again.

"Friday," I reply, my face in the hollow of his neck, breathing in his scent. He smells good.

"I'm going to miss you."

I pull back so I can look him in the eye. "I'm going to miss you too. But we can FaceTime and text. And we'll be back after spring break so Mom can look for a condo."

"I know." He rubs his hand along my thigh. I wish there weren't so many layers of clothes between us. "I've just gotten used to seeing you whenever I want."

I prop myself up on my elbow. When we went out for nachos, I avoided this conversation. I don't know how to have it—I'm afraid of it—but it's gotta happen. "I don't have any expectations of us, just so you know. You might meet someone else—"

He stops me by pressing his lips against mine. "I don't want anyone else. I'm not looking for anyone else. I want you."

Butterflies flutter through me. "How can you talk like that?"

"Honestly?"

"Vulnerable." I shake my head with a slight smile. "Don't get me wrong. *I* love it. It's awesome knowing how you feel. But . . . aren't you afraid I'll, like, hurt you or something?"

He shakes his head. "Not really, no. Are you afraid I'll hurt you?"

"Yeah." I thought that was obvious.

"There are a lot of things I want to do to you," he says in a low voice, "but none of them hurt." As if to prove his point, he kisses my neck. I shiver against him and feel his chuckle against my throat.

"Show me," I urge, wrapping my arms around him, tugging on his shirt until I can feel the warm, bare skin of his back. I trail my fingers along his spine and feel him shudder. I smile.

He does show me. Slowly, he peels away my clothes until I'm left in my underwear, and then he removes them too. Starting at my mouth, he kisses his way down the entire length of me—pausing in a few places to do more than just kiss.

Holy shit.

I watch him undress. There's no way I can touch him as much as I want, or taste him, smell him. There's not enough time in the world. But I try.

"Scarlet," he whispers, hands in my hair. My name has never sounded so urgent, so powerful before.

And then, I'm under him and he's inside me and my legs are wrapped around him, hands clutching at his waist. He looks down and our eyes meet. It's like looking up for the first time and seeing all the stars in the sky.

This is what they mean when they talk about sex with

someone you care about. How emotion makes it so much . . . *more*. It's amazing and it's terrifying and I don't care, I'm in it. He's been like a gift through all of this. An amazing, beautiful person that makes all the horror and shame of finding out where I come from fade into the shadows.

"Can't do *that* over FaceTime," he teases me later. We're still entwined, nerves tingling.

I laugh. My chest is tight, though, full of this new emotion, this awareness.

"I . . ." Words escape. I stare at him in the moonlight streaming through the window. There's so much I want to say. So much I *feel*.

Luke's expression changes, softens. "Yeah," he murmurs. "Me too."

And then he's kissing me again, and for the first time in my life I feel like everything I want is within my reach.

The next few months fall together in a blur. Mom and I pack up and return to Connecticut. My first day back to school is the week leading up to spring break. I'm thankful for the edge of excitement that takes the focus off of me.

It's good to be with my friends again. First day back, Sofie asks if we can talk. I don't know what to expect, but we find a quiet corner and she tells me that she's sorry for how things went down between us. She's on the verge of tears as she apologizes for how she treated me—how much she despised me for having Neal's attention. They are seeing each other now, but getting the guy she wanted wasn't worth alienating a friend. I appreciate it, I have to admit. I'm not even the least bit jealous about her and Neal. I'm grateful for her apology and give her a huge hug before heading to class. Having our little group back together means so much. It doesn't bother me to see Neal, but I'm even more glad we didn't have sex that night. That would be awkward.

Do people approach me about my father? Yeah, but it's old news. Ash is the only one who's interested in hearing about it, but she doesn't ask too many questions. She's helping me with the video series, though, and her knowledge about the psychology of all of this stuff is incredibly helpful. I can't even begin to explain how much she helps me process my father's psychopathy. Between her and my therapist, I'm doing really good. Like, surprisingly good. I hardly have panic issues anymore, and while I still like to imbibe every once in a while, I find I just don't want to drink or smoke up much anymore. I think a lot of that is because Mom has become so chill.

Our trip to England is amazing. Like, so much fun. It's like I've been given a new and improved Mom. She's still overly cautious about a lot of things, but not like she used to be. We spend spring break in London and driving around parts of England, visiting National Trust houses and historic sites. There's part of a Roman wall at the Tower of London. Boggles my brain how old it is. And there's graffiti carved into the walls of the tower jail.

We do the Jack the Ripper tour. Mom says we're not going to let Jeff ruin a perfectly macabre evening. I'm glad we do it, because our guide really knows his stuff, and it's just fun.

We shop. We drink tea. I try chocolate on my toast. I film a lot. It's the coolest thing I've ever done.

"Maybe for our next trip we'll do Paris," Mom suggests on the flight home. I'm in.

I text and talk to Darcy and Maxi as much as I can. They're

officially dating now. I won't be surprised if they're together for a long time. They have that kind of energy.

As for me and Luke, we're good. We text every day and Face-Time as often as we can. He's going to come up for a weekend soon and meet my friends. I can't wait to see him.

Mom's been talking to that guy she went to high school with, who is also divorced. They've made plans to get to-gether again when she moves back to Raleigh in May. She's already started packing. Me too.

I've finally come up with a plan. There are some good film schools in North Carolina, one of which I've already been accepted to. Thank you, rolling admissions. I'm going to start there and see what happens. I have other options—I've been accepted to schools across the country—but right now it's more important to me to put down some authentic roots. I want to get to know the family I'd been denied most of my life. I want to spend time getting to know Mom. Our rela-tionship has changed so much, and I don't want to walk away from that yet. Plus, there's still so much to do on the docu-series, and I need to be in North Carolina for interviews and filming.

And yeah, I want to spend more time with Luke. So, I'm going to school in NC and then who knows? If there's one thing I've learned since February, it's that you can't possibly predict the twists and turns life is going to take. I'm just try-ing to enjoy the journey. Make my life mean something.

They've identified the eleven bodies found in the storage container. My father did a good job of preserving them—and that's as much as I'm going to say about that. Dental records and DNA helped a lot. So, eleven more women who have been returned to their families. Eleven more for me to memorial-ize. From the number of trophies and journals found, Agent

Logan surmises there are a lot more bodies still out there, and a couple of cold cases may have been solved. I think about that whenever I remember my father and the time I spent with him. It was worth it. If it hadn't been for him, I might still be bitter and panicky and resentful of Mom. I'd still be that angry girl who had no idea who she was or what she was capable of.

Aunt Cat said Jeff wanted to have his ashes sprinkled over the grounds of the cabin, but there was no way she was letting that happen. Everly didn't fight her on it. She took the urn in to the nursing home where my grandmother Lake lives and left it with her instead. She told Mom she didn't care if someone stole it, so I guess I won't be surprised if the remains show up for auction on eBay.

My father was a bastard, but if he hadn't left that key for me, the ending to my story with him wouldn't be nearly so satisfying. He didn't mess me up. He didn't leave his mark on me. Knowing him made me stronger and gave me purpose. So, yeah. Fuck you, Jeffrey Robert Lake.

I've interviewed a lot more people for the series. And when we move back to Raleigh, I'm going to meet some face-to-face to film them. Meanwhile, I've filmed segments with Mom and of myself talking about our experiences. We talk about him as little as possible and try to focus on ourselves and the victims who weren't so fortunate to get out alive. Everly's agreed to an interview as well. A lot of people won't have sympathy for her. Hell, a lot of people won't have any sympathy for me or Mom either, but sympathy isn't the goal.

I have twenty-nine names on the list in my notebook, and Agent Logan will be giving me new ones to add any day now, I'm sure. My father told me he killed fifty-seven but I'll probably never know if that was the truth or another lie.

I don't need the list to remember them anymore. I have

their names written on my memory and in my heart. I know their faces. I know their stories. They were friends. Sisters. Mothers. Daughters. They mattered before they died, and they matter now. My father took their lives.

I'm going to give them a voice.

Acknowledgments

The idea for this book came to me after watching *Extremely Wicked, Shockingly Evil and Vile* on Netflix. It was the scene where Kaya Scodelario (as Carole Ann Boone) sits in the courtroom with her hands on her slightly rounded belly. I remember wondering just how surreal it must be growing up with Ted Bundy for a father. It made me feel for that kid, and it handed me the idea of Scarlet. So, I guess I need to thank everyone involved with that movie. I owe an even bigger thanks to Vicki Lame for making all the appropriate noises when I told her about said idea at our author-editor lunch shortly thereafter. Also, big thanks to my agent, Deidre Knight, for getting behind it, and for all my friends who weren't the least bit surprised when I said I was going to tackle this subject matter. A very personal point in all of this is that we (society) tend to put way more focus on the killer rather than the victims—something I would like to see change. The people these killers take away are far more important than the killers themselves will ever be. Each of them was a wealth of possibility robbed of ever reaching their potential, and too often they're reduced to being little more than objects of psychopathic obsession—an extension of the person who killed them, rather than an individual.

I also want to extend thanks to the readers who patiently waited for this book, and to those of you who read it. You know it's all for you, right?

And finally, a big thanks to my husband, Steve, who is always my light when I spend too much time in the dark. He has been my constant cheerleader, PR person, ego-soother, and best friend for more than half my life now, and I appreciate him more than I can say. Plus, he's funny and cute too, so that's a bonus. ☺